Slowly, almost reverently, he raised her till she stood erect. He loosened his hold, but didn't altogether release her.

Tara caught her breath as she observed the splintered brilliance of his mango-green eyes with their glittering purple shards. She felt drawn into the magical orbs.

'This is a hint of what to expect after we are wed. I'll expect a lot more when you share my bed, Tara.' Then he dropped his arms away from her.

His voice broke the spell, startled her back to reality. Collecting herself, she said, 'I refuse to bed with you until you've fulfilled your pledge.'

His face hardened into obduracy, eyes opaque. 'If you refuse then there'll be no raid on Motipur. Which is it to be?'

Tara's eyes wavered and flicked away from his. 'You force me to sin, Colonel.'

The hardness disppeared from his face and he grinned disarmingly. 'There'll be no sin; we'll be married, Tara. Think on it. Goodnight, fair one.' He sketched her a bow and abruptly left the tent.

Yvonne Purves was born in India and attended boarding school in the Himalayas. Alas, being deaf, she finished at the bottom of the class. Even so, she had always been an avid reader, and can't remember ever learning to read; it came naturally. She was at college in Delhi when Gandhi was assassinated and watched his funeral go by from India Gate. She came to Britain and married here. She has three grown up children and acquired a dog through the RSPCA.

She has been writing since 1980 and has two historical novels published. *The Burning Quest* is her first Masquerade Historical Romance.

THE BURNING QUEST

Yvonne Purves

MILLS & BOON LIMITED
ETON HOUSE   18-24 PARADISE ROAD
RICHMOND   SURREY   TW9 1SR

First published in Great Britain 1988
by Mills & Boon Limited

© Yvonne Purves 1988

Australian copyright 1988
Philippine copyright 1988
This edition 1988

ISBN 0 263 76179 7

Set in Times Roman 10 on 12 pt.
04-8809-73989

Made and printed in Great Britain

CHAPTER ONE

'I DARE SAY you're jesting, Father?' Tara jumped up from the divan, moved to the fretted window and twined her fingers round the lacy pattern of sandstone flowers. She stared up at the star-flung indigo sky, its tranquillity a contrast to her body simmering with wrath. 'It's not possible that you are serious about my marrying Todar Ram? You are as aware as I am that the man is loathsome!'

'Now listen to me, Tara.' Her father's cajoling voice caused her to tighten her fingers and lips in grim resistance to his persuasiveness.

'No, Father, *you* listen...'

'Stop!' Raja Rao Chandra's tall regal figure clothed in white muslin came to stand beside her, his familiar scent of betel-nut and sandalwood carrying agreeably to her nostrils.

In startled consternation Tara looked into his handsome face; he had never used that imperious tone of voice to her since her sixteenth birthday four years earlier.

'Hear me well, Tara,' he said sternly, his eyebrows coming together to express his displeasure. 'It is for the sake of our people that we must make sacrifices. Our army is no match for the Marathas, whereas Todar Ram's European-trained troops are. Besides, what we hear about him might well be distortion.'

'What of my feelings?' Tara cried. 'Must they be bandied about by that depraved creature? You yourself have raved against Todar Ram, condemned his morals and ruthless oppression of his people. Now, to suit yourself, you are finding excuses for him! What of me?' Her sapphire eyes filled with tears of rebellion. 'Must I be the white goat chosen for slaughter?'

'You exaggerate, my child. I'm not asking you to give your life . . .'

'Wait, Father,' Tara cut into his tirade. Her anger abated and she said in more sober thoughtful tones, 'You have pledged allegiance to the Mogul emperor. Why then do you not ask him for help?'

Chandra's laugh rang with caustic mirth. 'Mogul emperor, hey? What Mogul emperor? Now, in 1779, the Mogul empire is finished, Tara. Shah Alum no longer wields the power once possessed by the first six Moguls. You are aware of that.' He flung his beringed hands up in a gesture of hopelessness and, returning to the divan, flopped on to a heap of gold-tasselled bolsters and cushions of green and red silk. 'The emperor is virtually a prisoner of the Marathas and their mercenaries. He's of no use to me or any other princes,' he went on. 'But your marriage to Todar Ram will form an alliance, and together we can safeguard our lands. I fear it's the only way.'

She suppressed her impatience and joined him on the divan. 'Have you appealed to the British? I have no doubt that they'll give us assistance because Mother is English. And, remember, Thomas Orme is my godfather. You should have thought of him first.'

Chandra shook his head in despair. 'I've sent two runners with letters, not only to your godfather but to Governor-General Warren Hastings in Fort William, Calcutta. But they're so far away,' he sighed, 'and I have heard nothing.'

For a moment she brooded. As an idea materialised in her brain, she eyed Chandra thoughtfully. 'Father,' she said in a slow impressive voice, 'you could hire the services of the mercenary Colonel Markham and his Blue Cloaks. It's common knowledge that he's formidable enough to resist the Maratha Confederacy. There's no need to form an alliance by marriage with Todar Ram.'

Tara had never set eyes on Colonel Markham who, it was rumoured, hailed from North America and whose military prowess was famed throughout northern India. He was feared not only by the Marathas but even by the French, and respected by the English. Independently he had raised an army and hired it out to those princes and chiefs whom he thought needed protection from a foe of any nationality. His men honoured him with the title of Sikandar Sahib, a title once conferred on Alexander the Great after his conquest of the Punjab.

'My dear child, did you think I had not thought on that? I have appealed to Sikandar Sahib as well; he alone knows how weak our defences are. But a month has elapsed, and still no reply. His services are no doubt in demand by other princes who are afraid of losing their territory to the Marathas. Even the British are wary of them.'

'But, Father, why not summon help from other states? Why rely on my marriage to Todar Ram?'

'Because,' Chandra said tetchily, 'like the British and Sikandar Sahib, other states are too far away. Then they'll want advance payments for hiring out their armies, and by the time an agreement had been reached, the Marathas would have taken over here. Todar Ram is our neighbour. We can contact him within an hour by carrier pigeon...'

'Why haven't you used these birds to summon the British or Markham?'

'Because, Tara, my pigeons have not been trained to fly so far. Don't interrupt! Todar Ram has agreed to combine forces if you become his bride and on presentation of a—a large dowry.'

'Ah!' Tara rolled her eyes. 'I might have known!'

Chandra flicked Tara a sad smile and caught her small hand, studying its pale smoothness. 'Royalty, my child, does not entirely mean gracious living. We of royal blood who have the welfare of our people at heart are duty bound to make sacrifices for them, to shoulder our responsibilities. And the gods know,' he released a worried breath, 'Todar Ram may be smitten by your beauty and change into a dutiful monarch, if only to please you.'

His statement failed to console Tara. He was hoping Raja Todar Ram would succumb to her influence as he himself had done to her mother's. She withdrew her hand gently and viewed her reflection in the scalloped arched mirror on the opposite wall. Wide blue eyes filled with anger and fright stared back at her from the creamy pallor of her heart-shaped face. She chewed on her lower lip and touched the silver braid edging her apricot sari of transparent silk that offset the bronze highlights in her dark-brown hair.

'Have you spoken to Mother about this—this unwelcome proposal?'

'Now do not upset yourself unnecessarily, darling.'

'Unnecessarily? In truth, Father, you have just...'

'I know, I know, but nothing definite has been decided. I wanted to mention it to you first.'

Tara glared at him. Faceted gold bangles jangled on her wrists as she dismissed his words with an angry flip of her hand. 'That doesn't answer my question. Does Mother know?'

Chandra heaved a quivering and weary breath, rubbing his fingers across his lids. Dropping his hand, he said, 'No. As you are aware, your mother is with child, and the Jesuit doctor has remarked that her condition is unsatisfactory. Therefore she must not be subjected to anxiety, or she may lose the baby. We are hoping for a son.'

Tara shot up from the divan and faced him squarely, her cheeks flushed with rage. 'You know full well that Mother would not have consented to this marriage and that she will be upset. Otherwise, why keep it from her? I refuse to marry that obese, pleasure-loving tyrant. I'd rather kill myself!'

'Huh, foolish talk. I see now that I've spoilt you.' He stood up, and the cruel hardness of his dark eyes filled her with qualms. 'You are no true princess, or you would put the safety of the people first. Tonight, ponder on what I have said. View it thoroughly from all sides with a calm mind and give me your answer on the morrow.' He brought his palms together in a brief *namasta*, the Hindu salutation, and strode towards the archway leading out of the chamber, his ruby-studded slippers angrily slapping the mosaic floor.

But before Chandra could reach the beaded curtain, a servant dashed in and threw himself at his feet. The raja stepped away from the prostrate man. 'Has the devil possessed you? How dare you enter these chambers without permission! Get out, imbecile!'

The servant steepled his hands in a gesture of pleading. 'Raja Sahib, Highness, forgive me, I have grave news for you. I beseech you...'

'Then do it in a proper manner—through my ministers. Who allowed you in here?'

Tara knew her father would have shown more tolerance to the servant if he were not so annoyed with her.

'*Huzoor,* your honour, there is no time to lose. I entreat . . .'

'I said begone, man!'

'Father, wait.' Tara moved to his side and saw the terror on the servant's face. 'I think you should hear him. Something momentous has occurred for him to break in like this.' Ignoring her parent's surliness, she turned to the man and motioned him to rise. 'Speak, good one.'

He looked relieved and turned to her. 'Your Highness, the guards at the entrance to the bridge have been murdered. Their bodies have been brought to the courtyard by their brethren who have survived.' Tears spilled from the distraught man's eyes. 'My son is among the dead.'

'Murdered?' Tara and her father cried together.

'*Ji.* One of the guards lived long enough to tell that a group of men on horseback attacked them. My son lies out there in his blood, and my wife knows nothing.'

'I'm sorry you have lost your son. Before you go to your wife, please tell us what caused this tragedy,' Tara said in a sympathetic voice.

'The surviving guards said that they challenged some men on horseback who had arrived at the bridge, and were rewarded with gunfire. I do not know who these strangers were. The guards think they are Marathas.'

'I do not think they will return. It is merely an incident that we can deal with. I'll speak to the guards myself. You go home to your wife. My ministers will see that the kin of the dead receive compensation,' Chandra addressed the servant in kinder tones. On his departure, he spoke to Tara. 'You see how dangerous times have become, my child? We need Todar Ram's help, and he will give it only if you marry him.'

'All he wants is my dowry. And these.' She pointed to the state rings they both wore. 'These are priceless...'

'Enough, Tara! You weary me.' Chandra flung out of the chamber without bothering to glance at her.

Taking slow dejected steps, she returned to the divan, slumped on it, looked about her like a hunted animal searching for a means of escape and finding none in this opulent chamber. She yearned to run to her mother, so gentle, so beautiful, so kind and wise.

All proposals for an arranged marriage that Chandra had previously planned in accordance with Hindu custom for Tara, her English mother had swept aside, stating, 'She is a Christian and she'll marry for love as I did, or not at all!' And the raja had laughed and succumbed to her wishes as he had always done, even to the extent of discarding his Hindu wife and concubines before marrying her. Tonight all that had changed. With ruthless disregard for her feelings, her father proposed to offer Tara to one of the most bestial men alive.

The perfumed chamber with its silk and satin drapes seemed to hem her in, to stifle her. What she needed was to breathe fresh air and clear her mind of depressing thoughts, to think with cool logic and objectivity. She rose from the divan and went out into the walled garden to inhale the warm scented atmosphere, but did not linger. To walk here at night was dangerous; she had been warned that snakes sometimes emerged then to hunt. She climbed two flights of stairs to the roof of the palace and entered a pavilion fitted with fretted screens that overlooked the main courtyard. Often she came up here to catch a breath of cool air before retiring for the night. Once it had been the haunt of a yogi, who had died some years past, but now the wrought-iron door had become stiff, and she had been advised by the servant who cleaned the place not to close it because it might jam.

Tonight, in her distress, Tara disregarded caution and pulled the door to; perhaps an unconscious reflex to shut out her thoughts. She dragged out a bolster from a stack stowed beneath a stone bench and settling herself down on it, stared out into the darkness of the courtyard, thinking of the last time she had viewed her gross, repulsive future husband through similar fretted screens in the durbar hall.

She shuddered. On a number of occasions she had spotted him, but he had not as yet set eyes on her. In spite of Todar Ram's vile reputation, he and Chandra enjoyed an amicable relationship without interfering in each other's politics, although she was mystified as to why her father tolerated him. Now, of course, she knew. They had been engaged in negotiations over her dowry. It was intolerable that Rao Chandra, with all his wealth, should be compelled to rely on another state to defend his own! His negligence irritated her.

He should have considered it of prime importance to build up an army, to employ European mercenaries to discipline and train the young men of Chiriabagh with the proficiency of the sepoys of the Bengal army formed by the East India Company and controlled by British officers. Perhaps, she reflected, only they possessed the armed might required to resist and defeat the Marathas, the skilled guerrilla fighters whose first leader had been the great and humane Shivaji who had harassed and tormented the army of Aurangzeb, the last of the six most powerful Mogul emperors. After him, Mogul power had declined. Where the European fighters had the advantage, she acknowledged, was in the superiority of their weapons, no match for the obsolete and unwieldy arms of an Indian army, however brave.

Tara sighed. The blood of two nations, Rajput and English, flowed in her veins, and she believed she understood the mentality of both Indians and Europeans. That the former preferred to be ruled by men of their own blood, she had no doubt, and the powerful Maratha Confederacy might have had the backing of the Hindu millions, except for one thing: they no longer observed the long dead Shivaji's compassionate laws. Now, drunk with power, they defiled ruthlessly those armed or unarmed people whose territories they raided and conquered, whom they either massacred or cowed by crippling taxes. Unlike the British, Maratha chiefs failed to pay their troops regularly, and hence forced them to depend on plunder for their livelihood.

With the Mogul empire tottering, chiefs, nobles, land-owners—and not a few Europeans like Colonel Markham—carved out fiefs for themselves, minted their own coins and appropriated the revenue, consequently weakening the unity of the country; not that the peoples of the sub-continent were homogeneous. Since Indian nationalism did not exist, the present state of affairs was inevitable. Internecine warfare prevailed, and how it would all end, she had no idea. Rumours proclaimed that the British, the rising power in the country, with their superior weapons and disciplined armies, would eventually triumph. They had established paramountcy in Bengal, one of the richest provinces, that was at present flourishing under the rule of Warren Hastings, who was successfully combating the corruption once rife among Indian and British traders.

Tara's thoughts came to an abrupt halt. Sounds of a scuffle and muffled screams were borne to her ears. She leaned forward, gripping the fretted screen. Then, to her bafflement, she saw a group of mounted men dressed in black, their faces masked, carrying aloft blazing torches and galloping through the entrance arch. At the next moment, the main courtyard was crowded with horsemen, black turbans pulled low on their foreheads, their horses' hooves clicking, striking sparks on the flagstones. They dismounted, drew long, curved sabres that flashed in the torchlight, and rushed into the palace. Then horrendous shrieks erupted from all directions. Terror seized her, and her heart banged in her throat with the sudden knowledge that this was a raid!

She leaped from her seat and stumbled to the door, anxious to rush down and warn her parents of the danger, and to be with them. Dear God, help her poor pregnant mother! To her alarm, she could not open the door, no matter how much she tugged. The screeches of agony and terror rising from below made her hurl herself back to the screen, where she froze. In the courtyard, massacre raged.

In horror she stared at the carnage: men, women and children were being dragged out and ruthlessly butchered. She could not drag her eyes away; unable to move, unable to utter a sound. But when she saw her mother, her father and the Portuguese Jesuit priest, their arms bound behind their backs, being hauled out and forced to kneel, she screamed and raced for the door again, rattled it, tugged and hammered. Her screams were swallowed in the uproar below. She staggered back, and then she saw the decapitated bodies of her beloved parents and the good priest. In dazed helplessness, she sagged dry-eyed on the seat, oblivious of her clammy hands and sweat-soaked body. The terror-crazed cries petered out, and she stared down in stupefaction.

Then, having accomplished their grisly task, the masked men with flaring torches abandoned the courtyard, leaving it shrouded in darkness. Only the restless movements of tethered horses warned her that the killers must be at large inside the palace.

As she had feared, from the interior a voice yelled, '*Sub maro!* Kill all! No quarter!' More agonised cries for mercy followed.

Then silence. A deathly, eerie silence.

After a while, deadened footfalls sounded on the double flight of steps leading to the roof. At first Tara wanted to draw attention to herself, to allow the murderers to kill her; she believed she could not go on living after witnessing her parents' terrible deaths. But then an inner sense of preservation prompted her to think differently. She would live! She would live to find out who had committed and commanded this barbarity, and why.

The footsteps had now reached the second flight, and she spurred herself to action. She swept her frantic gaze round, and looked under the seat where the bolsters were stowed. Tearing them out, she scrambled into their place and heaped them against her, so that she lay completely hidden.

Moments later, she heard men padding round the pavilion and the door rattled. *'Non, mon capitaine.'*

French! Tara stopped breathing. She understood a little of the language.

'Do you want us to break it down, Captain?'

Tara's father had mentioned that French mercenaries were assisting the Maratha Confederacy. How soon they had moved to the north-east of Bihar!

'No. It is jammed, I fear. In all probability it has not been used in years. *Mon Dieu!* There is no one in there. Must we tarry? There's the risk that we'll be discovered. Remember Chandra's last words: that help is on the way?'

'And are we to believe the words of a desperate man? *Un moment.* I'll move my torch closer to the screens in case I can see anyone.'

Tara's heart leaped and tumbled, blood pounded in her head. She peered over the bolsters. Light wafted back and forth, and swiftly she dropped down. Scarcely breathing, but trembling violently, she prayed for her life to be spared for the purpose of inflicting a merciless revenge.

'There's a bolster on the seat, Captain.'

Tara swallowed, cursing herself for being so remiss. Go away, go away! she silently urged them.

'Come, André, *mon ami.* You worry over trifles. Let us collect the booty, and be gone.'

The light and the footsteps faded, and she was left in the black silence with her thoughts, unmoving, listening to men's voices coming from below issuing orders for the loot to be carried out and loaded on carts. Finally, the last horse galloped away. In the quiet, she released a long shuddering breath, and with it, lost consciousness.

'Oowah! Oowahoowah!' The howling of jackals brought Tara out of oblivion. At first she lay wide-eyed, staring up into blackness, feeling suffocated and streaming with perspiration. A heaviness weighted her down, and pushing with her hands, she encountered the bolsters. Awareness flooded in, bringing the memory of the horrifying massacre, the cruel deaths of her parents and her people. Yet she was so stricken with grief and a sense of unreality at what she had witnessed that she felt incapable of shedding tears. Part of her brain refused to accept that her parents were gone. It must all be a hallucination.

'Oowah! Oowahoowah!' The jackals were real; they had gathered in the courtyard below. She could hear them snarling, quarrelling over the dead. Choking back sobs, and thrusting aside the bolsters, she forced her cramped limbs out from beneath the seat.

A gentle breeze wafted through the fretwork of screens and chilled her sweating body. She rubbed the numbness out of her legs and painfully rose to her feet. For a while she gulped in the cool air. She had to get away from the sounds of snarls and howls down in the courtyard. She staggered to the door, her bones feeling as if they had turned to jelly. She leaned heavily against it and then started back, remembering that it had jammed. Oh no! She was imprisoned. In panic, she gripped the wrought iron, and heaved. It gave so easily that she was compelled to cling to it for support as it swung out. Some miracle has taken place, she thought, amazed. Perhaps the dead yogi's spirit has come to my help. She thrust aside the thought, and painfully recollected that her mother and the Jesuit priest had impressed upon her not to be superstitious. What, then, was the explanation? She frowned, trying to solve the mystery, and as she gave up with a shrug, the solution suddenly emerged: the iron had contracted in the coolness of the night. It surprised her that she could think of such a triviality while her brain was befogged with grief.

The starlight shone brightly enough for her to see clearly. She gathered her skirts up above her ankles and as softly as possible crept down the steps and hesitantly entered her chamber. A single lamp, left burning in a niche, showed the extent of the destruction. Wall hangings lay shredded on the floor, divans ripped and overturned, cushions scattered. Her carved *almirah*, where her clothes were once stowed, had been wrenched open and valuable saris and European-style taffeta and muslin dresses were gone. The caskets holding her jewels had vanished from the top of a wrecked dressing-table, and all the mirrors in the room had been smashed, their gold frames looted. Certainly she had not been suffering from delusions: the raid had occurred. But she could not accept her parents' murders. On reflection, she could well have mistaken other people for them. They had had their backs turned towards her so that she had not seen their faces. They must have been abducted, she decided; no one would dare to kill them! Even so, she would have to find them, and renewed her vow to wreak vengeance on all who had been responsible for the raid.

For the present, Tara forced herself to concentrate on one purpose: to change into simple garments and flee undetected from this palace of tragedy, a compulsion created by fear driving her on. As yet, she had no idea of to whom or where she intended to make her way.

She slipped into a side-chamber, where a beloved Punjabi servant had slept—perhaps she lay butchered in the courtyard—and in the wreckage, found cotton clothes strewn on the floor. She picked up dark blue pyjamas and a hip-length shirt, and changed into them. They would allow her ease of movement, unlike the restricting sari. Taking off her valuable jewellery, she knotted it into one end of a *chuddah* and draped the shawl over her head.

The grey of dawn brightened the sky when she stepped out into the garden. Today instead of birdsong greeting her, she heard the flapping of heavy wings. The ugly grey vultures wheeled, ready to swoop on the front courtyard and finish the gruesome remains left by the jackals. More vultures gathered above, and fright impelled her along the stone pathway. She dragged back the bolts and opened the wooden door in the wall of the garden. An embankment confronted her, which swept down to a moat.

She would have no difficulty in scrambling down and wading across, now that the level of the water had dropped in the hot season. What posed an impossibility was that the far side was too steep to climb, at least for her. But a few hundred yards away, a bridge on stone piers spanned the moat and led to a road. She kept on the narrow path and headed for the bridge, hoping to make her escape over it. Halfway there, she came to an abrupt halt and crouched against the wall.

She heard the galloping of horses, espied the riders, indistinct in the dawn, except for their bright blue mantles billowing behind them. These, she knew without a doubt, were the famous Blue Cloaks of Colonel Markham, and Tara opened her mouth to hail them, when the shouted command *'En avant!'* was borne towards her on the breeze.

She clamped her teeth together and pressed herself flat, out of sight. French troops had been involved in the murder of her father's people and the kidnapping of her parents, and she felt sure that these were Markham's mercenaries. Hatred for this man boiled in Tara's veins; she believed he had engineered the massacre and probably held her parents captive. She recalled her father's words: 'Sikandar Sahib alone knows how weak our defences are.'

This mercenary had taken advantage of the fact and now, on the pretence of helping, he had returned to clean up the wreckage and establish himself as the new ruler. More terrifying, if he knew she was at large, he would seek her out, and imprison her with her parents or kill her—to eliminate the last witness!

CHAPTER TWO

ONCE THE riders had entered the yellow-tiled courtyard,
Tara crept forward. She was shivering from the effects
of witnessing the massacre, but this did not prevent her
from thinking and planning.

There must be some method whereby she could cross
to the opposite bank without using the bridge. Perhaps
enemy guards were stationed at both ends, although from
this distance she could not be sure. Moats existed as a
means of defence, therefore bridges provided the only
access and exit to and from the palace and were guarded
by armed sentries. North of the citadel was another
bridge, but in order to reach it she would need to circle
miles of the protective wall, and by then she might be
discovered. No, she would have to utilise the nearest exit.

Taking deep breaths to try and control her shudders,
Tara moved quietly and peered with caution through the
grille of the side gate and perceived to her relief that the
yard was empty. She slipped in and, keeping to the
shadows, flitted to the main entrance, where there seemed
to be no signs of guards. From the direction of the inner
courtyard where the massacre had been executed, she
heard raised voices, but was unable to grasp what was
being said.

She had now arrived at the bridge. Without further
hesitation she sped along it, grateful for the noise-
lessness of her thin-soled slippers. On reaching the
shaded road, she leaned against a trunk to recover her
breath and relieve the twinge in her side, but the trem-

bling would not subside. Later, she pushed on, walking briskly, keeping to the side of the deserted and dusty road in the mottled shadows of flanking trees. Every so often she glanced back in fear to see if she had been spotted.

Her breakfast hour had long since passed, and although the thought of food sickened her, she yearned to quench her raging thirst. She ran her tongue along parched lips. There must be a village close by where she could request a drink. All her life she had lived within the confines of the palace, a town in itself complete with gardens and *maidans*, open spaces, therefore she had no conception of what lay beyond in the countryside. However, she did know that the state spread for fifty miles and that her father collected revenue from the villages within the area; but without a map, she had no idea of their locations. Raja Todar Ram's land encircled Chiriabagh. Now she cursed herself for neglecting to take an interest in her father's administrative work.

Slowing down, Tara took a quick glance round and observed that the bridge lay out of sight. Ahead, the road ribboned endlessly. On the left stretched vast expanses of sugarcane and fields of grain; on the right flourished bamboo thickets, jungle and forest. She had decided to cross to the left of the road and look for a path in the canefields, which she hoped would lead her to a village, when she heard the distant drumming of horses' hooves. She halted, raised her trembling hand to shade her eyes from the glare, and strained to obtain a view of the riders. Through a haze of dust, horsemen in blue cloaks were riding towards her. This must be another contingent of the mercenary army—and the thought created more violent shudders of apprehension

in her. Dashing behind the nearest tree, she pressed
against it, scarcely breathing.

Louder and louder came the galloping hooves and then
the horses rode past, leaving clouds of choking dust
hanging in the still, hot air; but she had noticed a woman
riding side-saddle, dressed in a European-style riding-
coat teamed with a full skirt. Her beautiful, discon-
tented face was visible beneath her wide-brimmed hat
that sported ostrich-plumes.

Too dangerous to use the road now, Tara reflected.
The idea of locating a village she soon abandoned, in
case Colonel Markham sent out a search-party for her.
Her only refuge lay in the jungle, where reptiles and wild
animals thrived. Staring at the dense growth confronting her, she wondered where to start looking for a
path. Her slippers would be no protection against snakes
and rough ground. Taking extreme care, she ventured
out on the road, and staying in the shade of the trees,
moved forward, her eyes scanning the bamboo barrier
for signs of a break.

Then she heard what sounded like stampeding cattle
heading towards her and darted behind a trunk and gazed
up. The tree looked easy to climb, with enough foot-
holds and low twisted branches. Without further hesitation she scrambled up, but in the process broke off a
brittle branch she had grabbed for support, and almost
hurtled to the ground. Finally she regained her balance,
settled in the fork of the tree. Breathing hard from her
exertions, she gazed below to observe what had caused
the stampede. The sound seemed to converge from all
directions, and then a herd of bison came thundering
towards the road, trampling down the bamboo. The
black beasts veered away, slowed down and returned to
the forest. The animals must have been frightened by

the galloping Blue Cloaks, and were satisfied that danger no longer threatened.

From her vantage-point she discerned a network of animal tracks through the jungle, and taking careful note of the distance to the nearest spoor, she climbed down and picked up the snapped-off branch to slash at the bamboos, bending them sufficiently to allow her to penetrate towards the track. It would lead her to water, she felt certain. At last she emerged on the rugged path and for a while fought for breath, wiping her streaming face with the end of her *chuddah*. She stumbled along, every so often tapping the branch on the earth, like a blind person, as a gesture to warn off reptiles. Although thirsty, and wilting in the torrid heat, she pressed ahead, refusing to rest, determined to survive, determined to avenge the massacred people, determined to find help to oust Markham—mercenary, murderer and abductor of her parents. Preoccupied with grief, bitterness and hatred, barely aware of her surroundings, she followed the spoor until she came upon a glade, and there sighted the most important thing in her life: water.

She ran towards the stream, crying out in delight, and dropped to her knees in the wet mud on the bank to drink thirstily of the clear liquid, then she bathed her face. Sitting on a rock, she kicked off her dusty, scuffed slippers and paddled her feet in the cool depths, sighing, and this time shuddering with pleasure.

When she had rested, she focused her thoughts on her next course of action. First I must find somewhere to shelter for the remainder of the day, she told herself, and decided to push on, conscious of the lurking danger of attack by wild animals that, come sundown, would relinquish their foraging and straggle to the stream. As though her thoughts, by some strange communication, had contacted the animal world, a wild boar appeared with her young, tails in the air, heading for the water. Grabbing her slippers and the branch, Tara hid behind a rock.

The mother grunted, and nudged her young into the stream, where they squealed, splashed and played. When they had drunk their fill, she snorted a command and the family headed back into the jungle. Such an endearing scene brought a faint sad smile to Tara's pale mouth. Animals' simple lives had to abide by the laws of the wild, with none of the complications humans created for themselves: always clamouring for power, surrounded by the scorching winds of war, by endless killings and massacres. She stiffened, her brain suffused with the terrible memory of the slaughtered people left to be devoured by jackals and vultures. Shudders racked her body. She shut her eyes, praying silently, saying the *De Profundis*, the prayer for the dead that the priest had taught her. Was that him and her parents? No, no....

She opened her eyes and said to herself, Like the creatures of the jungle, I too must submit to the law of the wild until I can assemble my thoughts and plan for the future. First, I need to find some kind of haven before sundown. With a weary sigh, she rose and ambled round the glade. After a while her alert eyes sighted another path, on which appeared to be human footprints. From the hacked bamboo canes and shrubbery bordering it, surely it must lead to a village or dwelling? A small surge of hope lifted her depression, and squaring her shoulders, armed with the branch, she moved deeper into the forest.

Trees arched high overhead, shutting out the worst of the burning rays. Around her, insects buzzed; perched on branches, green- and purple-necked parakeets screeched; other birds camouflaged in the undergrowth

rose and flapped as she thumped the branch. Ring-tailed
langurs loped up tree-trunks, baring their teeth and
hooting their annoyance. Every few paces she wiped the
beads of sweat gathering on her brow, brushed at sand-
flies hovering in front of her eyes, and staggered on. She
had no notion of how long she had been on her feet,
but when the track took her out into treeless open
country where black buck grazed and the sun's rays
hammered down, she observed from her stunted shadow
that it must be a little past noon.

Tara came upon it suddenly, hidden in a copse, a round
tower strongly built of red bricks. The footpath opened
onto a mud-packed space forming a yard in front of the
building. Excited fear pulsed in her temples as she moved
silently to the door. Black paint peeled off it, but it
looked sturdy. She conquered the impulse to peep
through the large keyhole. The solid wood did not budge
when she pushed at it. Tentatively she knocked and
waited, listening for footfalls. Her sharply attuned ears
caught the sound of a slow shuffling, then silence. She
drew in a sharp breath and again knocked, louder, her
heart rapping at an increased rate.

'*Kaun hai?*' a croaking voice asked from some distance inside. 'Who is it? What do you want?' It sounded
like an old woman.

The shuffling drew nearer, and Tara gulped, her shuddering increasing, and answered as calmly as she could,
'I am a lost wayfarer. I seek food and shelter.' She hoped
she sounded humble.

A long pause.

Tara moistened her dry lips to speak again, when she
heard bolts being dragged. The door opened a crack,
wide enough for her to glimpse a wrinkled brown visage
and a white eye. A blind person! It was a frightening

face, with wisps of grey hair straying from a sari-covered head.

'Who are you?' the old woman again enquired, this time sharply, revealing brown teeth between cracked, purple lips. 'Are you alone?'

'Yes, I am quite alone, good mother.'

'You are high-born—I gather so much from your speech—and you are young. The high-born do not roam the forest alone.' The door began to close.

'Please!' Tara pressed her hand on the wood, keeping the door ajar. 'I can explain, if you would allow me to speak, good mother.'

The old face peered out, hideous, with a great beak of a nose and flared nostrils. Cocking her head to one side, the crone appeared to be listening intently. 'I am old and have few belongings. There is little for you to rob, young one, if you are so minded. Yes, even the high-born steal!'

'I am no thief,' Tara retorted with a hint of indignation. 'All I ask is shelter and food. Or perhaps you can direct me to the nearest village?'

The crone's scoured forehead wrinkled in a frown. She shook her head and stepped back, opening the door wider. 'Come in. If you harm me, Raja Sahib will hunt you down as he does the tiger.'

Tara wondered if the crone referred to Chandra, her father, or to Raja Todar Ram. She thought it prudent to leave the branch outside and propped it noiselessly against the wall; it would not do to frighten the old soul. She slipped through the narrow opening the old one grudgingly allowed, then the door slammed and the bolts were pushed home.

It was cool and dark inside after the glare, and rainbow-coloured formations danced in front of Tara's eyes.

'Come,' the old voice cracked and snapped, 'follow me.'

Tara blinked, forcing her eyes to accustom themselves to the gloom. In front, the old woman, thin, bent, shambled along, and she followed, her ruined slippers sinking into layers of dust. She turned her head, taking in the surroundings, and vaguely glimpsed sacks stacked against the rounded walls where, higher up, geckos crept like miniature crocodiles. From the high ceiling hung dirty beard-like wisps of cobwebs, and the whole place smelt of sacking, grain and dust. The crone entered an adjoining, rectangular chamber partitioned from the large room by a split bamboo curtain. A string bed, covered with a dirty cotton quilt, stood against one wall.

'*Bhaito,*' the crone commanded, patting the air with an unexpectedly elegant hand towards the bed, and repeated her command to sit.

Never had Tara seen such a filthy room. A mat woven from coconut fibre sprawled at an angle in front of the bed, and bits of rice and food decorated it. Ants scurried across the dirty flagstone floor, flies were clustered on the rice and food and flew about the room, some settling on the dirty walls. The air smelt rank. She wrinkled her nose in distaste and perched fussily on the edge of the *charpoy*, while the old woman shuffled into another chamber, muttering discontentedly that she would fetch some food.

Flies harassed her and she brushed them off, but after a while they ceased to annoy her. As she lay back on the string bed her shivering grew less, and with the slight relaxation came the onslaught of tears and heartrending sobs. The scene of the carnage floated before her mind's eye, and she came to the terrible realisation that she had indeed seen the slaughter of her parents. Although she had tried to delude herself that she could not recognise them from the back, she could, of course; she had been too close to them in life not to know their physical appearance from every angle.

The sobbing gradually petered out, but her tears kept up a steady flow—she had no idea for how long. A profound lethargy seemed to draw her down into a nether world of gloom, and from somewhere above came the anxious enquiries of the crone, which made no impression on her and she made no effort to answer. Periodically she drifted off to sleep, only to be startled awake by nightmares of the massacre. Often she woke up screaming and weeping in grief. Then a dry cool hand would soothe her sweat-dampened brow until she sank into dreamless oblivion. Sometimes when she woke to stare unseeingly at the high ceiling, her mind a blank, the crone would offer her food and drink. But Tara pushed it away, turned over and wept again.

Suddenly one morning the mists of disorientation began to lift. Tara woke to full awareness to hear the woman clattering pans in what she assumed must be the kitchen. No longer did she weep or shudder. She finally accepted that her parents were dead and that she would have to live with the ache of grief for a long time, perhaps for years. But the healing tears had washed away the worst of the pain, and it was time she pulled herself together and offered to help the poor blind crone. But when she attempted to sit up, such a weakness overwhelmed her that, with a groan, she dropped back.

She heard the old woman approaching the bed from the vicinity of the kitchen. 'You called, young one?'

Tara stared up at the wrinkled brown face, and asked, 'Could I have a drink, please? Some water?'

A smile stretched the cracked lips. 'Ah, you feel better, young one! I am cooking *dal*. Would you like some?' The old woman looked pleased that she was showing signs of recovery.

'Thank you, if it's not too much trouble.'

'I will fetch.' The crone shuffled away.

Again Tara tried to sit up, and this time she experienced no dizziness. She was also aware of feeling dirty and sticky, and wondered how long she had lain on this filthy bed. Her hair had become a tangled mess, which she combed as best she could with her fingers, and managed to arrange the greasy tresses in an untidy knot at her nape. Her clothes smelt of stale sweat and stuck uncomfortably to her body. She would ask the crone where she could find water to bathe. Just then the old woman brought in a brass bowl of *dal*, thick lentil gruel, and a platter of chappatis, and gratefully Tara ate every morsel.

For the next couple of days she regained her strength, but the old woman rejected all help until Tara felt strong enough; she even brought in a bucket of cold water for her to bathe. The floor was so hot that the puddles formed from her splashing evaporated in no time.

Tara still bore the misery of grief in her heart, but now she could cope with it. Besides, she had a vow to fulfil: revenge. But at present that could wait.

After breakfast one morning, the old woman climbed into the centre of the *charpoy* and sat cross-legged while Tara perched on the edge.

'Now I think it is time you told me what has happened to make you so distraught, and why a high-born lady such as you is lost in the forest. What distress are you running from?'

'I was forced to run away, good mother.' Tara saw no reason to deceive the crone, who looked harmless; it was a relief to confide in someone.

'Come, tell me, my child. Share your troubles with me and I shall bestow what comfort I can,' the old lady said in gentle tones, her voice oddly cultured.

Tara hesitated, regretting her decision to unburden her soul and reluctant to reveal the horror she had witnessed and to live again the pain of grief, the emptiness of no hope.

'Who are your parents?' the crone enquired with soft insistence.

Taking a deep breath, Tara gave in. 'My mother was English. Twenty-two years ago she visited Chiriabagh with her merchant father, who wished to purchase top-quality sugarcane, spices and carpets for the East India Company. She and my father fell in love, but she refused to marry him until he had given up his Hindu wife and concubines. To please her, he sent them away, making ample provision for them. I often wondered who these women were and if they resented my father for discarding them.'

'Who is your father?'

'He *was* Raja Rao Chandra of Chiriabagh. He...'

'Raja Rao Chandra? Then you must be the Princess Tara Bai!' The crone sounded astounded.

'Yes. My father...'

'What has become of your parents, Tara Bai?' She unfolded her legs, dragged herself off the bed and stood head bent towards the girl, a look of consternation on her creased face.

'I'm trying to tell you, good mother. My parents, and the Jesuit priest who married them, were—were massacred.' She stifled a sob, brushed away a tear.

'How long ago was this, Tara Bai?'

'How long have I been here?'

'Three nights, my child.'

'They were slaughtered the night before I arrived here.'

She heard the crone's sharp intake of breath and her horrified whisper, 'Massacred!' After a stunned pause, she continued, 'You mentioned a Jesuit priest, therefore you must be a Christian.'

Tara nodded, then, aware that the old woman could not see, said, 'Yes. The priest baptised me and educated me in western culture. But I also had Indian sages to instruct me in the religions, customs and history of this country.'

'And where is your husband, Tara Bai? You must surely be married. Or was he also slaughtered?'

'No,' Tara said dabbing her eyes with one end of her *chuddah*. 'No. I have no husband, although I am now twenty years old. I wanted to marry for love, and my mother agreed. But before—before the killings, my father told me that I was to be betrothed to Raja Todar Ram of Motipur.' She saw the old woman stiffen, and wondered if she knew him. 'I refused to obey my father. We quarrelled. And that—that very night, he was slain.'

'Now I understand what ailed you. Do not blame yourself, Tara Bai. You were not to know that tragedy would strike. Your father would forgive you, and you must forgive yourself.'

'You seem to know much about my people, good mother. Who are you, and how come you to be in this tower?' Tara felt ashamed for thinking only of her own troubles when the old woman had to endure worse circumstances on account of her blindness.

The crone settled herself again on the *charpoy*. 'My name is Uma. I would not make suttee when my man died.'

'Suttee! But it is illegal in Bihar, which is a British domain. My father forbade the cruel rite in his state.'

Uma brushed the air dismissively. 'The Moguls too prohibited the rite, but it is still practised. Let us hope that the English will be more successful. I fear there are too few of them to maintain the ban.'

True, Tara acknowledged. 'I'm sorry to interrupt. Pray continue.'

'My man was cruel, you understand? He beat me every day, and I did not wish to save his soul by burning with him. If he had treated me well, I would have become a *sati*, a martyr. He was evil. May the god Vishnu return him as a rat! I told the priests that if they forced me to burn, I would curse them.' She smacked her lips, relishing her triumph. 'A *sati*'s curse is feared, so they let me go. It was decreed that I must not escape punishment, hence I was blinded and left in the jungle. Your father, Raja Sahib, found me and employed people to treat my eyes, but they could not restore my sight. Ever since, your father allowed me to live in this tower.' The old woman's voice quavered. 'Now the devils have killed him! Have you any suspicion of who his murderers are, Tara Bai?'

'A contingent of armed men rode into the palace at dawn after the massacre. They might be responsible; they spoke French, and there were Frenchmen among the perpetrators.' Tara went on to relate how she had witnessed the slaughter and how she happened to survive. 'I fear they have discovered I am missing and will start

a search. Do you think it's safe for me to remain here?
I might even put your life in danger.'

'Few know about this tower. I have remained here for
many moons, and only twice did your father come
hunting with three of his men. Now they must all be
dead, so who can know about it?' Then the crone began
to weep. 'Your father was a good man.'

Tara too wept. Her heart swelled with pity for the old
blind soul. It consoled her to know that another shared
her grief.

'My child,' the old one said, sniffing, 'sorrowing will
not bring back the dead. Assuredly we must not forget
them, but for the moment we must persevere on keeping
ourselves alive. The more so for you who are young and
have much to live for.' Without pausing, she asked, 'Are
you hungry?'

Hungry for revenge! Tara thought silently. And as
soon as I can think with cool logic, I'll make plans: keep
my pledge for retribution.

'Princess, I have some *dal* cooking, and chappatis.
That is all I can offer,' Uma admitted ruefully.

'Your *dal* and chappatis are delicious, but I fear I'm
not very hungry. If you tell me where the food is I'll
bring it.' Tara smiled drily to herself; at one time she
would have scorned such peasant fare, but now she ate
it with gratitude. In truth, God knew how to humble
the rich!

'No, I will bring it, Tara Bai. I know where all is kept.
You *must* eat something.' Old Uma ambled out through
a narrow archway draped with a dirty curtain.

Flies buzzed and settled on Tara, and with a grimace
and shudder of disgust she brushed them away. Now
that she had recovered from the worst of her shock, she
decided that in no circumstances could she accustom

herself to live in such filthy surroundings. As soon as she had eaten, she would clean and tidy this tower. Though she had never done housework in her life, she had watched the servants in the palace and had some idea of what to do. Old Uma was not to blame; she was blind and too old. Probably she occupied her waking hours in lighting a cooking-fire and feeling about for food to cook for herself.

Uma returned, bearing a loaded brass tray. Tara hurried forward and took it. 'Sit down, Uma, and I'll put the food in front of you.'

'No, Tara Bai, you eat first.' She caught the lobes of her ears and wagged her head. 'Never let it be known that Uma ate before a rajkumari!'

'I'm no longer a princess, Uma.'

Arguments ensued, and at last Tara grew quiet. Old Uma would be none the wiser whether she ate or not if she insisted in clearing up, but for the sake of her health she decided to eat something.

While the old woman consumed her share of the thick lentil mixture, she apologised for the state of the place. 'Raja Sahib paid one *chokra* to cook and clean for me, but that rogue of a boy stayed but two dawns, stole the few rupees the raja had given me and ran away. Without my sight, I cannot move from here. How could I go for help?'

'You seem to have done remarkably well. It is a marvel that you are able to cook and light a fire without burning yourself.'

'When one is alone, one is forced to help oneself, or perish. Is it not so? I prayed to the good god Vishnu, and he helped.'

When they had eaten, Tara asked, 'Er... Is there any
drinking water? No, do not move. Tell me where I can
get some.'

A barrage of protest followed, but eventually Uma
subsided under Tara's adamant attitude and pointed in
the direction of the dirty curtain. 'You will find it—pooh!
very dirty!'

Yes, in truth, the kitchen was appalling. The brick-
built stove, known as a *chullah*, was full of ashes.
Cooking utensils were unwashed. Soot covered the
ceiling, and grease, flour and spilt food were spattered
on the stone floor. Flies swarmed everywhere, and the
room stank of stale food and acrid smoke.

Tara grimaced, and placed the tray on the bricked-up
extension of the *chullah*, then lifted the wooden bars
securing the back door, and pushed it wide to allow the
hot but clean air into the room. She spotted the narrow-
necked sandstone goblet, secure in a wooden stand, and
lifting it out, poured cool water into her parched mouth,
and replaced the vessel.

She stepped outside on the hard-packed earth. At once,
the scorching pre-monsoon wind blasted her face and
she shielded her eyes from the glare. Beyond the clearing
grew shrubs that dipped downwards out of sight. She
followed a path to a slope, and there below flowed a
small river, a tributary of the Ghauri, she believed. So
this was where Old Uma collected water and managed
to survive. Then a clatter of metal made her swivel round
and climb back to the clearing. Uma was shambling
towards the path, bearing a pile of unwashed cooking-
pots, and Tara marvelled at her sense of direction.

'Leave those pots, Uma. I'll wash them later. First,
let me tidy up inside. Is there another *charpoy* I can use?

I've slept in yours for long enough and deprived you of many a good night's sleep.'

She tried to remove the utensils from the elegant wobbling hands, but the old woman protested loudly. Yes, there were beds stacked in the large room, Uma answered grumpily, for was this not Raja Sahib's hunting-tower? If Tara looked, she would find ample bedding and clothes in boxes near the wall.

After searching in the large chamber, she found what she wanted, but first she had to clean the place. As she had seen the palace servants doing, she swept out the dust and washed the floors, but unlike the servants, she worked slowly and clumsily. She threw the mat and all the bedding out into the sun, then flooded the floor of Uma's room, brushing the water out into the yard *via* the kitchen.

Uma wailed protests at Tara doing too much work, and generally made a nuisance of herself. Nevertheless she was thankful for the occupation and even the exasperating old woman, for they diverted her mind from her own misery. However, the nightmares did not leave her, and that night, she woke up screaming.

'Come, Tara, drink this.' Cool water touched her lips. She sat up and gulped from a rough clay cup held to her mouth by a shaking hand. For a moment she felt totally disoriented.

'It is I, Tara. You had a bad dream, I am thinking.' She recognized Uma's voice, which made her aware of her surroundings.

'Thank you, Uma.' She gently pushed the cup away and flopped back, exhausted. Perhaps she had worked too hard. Her eyes adjusted to the gloom, and she distinguished the woman crouching on the floor.

'I was dreaming of the slaughter. Why—why did God let my parents meet so cruel an end? Surely they did not warrant that? And will this grief ever leave me?'

Uma rose painfully and seated herself on the side of Tara's *charpoy*. Her thin hand felt for the girl's damp face, then moved up to stroke her dishevelled hair. 'My child, no one can question God's motives. What I have learnt from life is that few of us escape suffering. It is up to us to surmount our woes and seek to triumph over misfortunes or our enemies, lest we perish. You must not work to the pitch of exhaustion. Give yourself time to heal.' All the while Uma stroked Tara's forehead and smoothed her sweat-soaked hair, and the soothing movements sent her back to sleep.

In the following weeks the nightmares grew less, and the terrible vengeance she had vowed to wreak seemed a remote possibility. First, her enemy was the powerful Colonel Markham with a large army at his disposal. Second, how could she, a lone woman, carry out her pledge to destroy him without enormous help?

In the meantime, she had managed to clean out the tower, doing a little every day. In the late afternoons she particularly enjoyed taking refreshing baths in the cool stream, and used the soap-berries she had found in one of the sacks. After washing her clothes, she would wrap herself in a length of cotton she had purloined from one of many boxes.

Old Uma continued to insist on doing the cooking, and because she knew she had no skill, Tara agreed. The two women would eat in companionable silence seated outside on a *durrie*, a cotton mat. In the hot twilight, Tara watched flocks of birds and heard their noisy 'Charr! Charr! Charr!', their wings flapping as they flew to roost in the trees. After scrubbing the utensils with a wad of grass and river sand, again as the kitchen servants at the palace did, Tara would help Uma to bathe and then see her into a now clean bed. When darkness fell, Tara would retire to her own *charpoy* in the large chamber. Occasionally she woke from a nightmare and prayed for a way to avenge her peoples' deaths.

As the days wore on, she felt strong enough to work long hours in cleaning, and washing Uma's filthy clothes and the unused pile of musty-smelling male garments she had unearthed and kept for herself. A strong rapport sprang up between the two women, though neither of them discussed their pasts any further. Like many old people, Tara noticed, Uma went into details of her aching bones. Moreover, she grumbled about how loudly the *charpoy* creaked every time she turned over; about the howling jackals, the twittering birds; about the scorching wind and the noise it created; about the racket of crickets and the bites and buzz of the mosquitoes. 'Very noisy place this, Tara Bai!'

Tara smiled her amusement, letting the old woman rail on. She understood that the hearing sense of the blind became heightened. And so it proved, one hot night.

The women sat outside on a *charpoy* and Tara was preoccupied with how comfortable she had made herself, and guiltily thought it was time to move on and start making enquiries about the massacre. Tomorrow she would discuss it with Uma.

'Tara Bai, I hear horses!' Uma suddenly shouted.

Tara leaped to her feet and stood listening, but heard nothing. 'I can't hear anything. Are you sure?'

'I tell you horses are coming this way!' Uma pushed the sari off her head and cupped her ear. 'Hah, it is so!'

'Come in, quickly!' Tara helped the old woman down from the *charpoy*, and half carried her to the kitchen. She slammed and barred the door. Racing to the entrance, she shot the bolts. Then, remembering the branch she had left outside on her arrival, she unlocked the door, snatched the potential weapon in, and propped it against the wall. It might come in handy. There were open skylights in the roof, but no windows in the building. Trying to keep panic at bay, she lit a lantern and carried it into the large room. Ropes hung from the top and bottom frames of the skylights by which they could be opened and shut, and setting down the lamp, she pulled the frames closed, praying that no one could climb to them from the outside. At last, as she stood immobile, straining to listen, she heard the distinct sound of galloping horses.

'They are your father's murderers, I am thinking,' Uma wailed. 'They seek you, and they will kill us, Tara Bai. What is to become of us?'

Tara clamped a hand over Uma's mouth, and whispered, 'Quiet! If they cannot get in, they may go away.' She felt Uma's tears on her hand. Gently she removed it, hugging the trembling old woman to her, guiding her to the *charpoy* in the main room, where Tara slept. There they both sat down, huddled together.

Dousing the lantern, Tara focused her attention on the approaching sounds. The horses had now entered the yard in front of the door. Saddles squeaked, bridles clunked and jingled as men dismounted—they must be men! Tara's heart slammed like a door in the wind, her breath coming fast one moment and seizing up the next.

Male voices bawled orders. Tara heard horses pacing, making a circuit of the building. Some men had climbed on the roof, as she had feared—the flame of a torch was visible through the murky glass of the skylight. She dragged Uma to the floor and they both lay there, stunned.

Tara swallowed to relieve the agonising terror locked in her throat, suddenly recalling that in her haste she had left freshly-washed utensils at the back, also the *charpoy*, the *durrie* and some clothes spread to dry over the bushes near the river.

Then, cutting through the other sounds, came a deep and powerful male voice with a drawling accent, 'Open the door! We know the building is occupied. If you do not open up, we'll force our way in!'

CHAPTER THREE

TARA'S FACE turned cold and bloodless with horror when Uma shrieked, 'Go away, rogues! I am but an old, blind woman seeking to die in peace in my last refuge. Would you deny me such?'

A concerned but indistinct discourse ensued from outside and Tara tacitly congratulated the old woman for her bravery; no doubt she had spoken effective words. With luck, the riders might feel some compassion for the old one and ride away. The thought evoked in her a sense of shame and cowardice, and she rebuked herself silently for sheltering behind Uma.

'We shall not harm you, you have our word. Come now, old lady. Open, I say! Do not compel us to use force,' the deep drawling voice called again. These men had no compassion for the old, Tara thought acidly as the man continued, 'We are a hunting party, and we need this tower.'

Tara pushed herself off the floor. 'Let them in,' she whispered, struck with an angry curiosity to view the owner of the drawling voice and do battle with him. 'Either way, we cannot escape. If we enrage them there is every likelihood that they'll break in and harm us. But while they remain reasonably good-tempered, there may be hope.'

'All right; as Tara Bai wishes.' Uma breathed out a long resigned sigh and made to rise.

Tara had second thoughts. She helped Uma up, and pressed her to sit on the bed. 'I'll go.' Bracing herself, throwing back her shoulders and scooping in a deep breath, she moved somewhat unsteadily towards the door, her heart booming like kettledrums.

Just as she approached, fists hammered on the door. 'This is your last chance. Open at once!'

'Stop your noise!' Tara plucked up the courage to shout, although her insides were coiled tight with enraged fear. 'Move back while I draw the bolts. And don't think you can do as you please. Beware!'

A baffled silence followed, then, 'By God! How many of you are hiding in there?'

Before Tara could frame a reply, old Uma bawled, 'Her Highness Tara Bai, the ranee of Chiriabagh, and I, her old servant, dwell here! May the wrath of Shiva descend upon you if you harm us.'

Tara gasped her astonishment, and in despair clapped a hand over her eyes. Old Uma has betrayed me, she moaned. My fault; I should have warned her about this when we first met. Now, Holy Mother of God, what is to happen? There is nothing for it but to accept the consequences and pray that they may not be harsh.

'We await...er...your Highness.' A cynical laugh followed the words, bringing a sense of relief to Tara. Thank goodness this oaf disbelieved that she was the princess! Even so, his irony rankled, whipping her into a storm of resentment, adding momentum to an angry courage. Grabbing the branch she had left propped near by, she dragged back the bolts and flung the door wide.

A sudden flare of flaming torches blinded her and took her aback for a moment, but recovering rapidly, she blinked and, gripping the branch, drew herself up with all the aplomb she could summon and demanded in an imperious voice, 'What brings you here to disturb peaceful women at this hour of night? Why could you not wait till daylight to start your hunting?' Now that her eyes had adjusted to the light, she could make out a group of about six men.

For a while no one moved except the horses, who tossed their heads impatiently. Then the man to the fore, who had dismounted, stepped forward and, with lazy indifference handed the reins to a fellow rider. Tara saw the tall man quite clearly, and what she perceived shocked her a little, and caused her blue eyes, flashing hostility, to widen.

His indigo turban, wound round a cone worked in gold thread, ended in a pleated fantail, stiffened to stand erect near the crown of his head, adding to his considerable height, which Tara estimated at over six feet of lean, strong, male flesh. His high brown boots, worn over tan breeches, moved in studied deliberation so that he stood right in front of her, arrogance personified, feet planted apart.

'Your Highness?' Mockery edged the deep voice, and a smile curved the well-shaped masculine mouth. 'We are here for a purpose. But I do not feel obliged to answer your questions. You claim to be the ranee of Chiriabagh?' A thick, dark eyebrow was raised.

She lifted her chin and glared defiance at him. 'I am Tara Bai, daughter of his late Highness Raja Rao Chandra, Rajput prince descendant of Raja Birbal and ruler of Chiriabagh. Does that explanation satisfy you?' She was proud of her Rajput lineage going back to Raja Birbal, a favourite courtier of the Mogul emperor Akbar the Great. She was equally proud of her English blood from a line of distinguished London merchants imbued with the astuteness and intelligence required of successful traders. But she had no intention of giving him details of her family tree.

His mouth parted in a grin of amused incredulity, revealing strong white teeth. Turning his head slightly, without relinquishing his bold gaze at Tara, he addressed someone in his group. 'Why, Maurice, I'll wager you didn't expect us to meet a beautiful Rajput ranee—so she would have us believe.'

'*Non, mon colonel,*' the man addressed said, adding a chuckle.

A flush of mortification spread up Tara's neck and suffused her cheeks. Terror knotted in her abdomen when it suddenly hit her that this *mon colonel* could well be the vile Sikandar Sahib himself!

'And who, sir, are you?' she asked with a bravado contradicting her true feelings.

'Colonel Markham, ma'am.' His calm reply sent her heart rocking.

'You, Colonel, I assume, are the famous—and to me, the infamous—Sikandar Sahib.' Her voice rippled with scorn, surprising herself with her own daring, considering her inner fear.

Grinning easily, he sketched her a bow, the gold-fringed epaulets and frogging on his blue tunic shimmering in the torchlight. 'The very same, your...er...Highness. But tell me, why do you consider me to be infamous? What have I done that I should be branded thus?'

Tara's mind whirled. She had been reckless and imprudent in pronouncing him infamous, and she must rectify the error before he suspected that she knew he was the instigator of her parents' deaths. She thought rapidly, and improvised. 'To me, all adventurers are infamous.' She prayed she sounded convincing.

He shrugged. 'A trifle. And now...'

'And now, Colonel, I demand that you and your mercen—your men be gone this instant. You are trespassing on private territory. Mine!' Fiercely she flung out the branch she grasped and pointed to the jungle.

Colonel Markham straightened slowly to his imposing height, folded his arms across his wide chest and resumed his arrogant stance. Although his mouth smiled lazily, cold ruthlessness lanced from his eyes. 'Neither my men nor I are prepared to leave, lady. We waste time bandying words. Therefore I advise you to allow us to enter. Otherwise...' He fingered his square chin, and with pretended thoughtfulness eyed her slim figure in the ill-fitting masculine garb of baggy pyjamas and loose, collarless shirt.

His gaze roamed her waist-length dark-brown hair, smooth ivory forehead, angry sapphire eyes framed in thick straight lashes, small nose, mobile mouth and flushed cheeks. Then, to her increasing agitation, his bold appraisal concentrated on the rapid movement of her voluptuous breasts that even the loose shirt could not conceal. Nor did she miss the glow of desire in his eyes. She disregarded the racing of her pulses and refused to budge. She lowered the branch, but held it in a threatening position. Tightening her jaw, she challenged him, 'Otherwise?'

'Otherwise—this.' Easily he relieved her of the branch and threw it into the darkness, and in a fluid movement bent and scooped the astounded girl into his strong arms, cradling her against the hard wall of his chest. Laughter from the men following him rang in her ears burning with humiliation as he strode into the building.

His outrageous action stunned her into dumbness. The firm pressure of his arms, powerful muscles flexing round her body, alerted her to his strength and her own fragility. His smell of horses and sweat conveyed to her the coarseness of his type. So nonplussed and engrossed was she by his temerity that it did not occur to her to struggle or to offer token resistance until it was too late.

In the brief moment before he set her down on the *charpoy* beside the distressed and twittering Uma, Tara could not prevent herself from staring at Markham's face. His strong neck swept up to clean-cut jaws and a square chin, the nose slightly aquiline and narrow, the forehead broad and wide. Pale lines on the mahogany tan of his skin rayed out from the outer corners of his eyes. It was a powerful face, arresting in any crowd, immediately creating the impression of a strong personality, a leader of people and—to her—a ruthless killer.

Leader or not, she argued in her head, he certainly had no power over *her*. Not this common thug, the murderer of her loved ones. Uncouth swine, treating her as if she were no more than a sack of grain dumped in his path and to be pushed out of the way with minimum effort and disregard! No respect at all. But what could she expect from such as he?

Whether by accident or intention, his hand brushed her breast when he deposited her beside Uma, Tara was unsure. She shrank from him, shocked by the unexpected and unwelcome intimacy, but, immediately regretted her reaction. In truth, the best way to treat his boldness was to ignore it, to give the illusion that he left her unmoved.

Uma opened her mouth, possibly to accuse the colonel of the massacre but, guessing her intent, Tara squeezed her arm in warning. Thankfully, she seemed to understand and with reluctance clamped her mouth shut.

Tara's mind worked fast. If Colonel Markham suspected that she knew he and his mercenaries had per-

petrated the massacre, he would kill not only her but
Uma. She had grown to love the old woman too much
to be responsible for her death. Moreover, she wished
to live long enough to see Markham suffer as she did,
to fulfil her pledge made in the palace on the night of
the slaughter, to accomplish revenge.

'If you say you are the Ranee Tara Bai, what are you
doing here, lady?' he asked, adding with a grim set of
his mouth which she interpreted as cruelty, 'The raja
and his family have been killed.'

Yes, and you did it, you barbarian! She ached to fling
the accusation at him. She certainly would not relate what
she had witnessed and give him the opportunity of enjoying her pain. She said in even tones, 'Except for me,
Colonel. But I dare say you don't believe that I'm the
raja's daughter, so explanations would be a waste.' She
shrugged in apparent nonchalance, as though he were
someone of no importance. 'It doesn't matter to me in
the least what you believe.'

'In that case, the subject is closed. Meanwhile, my
officers and I are here on a hunting trip.' He glanced at
the men who had followed him in, winked and grinned
knowingly, then with a straight face, swung his gaze back
to Tara. Male laughter resounded in the high-domed
room.

Fury and resentment boiled in Tara. She knew perfectly well that Markham was insinuating that *she* was
the quarry. Her throat hurt as she tried to control tears
of bitter indignation. How dared they laugh at her and
make a fool out of her, these dregs of humanity: obnoxious   brutes,   probably   press-ganged,   illiterate
criminals!

Oh yes, she had heard French and English traders who
visited her father's court mention that both the English

Council of the Honourable East India Company in
Calcutta and the French Council of the Compagnie des
Indes Orientales in Chandanagore objected to their di-
rectors in England and France sending out criminals for
their European battalions in the East. She had gathered
from her beloved father that, fearing they might be returned to their respective countries after their term of
soldiering, to complete their sentences or perhaps to
hang, many of these troopers deserted and sold their
swords to various rulers in the sub-continent. They were
eager to taste freedom, exotic women, battle and adventure, plenty of which existed in this strife-torn
country.

It was difficult for Tara to control the powerful urge
to slap the smugness off Markham's face. This—this
American lout! What was he doing in India, anyway?
There was enough to occupy his time in his own country
that heaved with unrest, torn by civil war and, with much
of the West uncharted, scope for adventure. But that
was irrelevant. At no time in her life had anyone dared
to treat her with a suggestion of this degrading ig-
nominy. She clenched her teeth in formidable determination, and decided to use her eyes to quell these ruffians.
With imperious hauteur, she swept her gaze over them.

She noticed that all the men wore the same uniform
as their leader, except that there was less frogging on
their jackets. Three of the officers appeared to be
Europeans—French, she presumed—the other two she
recognised as Eurasians. All of them were attractive, in
peak physical condition, smart and insolent. What she
objected to most was their insulting appraisal, which affronted and frightened her into thinking that if they could
murder in cold blood, they could rape with equal brut-

ality. Hard though it was for her to suppress her terror, she fought to appear calm and unafraid.

Markham turned his back on the women and faced his officers. 'All right, find yourselves *charpoys* and get some sleep. Tomorrow we make an early start. The risaldar and his suwars should be here with the guns shortly.'

Risaldar, Tara knew, was an Indian cavalry officer and suwars cavalry troopers. She hoped that the guns were not meant to terrorise her and the old lady.

'Colonel Markham.' She eyed his broad back with dislike. 'I would like to know where Uma and I are to sleep tonight.'

A burst of ribald laughter greeted this.

'Quiet!' Colonel Markham roared to his men, and everyone, including Tara, jumped. 'You've had your fun, and that's enough. No more antagonising defenceless women. Now get those *charpoys*.'

The audacity! 'Fun' at *her* expense!

'Yes, sir!' the officers cried in unison, and with alacrity scrambled to pull down the beds upended against the curved wall of the tower.

Slowly Markham pivoted on his heel to face Tara's glare. For a moment she glimpsed ferocity on his face, which he immediately transformed to smiling ease, full of charm, but it affected her not at all. After poking fun at her, he was now trying to beguile her into thinking better of him. His protective attitude towards Uma and herself made not the least impression. He had assumed a façade to hoodwink her into believing him to be a gentleman. Huh! Yet she puzzled over why he should bother with the masquerade, and stared stonily at him.

'I'm afraid, ma'am, you and the old one will have to share that.' He waved a large hand in the direction of

Uma's tiny room, clearly visible since the curtain had been rolled up.

'It's far too small to accommodate another *charpoy*, Colonel.' And with overt sarcasm, Tara added, 'Can't you see?'

He ordered one of his men to light the lamp in Uma's room, and when the officer had done so and left, Markham strode to the doorway and scrutinised the cramped chamber. 'Hmm.' Turning, he slid Tara a sidelong glance alive with roguishness and insolence. 'In that case, ma'am, you'll have to share the old mother's bed. Unless...' His voice dropped to a near whisper, the firm mouth curving in a wicked half-smile.

'Unless what, Colonel?' Instantly she regretted voicing the question, knowing that he would reply with some distasteful witticism.

As she had foreseen, he said, 'Unless, lady, you care to share mine.'

Disinclined for humour, insulted by his lewd banter, she was about to utter a scathing retort when, to her complete amazement, old Uma started cackling, showing her ugly brown teeth, her nostrils, with holes for studs pierced in them, flapping like butterflies' wings. This added to Tara's chagrin. By the saints! The crone had succumbed to this unsavoury adventurer's charms!

'Shush!' Markham hissed, his eyes alight with mocking laughter. 'We don't want the men getting false notions.'

Tara compressed her lips in an angry line. 'Very well, Colonel, tonight I'll share Uma's bed. Tomorrow I hope you and your ruff—soldiers will depart and leave us to continue our peaceful life.'

Raising a thick brow, Colonel Markham leaned indolently against the wall of the doorless jamb. 'Oh, but I can't do that.'

'I beg your pardon?'

'I mean, I can't leave a beautiful lady here un-guarded' Now a thread of steel underscored his words. 'Sorry, ma'am. I must insist that you come with us when we go hunting. After that I invite you to be my guest at Chiriabagh Palace, my present residence—which you claim to be yours.'

'I'll do no such thing, Colonel.' Tara rose slowly, finding it an ordeal to keep her voice steady. 'I—I cannot leave Uma alone. As you can see, she's blind and needs help.'

What manner of man was this, merciful heaven, taking women on hunting trips? Her father would never have believed his ears if she had suggested she accompanied him on his hunts. Besides, she disapproved of the in-discriminate slaughter of animals. What riled her above all was that this mercenary had the gall to invite her as a guest in *her own* palace! She was torn between a desire to laugh at the black humour of the situation and fury at Colonel Markham's incredible effrontery.

'She'll come with us, too,' he said quietly.

'Look, Colonel, I...'

'Enough, lady.' And now his face hardened. 'If you please.' Gallantly he bowed, sweeping a hand to Uma's room.

Tara regarded him with distaste, finding it beneath her to continue the argument. Gently she helped Uma to her feet, and as she passed the colonel, she tossed him a scornful look that elicited a soft laugh.

'I'll be sleeping across the doorway, lady, on this bed, yours I believe, to see that you are safe.'

For answer, Tara gave the string securing the curtain a vicious pull and the *chik* fell with a clatter in front of him, just skimming his aquiline nose. She heard his low chuckle of amusement as he strode away. So he found her amusing, did he? She gritted her teeth. We'll see!

Tara lay beside the skinny Uma and listened to the hushed movements and whispers of the men in the large room; they were amazingly considerate for murderous thugs. With increasing perplexity she pondered on why they had shown no enmity to her and Uma, when they had slain her beloved parents and the residents of the palace with such savagery.

The creak of the *charpoy* across the threshold, accompanied by a deep sigh, told her that Markham had stretched out for what remained of a disturbing night. Unbidden came the thought to arm herself against these men. She was young and nubile, and no match for six virile young soldiers.

When all was still, Tara caught her bottom lip between her teeth and, holding her breath, slid off the bed. Barefooted she crept into the kitchen. She tried to lift the wooden bar across the back door out of its slot, but it creaked, and for a second or two she remained petrified, listening. Uma's snoring stopped and after seeming ages continued, and Tara breathed in relief. Carefully she lowered the bar, pushed open the door, stepped out into the warm starry night and moved towards a stack of lopped-off branches piled under a nearby mango tree and there saw the weapon she sought. She pulled out the chopper embedded in a block of wood.

Scarcely had she straightened up than fingers of steel clamped over her mouth, and the axe was wrenched from her grip. In panic she kicked, but her bare foot had no effect on the hard shin directly behind.

'Shush!' a voice hissed in her ear. 'Nod if you promise not to scream.'

Oh, she knew the murderous swine! He had followed her out to do her an injury. She nodded, but had no intention of honouring her promise. Did this wretch honestly think she would keep quiet?

Markham, she soon realised, was astute enough to doubt her and kept his hand firmly across her mouth as he manoeuvred her to face him. As he removed his fingers, she opened her lips to yell, but no sound emerged.

His mouth came down hard over hers and his arms crushed her to him. The insolent invasion of his tongue sent jolts of outrage shuddering through her. The more she struggled, the more he tightened his arms until she felt as helpless as a fawn in the coils of a python. Unable to fight, she lay limp in his arms and suffered his mouth to ravage hers. Frightened anger made her heart thump rapidly. At last he lifted his head. His quickened breath fanned her cheeks as he held her close for a moment longer, then slowly dropped his arms.

Able to breathe better now, she gulped in breaths of the warm night air. Speechless with fury, she glowered at him. She ached to rave and lash out at him, but that would waken the whole tower, and his odious henchmen would enjoy great amusement at her expense.

In the bright starlight, his face looked pale and taut. 'Go back to bed,' he whispered. 'Choppers are dangerous to play with.'

'I wanted it to safeguard Uma and myself, Colonel Markham. I don't trust you or your men.'

'You have no choice. But if I'd wanted to harm you, what's to prevent me from doing so?'

True, but, dear God, how could she trust her parents' killer? She said nothing.

He took her back to the kitchen, re-slotted the bar and led her to Uma's bed. Then he lifted the *chik*, and she heard him settle on the *charpoy* across the threshold.

She lay fuming beside Uma. How dared that devil treat her as if she were no more than a common whore! His invading kiss, so lustful and demeaning, had shaken her to the core; she felt defiled and smitten with an urge to wash her mouth. She now regretted not having hit him. It might have caused hilarity among his men, but he would know she was no cheap wench and that she opposed and abhorred his familiarity.

The clashing of pans, laughter and bustle from the kitchen startled Tara into wakefulness at dawn. Old Uma had already risen, sitting cross-legged on the mat, mumbling complaints.

'Those asses make much noise in stealing our food! May Raja Sahib's spirit haunt them... Ah, *Hazrat*, Highness, you are awake,' she said, as the *charpoy* wobbled noisily when Tara sat up. 'Tell the asses to go away and let us live in peace. They are going to starve us to death, I am thinking.'

Tara frowned. 'How did they enter the kitchen? I barred the back door. Did they come through this room?'

'No, Tara Bai.' The crone wagged her head. 'I heard them open door of the kitchen. Maybe the devil assisted them. For are they not the children of Satan?'

Tara jerked guiltily as she recalled her experience with Colonel Markham the previous night, and wondered if he had left the door open for his men. Then on second thoughts she remembered him securing the bar.

'I hear the women talking, Lal Das. Tell Sikandar Sahib. He wants to know when they wake,' a male voice said in Urdu from the kitchen, and remarked, 'I heard the sahibs talking last night. They say the young one is comely and fair-skinned like an English or French girl. She claims to be Raja Chandra's daughter. How can that be, when we know they are all dead?'

'*Ji*, it is as you say, Sergeant. I will tell Sikandar Sahib that the women are awake.'

Tara felt discomfited; she and Uma needed to bathe and change into fresh clothes, but how could they manage this when their privacy had been invaded by soldiers swarming in the grounds? Sighing, she splashed water on her face from a brass vessel that Uma kept in the room at night. Then, tidying her hair with a hurried brushing, she twisted it up on the crown of her head and draped over it the *chuddah* that contained her jewelry knotted at one end. A time might come when she needed these valuables, the most precious she had ever owned, and she marvelled at the sixth sense that had induced her to wear them on the night of the massacre. She could still claim to be a very rich woman.

Straightening her clothes, she sat on the *charpoy* and waited, ignoring Uma's ceaseless grumblings. The woman had not budged from the mat, making no attempt to wash or groom herself, on account of her worry, perhaps.

Harrowing thoughts swam in Tara's brain. She and Uma undoubtedly were prisoners of Colonel Markham. Perhaps when he forced them to return with him to Chiriabagh, he would fling them into the palace jail, there to rot for evermore. But first he would rape her; the torrid kiss he had forced on her was a warning of what was to come. No, this must not be! Her mind began to dwell on finding a means of escape....

'Ma'am,' Colonel Markham called from beyond the *chik*. 'May I have a word with you?'

My God, this man's hypocrisy amazed her; he sounded the epitome of a gentleman!

'Enter, Colonel,' Tara invited in a cold voice. She must not convey too much anger at his behaviour the night before and betray how adversely he affected her. 'We are decent.'

Markham lifted aside the *chik* and stepped in. 'Good day, ma'am.' He touched his temple in an informal salute.

Tara felt embarrassing heat start to rise in her face. He had donned a full-sleeved shirt and baggy pyjamas tucked into knee-high boots. Casually he ran his fingers through thick waves of copper-gold hair; its colour had not been apparent in the dark. And in the rapidly brightening room she noticed the dark green of his eyes, the shade of a glossy mango leaf.

'Is it your habit to ignore a greeting, ma'am? I feel sure that, for someone who claims noble birth, you would not be so remiss.' Laughter shone from his eyes as if he knew why she looked stricken.

She admitted to herself that he was indeed a handsome man, but knowing him to be a fiend, she was not impressed. Nevertheless, confusion reddened her flushed cheeks even deeper.

'Good day, Colonel.' To hide her discomposure, she demanded primly, 'How did your men get into the kitchen? Did you let them in?'

'Easily explained, lady. There's a gap at the side of the door, if you remember, through which one of them inserted a sword and lifted the bar.'

'I see,' she said with biting disapproval. 'Did it not occur to you, Colonel, that Uma or I could have been in the kitchen in a state of undress?'

'I do believe they gave fair warning. With the amount of noise they created, you would have had enough time to retreat here.'

'Uma and I wish to bathe and change, sir. We are accustomed to twice-daily baths. How can we manage with your army surrounding the place?' She sneered at his smile of teasing charm and shot him a look of what she considered pure venom. In no circumstances must she show this man a glimmer of friendliness.

'Do not disturb youself, ma'am.' A corner of his mouth lifted in an amused quirk, and she hated him for daring to flirt with her. Brazen fool! Did he really think she would welcome his lustful advances? 'A tent has been erected at the back, and inside are tubs filled with water. All is ready for your use. None of my men is permitted to go near it while you and the old one are in there.'

Good breeding compelled her to say stiffly, 'Thank you, Colonel.' She distrusted this ruse to get her more easily into his bed. God forbid, when her parents' blood clamoured for vengeance!

There must be some way she could strike back at him— kill him. No! The thought of murdering anyone horrified her. Mentally Tara groaned, O God, find me a means to revenge myself on this man!

CHAPTER FOUR

IF TARA had been allowed a mount of her own, she would have risked breaking away in a bid for freedom, but with cunning gallantry Colonel Markham had consigned the women to a tonga, canopied for protection from the onslaught of the sun and flanked by mounted suwars. He rode ahead of the vehicle, relaxed astride a spirited Arabian stallion, its coat blue-grey mottled with white, a gift from some grateful maharaja or nawab, she supposed enviously.

Markham laughed and joked with two of his officers riding on either side of him, yet managed to maintain the dignity required of a commanding officer. She needed to flee from this man who, she admitted, possessed a potent allure to draw women to him—except her; she saw him as a strutting peacock, an upstart, with evil locked in his heart. As soon as they reached their unknown destination, she promised herself, she must look for help, but how?

Earlier, before they set out, he had tried to worm himself into her favour by bringing her breakfast. After their baths, the women sat outside on a rug beneath a peepul tree, and it was there that Markham joined them. If he thought she would be grateful for his considerate gesture, he'd be disappointed! Tara nodded towards the tray he had placed before her, and with polite irony said, 'You needn't have troubled yourself, Colonel. I'm quite capable of preparing breakfast for Uma and myself.'

'I did it for a reason——' she might have known!
'—because I didn't want you to get in my men's way in
the kitchen. They have quite a number of people to feed.'

'And you are eating with us?' Her question held no
invitation.

'No. I've already breakfasted.'

He is shameless, she reflected, watching him settle
himself beside her on the rug. Can he not sense how
much I hate him?

'I decided to remain here and make sure that you are
fed and ready to leave when you've finished, ma'am.'

'Why so much haste, Colonel?' She drank some tea
and took a dainty bite of a rolled, buttered, wafer-thin
chappati. Alive to his eyes scrutinising her movements,
she prayed she would not disgrace herself by spilling her
drink and dropping her food. She wished she could
follow Uma's example and eat with easy enjoyment, oblivious of who looked on.

'As I stated last night, we are about to start on a
hunting trip.' He stared at the movement of her throat
as she tilted her head slightly to swallow. 'I don't ap-
prove of killing animals for sport, but one of the villages
is being menaced by rogue tigers. They have carried away
valuable livestock. The headman appealed to the palace
for help.' He took a chappati from a pile on a metal
plate, spread soft clarified butter on it and placed it in
Uma's hand, which was feeling about on the tray. 'Here
you are, good mother.'

'*Shukriyar,* Colonel Sahib,' Uma thanked him,
grinning her delight.

Tara closed her mind to his thoughtfulness and said
in a voice dry with sarcasm, 'Your fame has spread far
and wide, Colonel.'

'In truth, it has, ma'am.' His confident grin marked him as a conceited individual, and dragged him lower in her disfavour. 'As temporary ruler, I have promised to safeguard the Chiriabagh people and their property.'

The food almost choked Tara. What she gathered from his words was that he had now taken control of her father's domain. 'I suppose you held a durbar?'

'Indeed, ma'am. How else can the laws be promulgated?'

His brazenness smote her with a desire to hurl the tray and all its contents at his head: an inadequate retaliation for his crimes, and her childish action would brand her as a low-bred fool. It was so unfair, so frustrating! 'I— I think we are ready to leave, Colonel.' She clanked the metal cup on the tray with decisive force. My turn will come, and when it does, beware! she vowed in silent malice.

Colonel Markham had stayed by Tara's side as though he suspected her motives, and did not leave until he had helped her into the tonga. His touch on her elbow made her start away from him, but his mocking smile told her he found her amusing.

They now travelled on the cart-track, and the tonga bumped over ruts, going deeper into the thickly forested terrain. Behind Tara's vehicle came mules laden with dismantled tents, safari guns and baggage, flanked by more suwars. All the men had changed from uniform into cool cotton shirts, breeches and boots. The officers now wore solar topees, while the suwars retained their turbans. Their smart appearance intensified her feeling of shabbiness in the ill-fitting male clothes she had found in the tower. Although it was silly, really, she decided, since none of these men meant anything to her.

At midday the column reached a village surrounded by a mud wall with a rough-hewn wooden gate, where the colonel and his officers dismounted. He pulled on a bell-rope dangling from the gatepost.

After a while a man dressed in only a *dhoti* stepped out and brought his palms together in a respectful *namasta*. Tara noted with mild surprise that Markham returned a similar greeting. Europeans, as a rule, acknowledged such salutations with a nod, deeming the steepling of hands to be too demeaning. Perhaps Americans were different?

She watched him speak politely to the villager, who appeared to be delighted, eagerly inviting the colonel to enter. Markham said something more to the man, and indicated the rest of the party with a wide sweep of his arm. Nodding with enthusiasm, he indicated that everyone was welcome and expected, at the same time pushing wide the gate.

The officers remounted and followed the villager, but Markham rode back to Tara's tonga. 'I hope, ma'am, that the journey was not too uncomfortable for you and the old one.'

If Tara's opinion of this man had not been coloured by hatred, she would have acknowledged that he looked superb astride the stallion. His concern for her welfare did not deceive her. Although she had little experience of men and had led a life of opulent seclusion, she knew from her history lessons and books that the most notorious human beings were sometimes the most charming and solicitous in order to achieve their purpose. His purpose, she assumed, was either her seduction or the seizure of her throne—or both.

'It was as comfortable as can be expected in the circumstances, Colonel. Thank you.' Cold and distant were her voice and attitude. She added, 'May I ask where you have brought us?'

A dark eyebrow lifted. 'Surprising, lady, that you who claim to be the Princess Tara Bai should know nothing of your late father's domain.'

Tara's gaze slid away guiltily from the humorous scepticism mirrored in his green eyes. It was galling to know that this hateful man had the ability to make her feel ashamed of herself: of her inexcusable negligence to enquire into the welfare of her father's people—now, by right, hers.

Living in luxury, occupying her time in riding, feasting, idle entertainments, decking herself in fabulous silks fashioned in Indian and European garb, and jewels of incalulable worth, she regretfully admitted to being unaware, uncaring even, about the world beyond the palace walls. People like these villagers, through gruelling physical labour, provided the revenue that had contributed to her former lifestyle. She had bestowed nothing in return; on the contrary, she had lived like a parasite. Since the night of the massacre, she had found herself alone, unwanted, pitched into the cruel realities of Indian life. As though a jealous fate had dragged her out of a golden cocoon, decided she had lived in pampered wealth on other people's endeavours for long enough; eager to test her endurance in harsh conditions. Most humiliating of all, a bitter enemy had brought this to her notice, and it was because of him that she was forced to lead the life of a penniless fugitive in her own state.

Tara struggled to eliminate the bitterness in her voice, without much success. 'No, Colonel. I did not leave the vicinity of the palace,' she had to confess. 'There was no need for me to do so. Had I known that my parents would meet their—their deaths so suddenly and so...brutally, I might have taken more interest in the affairs of my father's domain.'

His eyes were filled with misgivings as he observed her through the mesh of black lashes. 'Strange,' he remarked, then with a dismissive shrug, proceeded to explain, 'This is the village I mentioned at breakfast.'

'Tigers have been pestering this village?'

'That's right. You shall rest here for the day, while my men and I confer with the village council, the *Panchayat*, I believe it is called, and find out how best we can be of use to it.'

'I see. Very well, Colonel.' She made it sound as if *she* were granting him a favour.

He threw her an amused smile, eyes dancing, then commanded the driver of the tonga to move through the gateway.

With round-eyed curiosity women and children ran out of their mud dwellings to view the newcomers. Outside a dung-plastered hut squatted a shrivelled old man clad in a thread-bare *dhoti*, smoking a rolled leaf filled with tobacco-dust. He placed it between the middle and third fingers of his clenched hand, which he lifted at intervals to his mouth, drawing in smoke only. Cattle were tied to posts outside the huts, and the odour of fresh dung and straw reeked in the hot atmosphere.

The villager, leading Colonel Markham and his column through the centre of the village, stopped outside one of the huts, calling out. A pale-skinned man emerged in a spotless white muslin collarless shirt and *dhoti*. Tara recognised him as a Vaishnavite Brahman, a devotee of the god Vishnu, from the white prong drawn on his forehead, divided by a red line denoting the god's energy. Each of the four castes had its own colour of distinction, and the Brahmans wore white. He steepled his hands in a quick *namasta* to Colonel Markham, and nervously fingered his necklace of brown seeds.

From where her tonga stood, Tara could not hear what was being said. She received the impression that the man was worried that Markham and his troops had come to take over his village; which might well be the case, Tara thought with a growing feeling of anxiety and resentment. But after some conversation, the Brahman's face brightened; he nodded and wagged his head, its black oiled hair scraped back into a tight knot above his nape.

Turning and pointing to Tara's tonga, Markham addressed an officer. He saluted and came over to her, respectfully doffing his hat.

'Mademoiselle, I am Captain Dupont. I and this man here,' he indicated the villager who followed him, 'will escort you to the hut you are to occupy, if you please.'

'Thank you, Captain.' She descended as serenely and elegantly as she could, and helped a bewildered Uma down. They followed Dupont and the villager to a vacant hut, where curious onlookers had gathered outside. 'How long do we stay here, Captain? Is it only for the day?'

'No, mademoiselle. My Colonel's orders are that you are to remain here until after the hunt.'

'I see.'

He shifted restlessly from one foot to the other, conveying that he felt uneasy in her presence. 'This man will arrange for one of his womenfolk to bring you food and see to your comfort. *Bonjour,* mademoiselle.' The young captain, who could not have been more than twenty-five, saluted and strode away. Watching him, Tara sensed his dislike and his distaste at having to supervise her welfare.

It was no cooler inside the gloomy hut, even though the walls had been dampened and gave off an agreeable smell of wet earth. A frayed mat woven from palm fronds covered the centre of the floor.

'I will send a woman shortly with food, Sahiba,' the villager said respectfully. She recognised him as a Sudra, from the peasant or fourth caste: the horizontal lines on his forehead signified that he was a Shaivite, a devotee of the god Shiva, the much-feared deity of production and destruction, and the colour black indicated his caste.

'*Shukriyar*,' Tara thanked him and smiled.

He made the *namasta*, which she returned politely. Beaming his delight, the man withdrew, shooing away the curious folk gathered outside.

'There is upset in the village,' Uma said, allowing Tara to guide her to a *charpoy*.

'It's hardly surprising, if tigers drag away their livestock.'

'No, it is worry of another kind. They say *dhamans* have drained their best cows of milk.'

Tara was aware of her keen sense of hearing, so that Uma concentrated on bits of gossip that sighted people invariably failed to absorb. '*Dhamans*? Do you mean those snakes that strike with their tails?' She shivered her revulsion. The poison developed not in the fangs but in the tails of these reptiles.

'*Ji*. They wrap themselves round the cows' legs and drain their udders. The poor beasts dare not move or make a sound, for they know the snake will lash them and then that part rots. But you should know about this, Tara Bai.'

'Yes, I do.' She scanned the room in dismay. 'Oh dear! I do hope none is hidden here.'

A woman entered then and placed a brass tray holding metal bowls filled with a vegetable dish cooked in *ghee*, clarified butter. On a platter lay a pile of fried wholemeal flat bread. Also included were a flagon of water and brass cups.

Tara wished she had a few rupees so that she could give the woman baksheesh, but the latter seemed content with her grateful *'Shukriyar,'* and performed a *namasta*, smiled shyly and departed. Though simple, the meal tasted delicious, hunger impelling Tara and Uma to consume every morsel.

During the afternoon rest-period, as she lay on a wobbly *charpoy* listening to Uma's contented snores from the opposite side of the hut, an idea suddenly surfaced. She stared absently at a niche where an earthenware lamp burned in front of the painting of Lord Krishna, a blue-skinned god wearing a garland of marigolds and a high gold crown. In another corner of the hut squatted the idol of Ganesh, the elephant-headed god of prosperity, and a favourite in every Hindu household.

Her brain blossomed with an ingenious scheme to escape with Uma before they were forced to travel to Chiriabagh Palace in Colonel Markham's train. Reassuring herself that her jewels still remained concealed in the knot at the end of her *chuddah*, Tara contemplated trying to bribe the serving-woman when she brought their next meal, possibly after sundown. Her ring, of priceless historic value, would have to be sacrificed to cover the cost of a cart and the hire of a knowledgeable driver willing to take them to a town where they could merge with the citizens.

Glancing at the old woman stretched out on her back, mouth open, lips flapping as she snored, Tara envied her ability to sleep in the heat, which was more ener-

vating here than in the tower. She had been accustomed
in the palace to the coolness of frames of roots, grass
or rushes kept wet over doorways, and overhead screen
punkahs, she recalled with yearning. In consequence, her
pampered body found difficulty in adapting to the ri-
gours of the climate to which the common people had
been inured since birth. However, at the moment, the
heat posed the least of her troubles in her emerging designs to leave Colonel Markham. If the serving-woman
did agree to accept payment and arrange for transport,
how would Tara and Uma be able to slip past the two
suwars undetected? The doorway they guarded provided
the only entrance and exit. She did not relish the idea
of testing the soldiers' loyalty to Sikandar Sahib by offering them money and hastily shelved the thought, considering this plan too risky.

Earlier she had overheard the suwars talking ani-
matedly about the forthcoming hunt. Markham and his
officers had gone with the village headman and a few
selected villagers to the spot where the tigers had dragged
and fed on the carcasses of two black buffaloes. Tonight, after the evening meal, a group with Markham in
the lead would tie a goat to a tree beneath a hide not
far from the buffalo carcasses to which the tigers would
return, it was hoped. The unfortunate goat would act
as a lure for the predators who would with luck emerge
and expose themselves.

Once the hunt was under way and Colonel Markham
and his men had left the village, Tara and Uma could
make their escape. It was a highly dangerous venture,
but in the circumstances Tara believed she had no choice.
Better a bid for freedom, however hazardous, than a
lifetime languishing in jail. To get rid of the suwars on
guard would prove to be the only drawback.

A little later, Uma woke with a snort. Tara crossed to the old woman's *charpoy*, and kneeling beside it, outlined her plans in an excited whisper. But the crone showed no keenness.

'I am too old to roam the countryside, Tara Bai. If we go to jail, we will be fed. Out in the jungle we can starve to death.'

Tara scowled her impatience and felt deflated by the woman's lack of enthusiasm. 'That's what you think. That cruel mercenary might have us killed.'

Uma wagged her head. '*Nahin*. What you say does not make sense. If he wished to kill us, he would have done so in the tower. Why waste rupees feeding us only to slaughter us later?'

Tara had to admire Uma's sound reasoning. Even so, it was imperative that she escape from Markham and arrange for an army to march on him and regain her kingdom.

'Then I must go by myself. You forget this man savagely killed the raja, my father, who gave you shelter.' Immediately contrite by a sudden thought, Tara put an arm round Uma and hugged her. 'I'm sorry, old one. You have repaid Chandra amply by giving me refuge in the tower. Forgive my ingratitude. Perhaps you will be safe with this Sikandar Sahib. I, on the other hand, must leave.'

'Leave for where?'

'For Motipur.'

'Motipur?' Uma emitted a startled gasp, but soon gained control of herself, and Tara detected more interest in her voice. 'You cannot travel alone, Tara Bai— I shall come. Do not speak with the servants, but leave the talking to me. Few in Hindustan live to be as old as I, but those who do are respected. Where is your ring?'

Tara gave Uma a grateful squeeze and from the knot at the end of the *chuddah* produced the emerald ring set in a circle of Burma rubies and Golconda diamonds, a replica of the original Chiriabagh state ring that her father as ruler had worn, an heirloom handed down to the eldest son ever since the sixteenth century. Tara had been so enchanted with the jewel that her father had ordered replicas for her mother and herself.

The serving-woman received the ring with many salaams when Uma handed it to her during the evening meal and stated what they required.

'Do not worry about the suwars, *Materji*. I will give them drugged palm wine,' she whispered. Having listened to all the instructions relayed in undertones, she nodded her understanding.

The hours seemed to drag and Tara became jittery; her mind harboured suspicions. Supposing the serving-woman vanished with the ring? Such a priceless object would be a great temptation to a villager, who could disappear in this vast country and live the remainder of her life in luxury. Tara or Uma could not complain about the ring having been stolen without betraying themselves. Oh, what had she done? But, to her relief, the woman came in the darkness, long after the hunting party had left, and beckoned the captives out. Holding Uma's arm, Tara slipped past the drugged suwars, and followed the woman who lit the way with a feeble oil-lamp along a dusty lane to a small door in the mud wall that circled the village. Outside waited a single bullock yoked to a covered cart. The driver, in turban and *dhoti*, jumped down from his perch and lifted the back flap for the two women to climb in.

'May the gods go with you,' the serving-woman said in farewell, steepling her hands in a quick *namasta*. She turned and vanished through the door in the wall.

Blackness and heat enveloped the interior of the cart, so Tara parted the back flap. Bright starlight enabled her to see the rutted path on which the vehicle creaked along. The serving-woman had mentioned that it would take at least four or five days to reach Motipur, the state capital of Todar Ram, the ruler to whom Tara's father had pledged her in marriage. She felt uneasy about trespassing on his domain because of her intense dislike of him; but for now her plans could wait till her arrival at Motipur. First, she must put as much distance as possible between herself and Colonel Markham. The ravaging kiss he had forced on her the night before warned her of his lustful intention.

The rhythmic roll of the cart soon lulled Tara and Uma into slumber. The girl's last thought before she drifted into oblivion on the hot quilt was that the escape was proving a lot easier than she had anticipated. Until...

'*Arre bap!* Oh, father!' The cart-driver's alarmed shout brought Tara wide awake.

'What goes on?' asked Uma. 'Why are you making noise? Why have you stopped?'

'There is buffalo on path. It will not move, I am thinking. How can I get my cart past?' He bawled at the animal obstructing the way, '*Hutto!* Move!'

Pushing aside the front flap, Tara peered out. A buffalo stood motionless across the path, looking as though it were carved from black marble. The driver muttered a curse, jumped down, and moved to investigate. He raised his stick to wallop the animal, then slowly lowered his hand and warily, keeping a fair distance, circled the beast.

The next instant, he let out a yell and came racing back to the cart. Breathlessly he burst out: 'There—there is *dhaman*...wrapped round its legs...drinking from the udders.'

'By the gods!' Uma shrieked, patting her quilt in distress. 'It is ill omen. Is there no other path we can use?'

'There is forest, respected mother, but much undergrowth. Cart cannot move over it. We must wait till *dhaman* leaves. Then only will buffalo get out of way.'

'Can you not remove the snake?' Uma asked querulously, while Tara shivered her disgust at the whole loathsome business.

'*Nahin!* It will lash not only buffalo but me as well. I do not want to lose my limbs. Let us wait.'

They suffered in an uneasy silence that stretched endlessly. Then, what seemed like hours later, Tara heard the buffalo bellowing in fear and thudding away. She wondered with a shudder whether it was dragging the snake along.

'Ah! Now way is clear.' The driver sounded jubilant, and the cart rumbled forward.

Despite a feeling of queasiness, Tara let out a long, slow breath of relief. Now they could proceed in peace. The cart had barely done half a dozen turns of the wheel when she felt Uma's bony fingers gripping her arm. 'I can hear something, Tara Bai.'

Tara's body tightened. 'Now what?'

'A roar. Can you not hear it?'

Tara listened, her apprehension growing. All she could hear was the creaking of cart-wheels. 'No.' She shook her head, but the prickling of her flesh presaged impending danger.

'It is the snarl of the tiger. It has smelt the buffalo.'
Uma had barely spoken when their yoked bullock lunged
forward, breaking into a gallop, bellowing in panic.

The cart rocked from side to side, hurtling the women
about, throwing them all into a confusion of shouts and
screams. And now Tara heard the vibrating roars growing
louder by the moment.

'Arraaoum! Rrraaoum!' The sound resounded
through the jungle.

In a flurry of skinny arms and legs, the driver hurled
himself from his seat in a somersault into the interior
of the cart. 'Do not make noise. Do not show yourselves.' His voice squeaked and trembled.

Do not make a noise? Tara could have laughed if the
situation were not perilous. The tiger and bullock were
making enough noise to attract every creature in the
forest. Monkeys coughed, owls hooted and parrots
shrieked. The two women huddled together, rocking and
shuddering in terror.

'Arraaoum! Grraaoum! Grrraaoum!'

Beloved Jesus, there were *two* tigers! Tara resorted to
prayer. Nothing else could save them! She finished the
'Our Father' and was halfway through *Ave Maria* when
the cart swerved, bumping over uneven ground. She
could hear the snapping of twigs and scraping of
undergrowth as the wheels wobbled over them, and her
sympathy went out to the panic-crazed bullock. Heavy
pads loped beside the cart, and the nearness of the roars
was deafening.

Then shots erupted, and a roar of pain-induced rage
followed. Enormous claws caught and ripped the cover-
ing off the cart. Uma screeched. Tara's throat dried up.
More reports reverberated. From the now open wreck
of the cart Tara watched, stricken, an enormous tiger

leap into the air, snarling with enraged agony. She could smell its rank breath. It curled up in a large striped ball, and then fell with a thud alongside the cart, which trundled past. More roars, more shots. Then the forest seemed to subside and the only sounds came from the bullock, the cart and the distant drum of horses' hooves.

The driver leaped out, and dragged at the ropes securing his animal. Screaming and sobbing, he reined in the frightened beast and brought it to a quivering halt.

No sooner had the cart rocked to a standstill than a group of horsemen materialised, carrying blazing torches, and surrounded the vehicle. In the firelight Tara spotted Colonel Markham, a portrait of splendid fury. His shirtsleeves were rolled up above his elbows, revealing muscular arms glistening with sweat. Across the saddle he held a smoking gun. His mouth was set in a grim line, and his eyes shot gleams of rage that scared her as much as the tigers had done.

'Thanks to you, your Highness, we bagged both tigers.' No gratitude in his tone. Tara had never heard such hard anger in a man's voice. Even so, what disturbed her more was that he had addressed her as 'your Highness' as though he meant it. What had convinced him that she was indeed a princess?

CHAPTER FIVE

TARA DID NOT feel like 'your Highness' at that moment: more like a criminal escaping from some misdeed. And it was Markham, she fulminated, who had provoked this unwelcome attitude in her, despite her belief that her attempt at running away was fully justified. But the fact that she had been compelled to act in a furtive manner made her conscience uneasy.

Oh, nonsense! He had no right to cart her around as if she were an inanimate piece of his baggage incapable of possessing a will of her own. She had done no wrong. Well...perhaps a little, she conceded grudgingly. Like any free person, she reflected, she had paid for transport to a destination of her choice. True, the arrangement fell short of honesty, considering the drugged suwars, which aroused her sense of guilt, but they had come to no harm—she hoped. Furthermore, she was certainly under no obligation to remain with Colonel Markham and his ruffians; she had a right to go where she wanted.

Satisfied that she had done nothing of significance to be ashamed of, Tara pushed back the untidy strands of hair that had worked loose from the thick coil on her nape. She marvelled that the knot had stayed in position and not tumbled down in their ordeal. Why, she wondered, did her mind dwell on inconsequential factors when she was surrounded by danger?

By now Uma, still trembling, had been helped down from the vehicle by the shaken driver, and Tara, controlling her own quivering limbs, followed with dignified sedateness, her blue eyes sweeping over Colonel Markham with frosty disdain.

He dismounted, and moved to stand in front of her. 'I wouldn't advise you to try any more foolish and dangerous escapades, your Highness.' From his little finger he pulled off a ring and offered it to her on the palm of his hand. 'Yours, I believe?'

She stared in astonishment at the trinket she had given the serving-woman. 'It—it *was* mine, Colonel.' She strove for equanimity, making no move to retrieve the jewel, its emerald and rubies seeming to sparkle accusation at her. 'I gave it in payment for...' With an encompassing sweep of her hand she indicated the wrecked cart and frightened driver. 'So I suggest you return it to its rightful owner.'

Markham assumed a bland expression. He viewed her lazily through meshed lashes, a gleam of mockery apparent in his green eyes that exacerbated her annoyance. He delighted in treating her as if she were a recalcitrant child. 'Payment?' he asked. 'Don't you mean bribery?'

'I mean nothing of the sort! I refuse to be your prisoner, Colonel, and...'

'Guest, lady, guest.'

'*Prisoner*, and within my rights to go where I choose, how I choose and when I choose, since I have paid for them.' Drawing herself up to her full height—which reached his chin—she eyed him haughtily. It was a difficult accomplishment, owing to her shabby appearance.

'Why didn't you ask me? I said you were a guest, not a prisoner.'

That defeated her. She could not understand this man. Did he honestly expect her to ask him? Could he not sense how much she hated him and that she would not deign to seek his help?

'Would you have consented to have Uma and me escorted to Motipur, Colonel?'

'Perhaps. Perhaps not. Depending on circumstances.'

His non-committal reply surprised her not at all. 'But I have no desire to remain here, sir. Therefore I would be grateful if you would leave my companions and myself to continue our journey.'

His face hardened into inscrutability. Only his eyes flashed irritability, impatience. 'I'm afraid that's out of the question, lady. As you have witnessed and experienced for yourself, the jungle is no place for unarmed people, least of all women. And you seem unconcerned that one of you is both old and blind.' In measured tones he drew Tara's attention to her selfishness, bringing stinging heat to her cheeks. She resented him for embarrassing her in front of his miscreants. She resented him for any number of reasons! She glanced at his men. They looked on with impassivity, evidence that they and their commander were capable of gruesome slaughter, she reminded herself. A sharp order from Markham would leave her as dead as the tigers slain not far from the cart.

His tender regard for Uma deceived her not in the least: it was just a front to force herself into doing his bidding. Conscious of his position of power, she considered it unwise to arouse his antagonism further and maintained an angry silence. He probably interpreted it as surrender, judging from his slow smile of triumph which affected her with frustration and bitterness, aware of her impotence to flout his orders.

'For your own safety, lady, I'd advise you to climb back into the cart,' he said with quiet authority. He tossed Tara's ring once or twice on the palm of his hand, and then pushed it on to his little finger.

She watched his actions through narrowed eyes glittering with outrage. Faith, this man had openly stolen the ring from a poor village woman who had risked much to help Uma and herself, and probably had spent her meagre store of rupees to pay for the hire of the cart and driver until she could recover the money from the sale of the ring.

'That ring doesn't belong to you, Colonel.'

'True, it doesn't. But I did offer it to you.'

'It belongs to the serving-woman now. You have taken advantage of her inability to keep the jewel, and stolen it from her!'

A frightening silence settled. She could sense the fury radiating from Markham, saw the pulse hammering in his jaw and watched his fist clench and unclench.

'She has been amply compensated, I assure you, lady. Now, please, get back in the cart.' His voice cut like a steel blade.

Tara thought it prudent to obey; indeed she had no choice. 'Very well, Colonel.' Turning her back, she wondered how she could perform the clumsy action with aplomb.

She did not have long to wonder. As she hesitated, his hard hands enclosed her slender waist, lifted her with ease and gentleness up on the cart, and did not release her until she was seated stiff-backed, her legs curled to one side. She wanted to tell him not to touch her, but it would seem childish, since all he was apparently doing was to give her a helping hand.

Instead, she said, 'For the time being, Colonel, I'll ignore the matter of the ring, although I'm not satisfied with your explanation of the so-called "ample compensation" you paid for it. You, I assume, are ignorant of the fact that the ring is priceless.'

He sighed with boredom. 'I know, lady. That's why I'm puzzled that you gave it to the woman. But we delay.' Ordering the cart-driver to return to the village, he immediately sprang on his horse and rode ahead, giving Tara no chance to argue unless she resorted to shouting, which she considered too lowering.

Voices, other sounds and activities washed over her as fatigue took its toll. She slumped down on the quilt and slept.

In consequence, on returning to the village hut she lay on her *charpoy* wide awake. Her brain teemed with doubts, branched out in an alternative direction from her firm conviction that Markham had been responsible for the massacre. Had she been mistaken in basing her opinion of him on mere conjecture? Because he and his officers spoke French, it did not necessarily mean that they were guilty of murder. Undeniably the palace raiders had spoken French, but what did that prove? To her knowledge, many rulers and Maratha chiefs employed European mercenaries.

She knew nothing about Colonel Markham's background except that he came from North America, where the colonists, enraged by the imposition of stamp duty and the raising of other taxes, were fighting for secession from the British Crown. They had shown their objections by masquerading as Red Indians and tipping the entire cargo of tea brought in by three East Indiamen into Boston harbour, an episode derisively known as the 'Boston tea-party.' In July 1776, their Congress headed by George Washington had signed a Declaration of Independence. They no longer considered themselves colonists but Americans, and referred to colonies as states.

Many colonists, she had learned from the priest, upheld the sovereignty of the British Crown; many did not. Not only those of English origin but Irish, Scots, French, Spanish, Dutch and people of other European nations had settled in America, consequently a substantial proportion of the population saw no reason to owe any fealty to an English monarch. But all these political factors provided Tara with no clues to Colonel Markham's character, or why he had left his country and taken up arms in India.

Although she experienced misgivings about his involvement in the palace massacre because she lacked proof, she still felt resentment towards him for daring to establish himself as ruler of Chiriabagh: *her* domain, *her* inheritance. As the only surviving member of the royal house of Birbal, she was the legitimate heir to the throne, hence the ranee of Chiriabagh. She drew in her breath through clenched teeth. There was no justice in this world!

'He is no murderer, Tara Bai.' Uma's voice from her side of the hut cut short Tara's thoughts and startled her. So she too was thinking of Markham and had revised her judgment of him.

'Are you talking of the colonel?'

'*Ji,* Tara Bai. And assuredly Sikandar Sahib will not put us in jail.'

Tara was not as certain as Uma that they would evade imprisonment. She sighed. Mentally and physically exhausted from the effects of the attempted escape, she had little stamina and no inclination to argue. 'Go to sleep, Uma,' she murmured, and turning on her own *charpoy*, immediately fell asleep.

It came as no surprise when she and Uma were confined to their hut and not invited to join in the festivities celebrating the triumph of the tiger hunt, after sundown next day. But they had not been neglected: a water-carrier brought in a large metal tub and filled it with cold water from the buffalo-skin he carried on his thin back, for their baths. The guards brought them in tasty vegetable meals.

All night long drums beat, and tuneless voices wailed in monotony. Tara had been sure, as she lay on her *charpoy*, that the exertion of the escapade the night before would have fatigued her sufficiently to send her into instant sleep oblivious of the rowdy revelling. On the contrary, her mind again dwelt on whether Colonel Markham had been involved in the massacre.

The next morning, a different servant brought breakfast to their hut. Tara had assumed that the same woman would bring their meals after the celebrations were over, and this disturbed her, suddenly mindful that both the previous serving-woman and the cart-driver might undergo punishment for their part in assisting her. She felt responsible for their actions, and determined to have the two people absolved from all blame. She had to speak to Colonel Markham, and alone, not with his men creating an audience ready to ridicule her. Perhaps she could send one of the guards with word to him. The suwars on sentinel duty had been increased to four: two at the entrance of the hut and two doing the rounds, she perceived with concern.

'Uma, I must speak with the colonel. I can't allow our serving-woman and the driver to be punished for what is really my fault. I'll talk to the suwars.'

Uma swallowed some fruit-juice before replying, '*Ji,* that is good talk.'

Her immediate compliance surprised Tara. Uma usually argued or grumbled about the futility of Tara's plans—which she had been doing intermittently throughout breakfast, reminding the girl of her folly in trying to escape. 'You said you hated the raja of Motipur and all his relatives. Why, then, do you wish to go there?' she argued. So now when she concurred with her, Tara felt pleasantly encouraged.

'How does one address suwars, I wonder?'

'*Nahin,* Tara Bai,' Uma objected, wobbling her head. 'Let me. It is not done for a rajkumari to speak with common soldiers.' Before Tara could protest that it made no difference whether she was a princess or a commoner, Uma yelled, 'Good suwar, my brother, I would speak with you!' Uma rose in slow painful movements from her cross-legged posture, grunting the while. 'Come inside, good man.'

A suwar at the entrance muttered something to his companion and entered the hut, eyeing the women with suspicion. Understandable in the circumstances, Tara acknowledged, since his predecessors were probably nursing aching heads after imbibing drugged toddy. She was a little surprised that he had bothered to answer Uma's summons at all.

'*Ji,* respected mother?' he asked a trifle dourly, at the same time maintaining a respectful toleration extended to the old.

'What has become of the serving-woman and cart-driver we bribed, good man?' Uma's blunt question brought red shame sweeping into Tara's face. She might have used the word 'paid', instead of the vulgar 'bribed'!

'The *Panchayat*, the council, were of a mind to place them under guard and try them for treachery. But it was the poor woman's buffaloes that the tigers had dragged away and eaten, and she had no money to replace them. That is why she took the ring. On hearing this, our

Sikandar Sahib, the gods bless his good heart, has asked that she and the driver be spared. He has given them both money, and the woman extra rupees to buy more buffaloes.'

Markham had, after all, told the truth about compensating the woman and the driver. 'Thank the good Lord!' Tara sighed out her relief, forgetting that Uma was meant to do the talking, and the old woman snorted disapproval.

The suwar changed his tone to one of esteem. He brought his steepled hands to his forehead, bowed, and addressed Tara. 'Is that all, *Hazrat*, Highness?'

'That will be all,' Uma snapped, asserting her right to answer him, and the suwar flicked her an acid glance before withdrawing.

Tara pondered on the suwar's respectful address. Obviously Colonel Markham was now convinced of her true identity and had told his men so. What had assured him that she was indeed the late Raja Rao Chandra's daughter? The ring? But he would not accept blindly that it belonged to her without making enquiries or logical deductions. She could well have stolen it, and was now posing as the princess. Instinct warned her to be on her guard against...what, she was not yet clear.

No sooner had the suwar withdrawn, than she heard both guards click to attention and thump their boots. In marched Captain Dupont, who turned to Tara and saluted. Although his bearing was correct, she sensed that he disliked her more than ever. Perhaps he disapproved of troublesome women.

He doffed his topee, his forehead beaded with perspiration. '*Bonjour,* Highness.'

'Good morning, Captain.' Tara inclined her head coolly. He was not the only who could show dislike.

'Colonel Markham will be leaving within the hour, Highness.' This last with a hint of a sneer. 'And he has requested that you be ready to ride in the tonga waiting outside. We are returning to Chiriabagh Palace.'

'We'll be ready. Thank you, Captain.'

'My pleasure, mademoiselle.' So polite, so cold. Pompous wretch! Dupont replaced his hat, saluted, and was about to retreat when Tara spoke.

'And, Captain...' She favoured a regal tone, looking straight into his cold grey eyes, her own imparting contempt.

'Highness?' His glance wavered and slid away from hers. She rejoiced at his uneasiness, boosting in her a sense of malicious satisfaction.

'Is it possible for me to speak with Colonel Markham?'

'Your Highness shall have the opportunity. My Colonel will be escorting you, riding beside your conveyance.' His tone of voice implied that he objected to such an arrangement, regarding her as too lowly to enjoy the honour.

'Thank you.' She dismissed him with a condescending flip of her hand, and almost smiled in triumph on observing his face suffuse with scarlet indignation.

Tara's mind did not linger on Captain Dupont, a man of no importance as she judged him to be. She found herself eager to start the homeward journey, for, despite the massacre, the palace was the home where she had enjoyed a happy life. On familiar ground she could regain her sadly depleted confidence and stand up more firmly to Colonel Markham. She hurried through her refreshing bath in the tub placed behind a partition in the hut, and put on the clean but ill-fitting garments. She yearned to wear one of the English-style dresses her mother had ordered to be made from sheer muslin draped over silk embroidered petticoats. She had worn it last when her godfather Thomas Orme had visited the palace, but all her dresses had been destroyed in the raid. Dolefully she examined the drab pyjamas and shirt that did nothing to enhance her figure and stared at the well-washed *chuddah*, and grimaced.

By mid-morning the Blue Cloaks trotted out of the village to the accompaniment of drums, the chanting of '*Shabash!* Well done!' grateful cheering and blessings.

Colonel Markham, astride the grey stallion, rode on Tara's side of the tonga, and when the column were well on their way, he spoke. 'I believe you wished to speak with me, Highness.' Gone was the irritating mockery, and he addressed her with unemotional respect and the adherence to protocol reserved for eminent personages.

She was pleased to see that they were well out of earshot of his men, though the conversation would not be altogether private because of Uma seated by her side. Since the discourse was in English, she doubted whether the old one would understand, but if she did, it would not matter.

'Yes, Colonel. What convinced you that I am Rajkumari Tara Bai?' Her real title as authentic ruler was 'ranee', but at the moment she did not feel easy with the rank. 'My English mother would have called me Princess Tara.' She slanted him a quick glance, but he stared ahead, eyes narrowed against the glare, face hard, shadowed by the jutting brim of his topee.

'The ring, ma'am,' he replied abruptly.

He *did* believe it was hers! She recalled that no one in the state of Chiriabagh was permitted to copy it, a privilege accorded to the immediate members of Chiriabagh royalty. Whoever had handed the jewellery to Markham had probably explained this to him. For a moment her gaze rested on it sparkling on the little finger of his hand which held the reins with casual expertise.

'Simple, ma'am. The woman handed it to her husband. He, alas, recognised its worth and showed it to his father, who happens to be a member of the *Panchayat*. The old man realised the ring was royal property and passed it to the headman, who promptly set out to contact me at the hide. That's how it came into my possession.' A trace of laughter hovered in his eyes as he swept her a sidelong glance. 'He thinks you are my concubine and that you stole the ring from the finger of a slaughtered member of the royal family.' A pause. 'He suggested that I beat you.' He laughed softly.

'But, from your attitude, I gather that you are definitely convinced that I am Tara Bai and not some common thief,' she said in a stiff voice, ignoring what she regarded as his crude joke. Concubine, indeed! She arched a slim brow and angled her head, gazing into his face with unabashed directness in the hope of unsettling him.

He looked at her squarely. He was not at all as easy to disconcert as Captain Dupont! 'Yes,' he said.

'Why? The ring doesn't establish my identity.'

'First, your English is accentless, proof that your mother was indeed English. Second, from the portrait the headman has of your father and mother, you closely resemble that lady.' His jaws tightened for a moment, then switching his gaze to the road, he said, 'If you had stolen the ring, then you'd have also stolen those from the ruler's and his wife's hands. It was I who removed their rings.'

Tara gaped at him in horror, her breathing shallow, but he did not take his eyes from the dusty road, unaware of her reaction to his words. All doubts vanished from her mind. His bald confession of appropriating the jewels proved that he had killed her people. She quickly lowered her eyes to shield the horror manifest in them. Why had he told her this? Was he warning her that any misbehaviour on her part could bring about her death? Now more than ever he must not suspect that she knew of his complicity in the massacre, thus putting her life in jeopardy. This handsome Adonis, this seed of Satan, would have no mercy on her!

Once they arrived at the palace, she must find some way of escaping to Motipur, Raja Todar Ram's capital, and fulfil her father's wish and marry him. She stared at her hands working at a feverish pace, twisting in her lap, her heart frozen with hatred, her skin a-shiver.

She would persuade Todar Ram to launch an assault on Chiriabagh, and recover her kingdom, even if it meant razing the palace. Then...she swallowed... Then she would kill Colonel Markham. Kill him in cold blood!

CHAPTER SIX

ROGER MARKHAM gazed down at Tara from his perch astride the Arab stallion Galaxy, named for his blue-grey coat and white spots resembling faded stars in a dawn sky. As he rode alongside the tonga, he watched the girl's fine features tauten, her skin whiten. Her eyes, framed by straight black lashes, dropped to study the restless movements of her hands. He knew he had taken her aback.

The kiss he had forced on her at the tower, because he could not help himself, had aroused a strange emotion in him that surpassed the physical. He strongly disliked the sway she held over him in that she made him feel inferior, uncouth and unworthy of a proud regal woman—herself. Goddamn her—he was not going to tolerate her snobbery!

Despite her aloofness, this beautiful princess fascinated him more than any woman he had known, and he had known many, bedded a number too. None, however, had sent his heart dancing with just one look, as this girl did. And that look was not in the least provocative. He mused on what she would be like, ready and willing, in bed, and a ripple of arousal circulated throughout his body. Those shabby clothes she wore deceived him not at all; he had felt the firmness of her full breasts against his chest and the slimness of her waist when he had kissed her. The ill-fitting garments hid a rare beauty to match her face. Unadorned, it revealed refinement, intelligence and mystery.

Mystery there was. He puzzled over how she had escaped the massacre. The easiest way to find out would be to ask her, he thought drily, yet he refrained from doing so, sensing her restraint and hostility towards him. In the mood he judged her to be in, he assumed her answer to his question would be a blunt refusal to discuss the subject. Now was no time for interrogation. Later, when they had both rested and were in comfortable surroundings, he would probe for details.

Galaxy sidled and snorted with impatience. Heat or no heat, this highly-strung Arab needed an hour's vigorous galloping to calm him down. He flaunted his arrogance, objecting to mild trotting beside a tonga pony, Markham sensed with amusement. He was a snob, like her Highness Tara Bai!

Markham pulled on the reins. 'Quiet, boy! We'll be home soon, and then you can have the run of the *maidan*.'

He felt the girl's withering glance flick over him. She probably objected to his use of the word 'home' as if *he* owned the palace. He ignored her, staring ahead at his vanguard of Blue Cloaks surrounded by swirls of dust kicked up by their horses' hooves. Again he felt the power of her gaze exciting him, and he marvelled.

Her beauty had had no effect on Dupont, who had voiced his dislike of Tara. 'You expect me to bow and scrape to that half-caste, Colonel? I regret, monsieur, that I must protest.'

Markham had contained his rage with an effort, resisting the powerful urge to smash his captain's jaw. 'She happens to be royalty, Dupont, and in this country, royalty is respected. Therefore I command every one of my men, officers and rankers, to show her respect. Her Highness Tara Bai is no cheap whore from the bazaar!

And you'll not on any account speak of her in that de-rogatory manner in my presence,' he had told him in a stern voice the night before in the village hut. Dupont had entered when Markham was alone and on the point of preparing for bed after the celebration of the hunt.

'Céline will not agree to her being in the palace, Colonel.' Dupont stood defiantly in front of the *charpoy* where his commander reclined.

Ah, Céline, Dupont's voluptuous half-sister who had designs on a wedding, Markham remembered, stifling a yawn of boredom. She had pestered him to sell his land in Oudh, a gift from the nawab for fending off raiders. She had wanted him to marry her and return with her to France. 'We'll spend our honeymoon in Paris, *mon chéri.*' The woman had not been content with the jewels he had lavished on her. She bored him with her constant whining about the heat, the people, the country about which she knew nothing, and made no effort to do so. Her conversation, limited to the shallowness of a coquette, lacked intelligent curiosity, a stimulus which would generate interest in India and therefore provide the means to enjoy the best the country offered. He could imagine Céline's tantrums if he mentioned that he had no intention of marrying her! But why evade the fact? At his age of twenty-nine, he had not yet met a woman he loved enough to marry. 'I'll remind you, Captain, that Céline is not my wife.'

Dupont's pale skin took on the ruddiness of anger. 'But, Colonel, Céline told me...'

'Goodnight, Captain,' Roger said firmly, pushing his fingers through his hair and exhaling a tired sigh.

'Monsieur, Céline is my sister, and I can't allow her to be treated as a mere mistress of yours. We come from a respectable family.'

'I think Céline is old enough to speak for herself. She is no longer your concern.'

'Colonel...'

'That will be all. Goodnight, Captain.'

Dupont made a choking noise in his throat and only at the entrance of the hut remembered to salute. His near insubordination was becoming irksome, and Markham cursed himself for becoming involved with Céline. He supposed he could have tolerated her for a while longer. Now if she had been like Tara... He frowned, disliking the trend of his thoughts.

Relaxing back on the rickety bed, creaking from his movements, he curved his mouth in a sardonic smile. He recalled Dupont's prejudiced remarks on Tara's mixed blood, and laughed softly. What would be the captain's reaction if he knew that in his commander's veins flowed the blood of an American Indian?

The vanguard had now arrived at the bridge leading to the palace, and a cold shiver ran through the colonel. For him, the place had a haunted atmosphere as a result of the massacre. Who had been responsible? A pity he had received Rao Chandra's message too late. The raja's courier had been badly beaten, but left with just sufficient strength to crawl into the camp at Oudh and gasp out the raja's message, then lost consciousness from which he failed to recover.

During his five years in India, Markham had witnessed much bloodshed, the effect of straightforward fighting in which both sides were armed and equally matched. To be confronted by the unexpected and gory sight at dawn of the decapitated bodies of defenceless men, women and children sprawling in the courtyard of Chiriabagh, half eaten by jackals, picked at by vultures, had made his stomach heave. The outrage was not the work of Marathas, he was sure. They and the French had allied themselves with Sultan Hydar Ali, ruler of Mysore State to the south, against the British troops of the East India Company who were concentrating on collecting a grand army in preparation for the warclouds to burst.

Although Bihar province had been officially declared British territory by conquest, the British were too busy preparing for another war to have either the time or the inclination to interfere with independent states in Bihar that managed their affairs peaceably, he knew from reliable sources. Nor did they have sufficient troops to deploy in the defence of their Indian borders. In consequence, he concluded, the killings might be the outcome of a neighbourhood feud.

Markham glanced at the girl, who was gazing with a frown at her blind companion who coughed spasmodically, and a staggering thought entered his mind. Unless...!

He jerked at the reins, astounded by the sudden revelation, and Galaxy pranced, and whinnied resentment. Hell! It could be! He stroked the Arab's neck in apology. Supposing Tara had organised the raid? Not an impossibility, if one considered that her parents' deaths entitled her to inherit the throne of Chiriabagh, a small but wealthy state. Intrigues of this kind were rife among the nobility, and he wanted no part in them. Possibly Rao Chandra had planned to rid himself of Tara by marrying her off and leaving the throne free for his unborn child. The pregnant body of the raja's slaughtered wife had not escaped Markham's notice.

Surreptitiously he studied the proud tilt of Tara's head, and her regal bearing despite the shabby garments. He judged her to be a woman of high intelligence, capable of devising clever plots, accustomed to giving commands, perhaps imbued with ruthlessness and skilful at hiring thugs to carry out a crime advantageous to herself. Her kindness to the crone was probably a cover designed to deflect suspicion. The night before, he recalled, she had used bribery to leave the village in an attempt to contact her allies in preparation for ousting himself from Chiriabagh. He had no intention of leaving until he was certain that she was free from guilt. What she had miscalculated was her father's appeal to him, Markham, for help. Or perhaps the raja had not confided in Tara, because of his distrust of her. Had she somehow found out about the courier and tried to eliminate him? It could be, it could very well be. On the other hand, it could be simply his own wild conjectures. He sincerely hoped so, and suddenly wished he had never set eyes on her. This woman meant trouble!

But his thoughts would not be controlled. There were flaws in his reasoning, he reflected. Why was she at the tower alone with the crone? Where were the assassins she had hired? There must have been a whole army of them. Had she paid them off on the night of the massacre and headed for the seclusion of the tower? She had probably intended to wait there until the uproar had subsided, and at the right time to emerge and claim the Chiriabagh throne.

Roger Markham—he was aware that some of his officers had corrupted his name to *Raja* Markham—decided against questioning Tara as a suspect. She would deny her part in the slaughter whether she were guilty or not. He would have to find some other means of investigation.

If she insisted on leaving the palace, he could let her go, but keep track of her movements. In no circumstances must he allow her to beguile him with her charms. Not that she had tried to do so yet; in fact she seemed unaware of her attractiveness, which, he owned, heightened his own awareness of her. Tara's beauty had stunned him when he had first beheld her in the doorway of the tower, and in spite of the ill-fitting male clothing, her allure had been captivating. He smiled drily as the cavalcade clattered over the bridge. Instinct warned him that this beautiful princess, prone to ruthless ambitions of power, was not for him.

In the courtyard the column dispersed, the riders heading in the direction of the stables. Markham dismounted, and helped Tara down. Her hand lay passive in his and he curbed the roguish impulse to squeeze it; his delight in her angry reaction, the flash of her sapphire eyes, the flare of her delicate nostrils, the tightening of her lips that he ached to kiss again. But, he admitted, his feelings for Tara bordered on respect and seriousness; not the dalliance he enjoyed with coquettes like Céline. If she were innocent of the massacre, this princess or ranee was a woman he could . . . love? Whoa! He was suddenly surprised at the depth of his attraction to Tara.

As she turned away to help old Uma down, he called out to a Eurasian officer, 'Lieutenant Pullen!'

The young man handed his reins to a syce and ran up to the colonel and saluted. 'Sir!'

Markham looked Pullen over with approval. He had coaxed the young officer away from the army of the Maratha chieftain Sindhia, with the promise that he would not have to fight against his former employer. A handsome man, Pullen had inherited his English father's fair skin and his Rajput mother's noble features, dark eyes and black hair.

'Lieutenant, will you escort Princess Tara Bai to the zenana quarters? See that she is installed in the largest apartment.'

'Yes, sir.'

Tara flicked the young officer a cursory glance and then gazed with cool steadfastness at Markham. 'Colonel, the zenana has not been in use for years. The rooms are probably infested with vermin and snakes. Or am I to be treated like a common felon, and expected to sleep on straw?' In her eyes he saw contempt. He wondered what he had done to incur her aversion to this extent. Perhaps she was afraid he had guessed her part in the carnage!

'I recall, ma'am, that I invited you to be my guest.' His voice held a chilling edge to it. 'You can rest assured that the zenana apartments are now habitable. You'll find everything you need.'

Her blue eyes widened in mock astonishment. 'Guest, Colonel? Don't you mean your *"jest"*? I would remind you that this palace is *my* home and *you* are the intruder. I demand that you take your army and depart from here as soon as possible.'

A slow contemptuous smile curved his lips. 'And you intend ruling without experienced ministers, without knowing anything about administration? In truth, have you any idea where the villages in your realm are? Your dead father did ask for my help, and I intend to accede to his plea until I feel you are capable of ruling Chiriabagh.'

'*I* don't need your help, Colonel! I'll find wise ministers to replace the slaughtered ones.'

His impatience was surfacing fast. He sighed. 'Ma'am, this stifling courtyard is no place for carrying on an argument. Please, after you've rested, let us discuss the matter further.'

'Very well,' she agreed reluctantly. 'I'd like old Uma with me. She does not appear to be in the least well.'

Markham was not troubled about the crone's health at the moment. He was preoccupied by the stab of jealousy he felt watching Pullen's rapt gaze on Tara. 'Of course, ma'am.'

She flashed him a false smile. 'Thank you, Colonel.'

He eyed her broodingly as she guided the old woman and followed Lieutenant Pullen to an archway beyond which lay the zenana apartments. He noticed pain in the girl's eyes as she briefly surveyed the courtyard where the killings had occurred. Was she regretting her heinous crime?

'*Mon chéri!* Colonel!' A feminine voice arrested his thoughts.

Markham closed his eyes and groaned to himself, then turned to look up at the woman posing at the top of the broad flight of steps leading to the arched entrance of the main palace.

Dressed in green muslin draped in the polonaise style, over a wide petticoat of bronze shot silk, her shoulders and a generous portion of her pink breasts bare, she presented an enchanting picture to most men, but not to him. Faith, how she bored him! The hunt had been a pleasant relief from her overpowering presence.

'Céline.' Markham bowed and slowly mounted the steps.

'Colonel, did you kill the tiger?' she asked gaily, twirling a gold ringlet lying on her shoulder, and gazing provocatively at him.

To Markham, Céline's amber eyes were reminiscent of the tiger's, and, like the animal, she was beautiful and fierce, though her fierceness held no terror for him. Her half-brother Dupont was her victim who suffered the lash of her tongue and the tearing of her claws, yet he adored her. Markham believed the adoration was incestuous.

She touched him lightly on his arm and smiled into his eyes when he came abreast of her.

'We killed two. We brought back only their skins. But if you'll excuse me, mademoiselle, I must have a bath. The journey was hot and dusty.' A year ago he would have whisked her off to share his bath, but much had happened since then.

One day he had caught her whipping a woman servant who had accidentally tugged her hair while dressing it. He had arrived in time to snatch the lash from her hand before she had half-killed the servant. Although afterwards Céline was sorry, Markham's feelings for her had cooled. And now, by his reckoning, another ruthless woman was making sensuous inroads into his heart, except that she was doing it unknowingly and without any encouragement. On the contrary, she scorned him.

'So it is "mademoiselle" now, is it? No more "*Ma chérie*", hmn?' She tightened her hand on his arm, her face hardening. Anger did not become Céline; it transformed her beauty into ugliness, he noticed, the flawless skin became mottled, the mouth paled and thinned. 'Huh! I see why. You brought back more than the skins of two dead tigers, Colonel.' She cast a withering glance in the direction Tara had taken. 'That—that dowdy creature! Who is she? Your new toy? You are tired of playing with me, are you not? Now you choose her!'

From the corner of his eye he saw that his men had dismounted and instead of moving on to their quarters, were milling around, apparently listening to Céline's shrill tirade.

'I don't wish to discuss anyone with you, mademoiselle.' His eyes, cold, opaque, looked pointedly at her hand clutching his arm. 'If you'll excuse me.'

'A moment, Colonel.' He let out an impatient breath. 'Is she important to you?'

'She is important.' Did this goddamn woman not see that she was causing a scene?

'To you, monsieur?'

'No, to Chiriabagh.'

'It is a mystery that you concern yourself with this native state and its people with their numerous gods. You use your own money to help them. Why do you not *extract* revenue from them, as European nobles do from their tenants?'

He could tell her that Eastern nobles did the same, but that after the tragedy and pillage of Chiriabagh Palace, many ordinary people who depended on the royal family for their livelihood and who lived outside the precincts were now without jobs. Markham had put them all to work on the restoration of the palace. He was disinclined to discuss the issue with Céline; he was not interested in her or her views. So he remained silent.

Céline dropped her hand, frustration and crossness distorting her face. Markham tipped the brim of his hat and strode away into the cool interior, her voice shrilling after him. 'I'll find out who that woman is. You think to deceive me, bringing whores? *Mon Dieu!* Now, like the common soldiers, you have acquired a taste for the native women, do you dare to bring in strumpets while I am here? You think . . .'

He closed his ears to her diatribe. He had become inured to Céline's jealousy and tantrums, tolerating them only for the sake of her brother. In spite of his bigotry, Dupont was an able soldier and officer.

Closing the door of the raja's apartment, which he had taken over temporarily, Markham handed his hat to a hovering servant dressed in white muslin. 'Sunyal, I need a bath.'

'*Ji,* Sikandar Sahib, cold water awaits you in the bathroom.'

He thanked Sunyal and headed for the large bathing area of polished stone. Peeling off his clothes, he tossed them on a stool and placed his boots outside the beaded curtain in the doorway for the servant to collect for cleaning. He stepped behind a waist-high wall and scooped up water in a brass vessel from a metal tub placed on a high pedestal. The cascade was refreshingly cold, making him gasp with pleasure.

It reminded him of his childhood in Virginia, when he had splashed and swum daily in the stream that flowed beside the Indian encampment in the Rappahannock region where the tribe lived, and where he had shared a teepee with his half-breed mother Green Water, named for the colour of her eyes. She had called him Cougar Paw, and to honour her he used a lion's paw, claws extended, as the emblem on his blue standard. He remembered his mother vaguely as a cheerful woman. Then one morning he could not wake her, and the chief had told him that the Great Spirits had taken her soul. He had wept bitterly. Days later, a tall Englishman rode into camp, handed the chief some beads and money, and took Cougar Paw away. The man who had bought him called him Roger, and claimed to be his father, David Markham, a wealthy tobacco-planter with sprawling plantations on the banks of the James River. But it was his father's French wife who had made life miserable for him, taking the whip to him for little or no reason. Céline's ill-treatment of her servants had reawakened his own suffering at his stepmother's hands.

His stepbrother François, a year older than he, received similar harsh treatment from Roger's father, and the boys had saved each other on a number of occasions. A rapport had sprung up between them and they had grown fast friends. Their tormented lives stopped when Roger's father decided to send the boys to a boarding school in Jamestown. After their education, François was set to oversee the slaves on the plantations, and Roger was sent as an officer cadet in his father's trading vessels. When he attained his majority, his father had entrusted him with the captaincy of his merchantman *Markham* to transport tons of tobacco to France. Meanwhile, François had become embroiled in deep trouble, and to save him, Roger smuggled him aboard. When the ship docked at Cherbourg, he pocketed the money from the sale of the tobacco and the two men had taken a bone-shaking journey across France to the port of Marseilles, where they bought passages to India. But François had died...

'Sikandar Sahib, *Huzoor*,' Sunyal called, breaking Markham's thoughts.

'What is it?' he asked, drying himself and wrapping the towel round his waist.

'One risaldar has brought message,' the servant replied. He was a thin, short man, always eager to please, which Markham found endearing.

Markham emerged from the bathroom, bare-bodied except for a towel draped round his waist, the hair on his head and chest wet and tousled. He took the sealed scroll, wrapped in silk, from the platter the servant held out. 'Ask the risaldar to wait a moment, please.'

He put the unopened scroll on a low table and proceeded to dress. Pulling on a clean shirt and breeches, he lounged on a divan, eyeing the scroll with curiosity. 'Bring in the risaldar now, Sunyal.'

The cavalry major marched in and saluted. Markham recognised him as Risaldar Azamuddin and acknowledged the salute with a polite nod, invited him to be seated and offered him lime-juice, which he refused, saying that he had slaked his thirst.

'Who brought this?' Markham indicated the scroll.

The tall copper-skinned officer fingered his beard and replied, 'A man claims that he has come from a prince, Rajkumar Nagandra, who urgently needs your help, Sikandar Sahib. He, the messenger, explained that he went to your camp in Oudh and was told you had come here. He is tired and hungry, sahib, so I ordered that he be taken to the suwars' barracks and fed.'

'That was thoughtful of you, Risaldar. You did well. See that he has plenty of rest.'

The risaldar looked pleased, and nodded. 'I brought the message myself so that I can assist if it is written in Persian or Urdu. I know that you are fluent at speaking these languages, but cannot read or write them.'

'Quite. They're difficult languages for English-speaking people to grasp.'

Markham slipped off the silk wrapping, broke the seal and unrolled the scroll. Emitting a defeated laugh, he passed the parchment to Risaldar Azamuddin. 'You're right, I'll need your help. What does it say?'

The risaldar interpreted: 'Rajkumar Nagandra claims that he is the elder brother of Raja Todar Ram, hence the rightful heir to the throne of Motipur.'

'Wait. Where is Motipur? This is the place I'm anxious to locate. I received vague information that it lies north of Chiriabagh.' That was where Tara had been heading in her attempt to escape from the village, he recalled. He cocked his head, listening with deepened interest.

'It is about fifty *koss* from here, Sikandar Sahib. A large estate, I am told.'

'Fifty *koss*; that's about a hundred miles, isn't it? Go on.'

'Prince Nagandra wants your help to oust his brother.' The risaldar perused the scroll for a while in silence, then looked up, his face beaming. 'Sikandar Sahib, he writes that if you defeat Todar Ram, he will give you his estate where he is exiled at present, in a small valley in the Himalayas.'

Smiling at the irony, Markham rose to his feet, hooked his fingers into the waistband of his breeches and strolled about the apartment. Dwellers in the burning and war-torn plains dreamed of the cool Himalayan valleys. He understood the risaldar's yearning at the thought of a peaceful life in idyllic conditions, once the hazardous journey over the mountains had been overcome. He himself felt the same on occasions. But he was not given to hasty decisions. Prince Nagandra's claim might not be valid, his motive perhaps one of greed, possession, power. Raja Todar Ram might be the rightful heir to the Motipur throne. What proof was there that he was not? Besides, Markham's interests lay in finding the perpetrators of the massacre, not in becoming embroiled in wars of succession.

Coming to a halt in front of the risaldar, he said, 'You know my motto: Defend and not attack. If this Nagandra, prince or whatever, had asked me to defend his realm as Rao Chandra did, I would have considered his request. But it's against my principles to attack another ruler unless I have proof that he is a usurper.' He pointed to the scroll. 'I want to know more about these brothers and their feud.'

'The messenger can give us news, Sahib. Shall I bring him?'

'No, let him rest.' He settled on the divan and immersed himself in thought, gazing with absent eyes at the marble wall once draped with embroidered silks. Tara's face rose unbidden in his mind.

The sapphire eyes that had viewed him with contempt had disconcerted him more than he cared to admit. It occurred to him that she was the only survivor of the carnage and, whether guilty of it or not, she could impart the information he required if he conducted the interrogation with adroitness and discretion.

'Risaldar, the Ranee Tara Bai, as she claims to be, may be able to help us. I'll ask her to dine with me tonight.' He kept his voice casual, but his heart quickened with excitement. He yearned to see her alone. God's mercy! He was becoming a besotted fool!

'That is very good idea, Sahib,' the risaldar said, rising. 'I had not thought about Princess Tara Bai.'

Markham smiled drily to himself. And I have thought about little else.

CHAPTER SEVEN

MARKHAM READ her note several times. Formal and to the point, she had written in a clear rounded hand:

> Dear Colonel Markham,
>   Thank you for the invitation to dine alone with you tonight. You are aware that there are matters of importance I wish to discuss, therefore I look forward to seeing you at eight of the clock.
>   I am,
>   Yours sincerely,
>   Tara Bai.

Folding the letter, he tucked it into an inside pocket of his cutaway blue coat. He glanced at himself in the wall mirror in a gilt frame shaped like a domed arch. It had been cracked in the recent raid, but not sufficiently to mar his reflection. Gold epaulets and frogging gleamed in the candlelight of branched holders of European origin. The spotless starched cravat matched the frilled lace protruding beneath his jacket cuffs.

Turning away, he surveyed the chamber. His men had brought in some divans and tables that had escaped destruction. In the centre of the room stood a low fretted sandalwood table, and round it on the floor lay heaped cushions of blue, orange, violet and yellow silk, tasselled in gold.

Markham frowned, wondering if he had made the right choice of food. Considering that Tara's mother was English, she had possibly acquired a taste for that kind of fare, although her preference might be for local dishes. Since his army cooks were adept at curries, he had decided on an Indian meal of meat and vegetables. Most Europeans in India, he had noticed, relished the country's food. 'It burns out the palate,' one of his officers had joked, 'so anything else tastes insipid.' His mind wandered back to Tara. She might be a Hindu. She might be a Christian. She might be the instigator of the massacre—she might be a ruthless killer! As such, she would be determined to leave the palace with or without his consent, and she would return to try to throw him out. He was surprised at the spasm of pain he felt, occasioned by the thought of her departure and never seeing her again.

He squared his shoulders. Markham, reason must dominate emotion! By subtle means he would extract from Tara how she had escaped the massacre, and draw his own unbiased conclusions. His personal feelings must not be allowed to intrude. Egad! Women had made him suffer enough.

Just after Tara had completed dressing for dinner, a European woman of indeterminate age entered the chamber unannounced, and her blue eyes widened. She had seen this person before! The woman glided across the room and with smooth audacity subsided on Tara's divan, settling her bell-shaped skirt of russet silk with fussy exaggeration around her.

'Who, pray, are you?' Tara asked, more bewildered than annoyed.

'Tch, tch! Do you speak *le français*, mademoiselle?' she countered with a laugh that shrilled and jarred on Tara's ears.

'Yes, I speak a little French.' This was not going to be a friendly conversation, instinct warned her.

'*Bien!* This English—how is it you say?' She fluttered white hands and grimaced her distaste. '*C'est*...ah! vulgar. *Le français*, it flows like the music.'

Where have I seen this woman? Tara asked herself, and said to the woman, 'Who are you, mademoiselle?'

For a moment the French girl looked startled at Tara's sharp tone. Then her amber eyes narrowed, rippled over Tara and her glance dismissed her in a side-long sweep of disdain. 'The colonel, he has not mentioned me?'

'No. We scarcely know each other. Mademoiselle, I have a dinner invitation, and I do not wish to be late.' This woman irritated her and she wanted to be rid of her, also to be done with the wretched dinner. She hoped to leave this palace of tragedy; she felt the agony of unquiet souls crying out for vengeance and this could be accomplished only if she sought outside help.

'I am Mademoiselle Céline Dupont!' the Frenchwoman stated with a flourish, as if she had pronounced herself queen of France. 'Sister of Monsieur le capitaine Antoine Dupont!' As if he were king of France! 'Do you know him?'

'I know him.' And I dislike him as much as I dislike you! Both pompous asses, Tara yearned to say aloud. 'Now, if you'll pardon me...'

'Ah! But I am much intrigued to know who it is you are to dine with, *ma petite*. Is it the handsome Monsieur Pullen?'

'No, with Colonel Markham. Now if...'

'What!' Céline lunged to her feet and gripped the startled Tara's arm. Her eyes narrowed, lower lids quivering with fury, her breath erratic, spurting through flared nostrils. A tigress enraged!

Then it came to Tara that this was the woman she'd seen riding with Colonel Markham's Blue Cloaks towards Chiriabagh Palace on the morning following the massacre when she had made her escape. She stumbled back, wondering what she had said to earn this woman's fury. She wriggled her arm, striving to wrench it from Céline's grasp. 'Will you unhand me, mademoiselle! Have you lost your wits?'

Céline gave Tara's arm a vigorous shake before releasing it, and suddenly the French girl's anger evaporated. She smiled, the corners of her mouth dimpling, teeth white and even. Her gold hair shone in the lamplight, and Tara was forced to admit that she was indeed beautiful. The only visible sign that her anger remained was the heaving of her breasts.

Céline resettled herself on the divan. 'Pardon, *ma petite*. I was enraged that a young innocent like you has been enticed by that rakehell colonel! He is not for you. He is also the mercenary, very ruthless. Understand?' Not waiting for an answer, she dashed on, 'He left America with his stepbrother François and sailed for France.'

Céline rose and studied her reflection in the mirror, talking all the time. 'Alas, they found the civilised life of the French not to their liking and bought passages on a French India merchantman sailing from Marseilles. I was on it with my brother; we heard of the riches to be made in India. *Mon Dieu!* If I had known how hot and filthy this country is...' She sighed fretfully.

'François, the colonel's brother, died of a fever in the French settlement of Pondicherry, where we disembarked. I thought then that Monsieur Markham and my brother would want to return to France,' she said bitterly, 'but the colonel, he raised his own army of mercenaries and made my brother his captain.' Céline returned to the divan.

'Mademoiselle Dupont, I'm not interested in Colonel Markham's life.' A lie, Tara owned; she was very interested. One is always intrigued by the actions of one's enemy!

'Hear me out!' Céline snapped. 'He is a man of the world. Do you not see? I can manage men like him. Not you. Most important of all, I advise you to take heed, for he is my betrothed.'

Tara said nothing in the hope that this woman would sense her boredom and leave.

'We are to be married after Christmastide,' Céline continued, her amber eyes scrutinising Tara's face, as if hoping to disconcert her. 'I warn you that he is using you. He thinks to make me jealous with a little dalliance. La! Do not be fooled, *mon enfant*, if you have the pride of the ranee you claim to be.' With a laugh of malicious triumph, she gathered up her skirts and swept from the room.

'Sikandar Sahib! The Rajkumari Tara Bai,' one of the suwars sent to escort Tara announced from beyond the hanging mat doused to cool the interior and placed over the entrance.

'Enter!' Markham commanded.

She heard his quick indrawn breath as she came into view, her slim figure swathed in a blue sari spangled with gold stars and edged with gold braid, with a short-fitting bodice to match. After her escort had been dismissed, she stood uncertainly just inside the doorway, patting the coil of her rich dark hair in a gesture of awkwardness.

Moving towards her, Markham abandoned the Indian *namasta*. He lifted her hand to his mouth, and she felt the movement of his lips on her rose-scented skin. Her dislike of his contact was conveyed by the trembling of her hand. 'Good evening, Highness.' He did not release her fingers until he had led her to the table.

Her eyes wide, Tara studied him with suspicion, her face pale, taut and beautiful. 'Good evening, Colonel.' Her voice was grave and controlled, and hid the fear she experienced; she did not trust this man at all.

He smiled, exerting his charm to put her at ease, she suspected, politely indicating the divan against the wall and waited until she had seated herself before settling beside her at a respectable distance. 'May I offer you some Madeira wine, ma'am? I assure you it is of the finest quality.'

'No thank you, Colonel. I am not partial to wine.'

'China tea, perhaps?'

'No, thank you. It's too late for tea. But please don't let my presence prevent you from drinking what you wish.'

She saw she had impressed him with her good manners and hoped he considered that it stemmed from good breeding, so that he was not free to treat her as an ill-bred doxy. She watched him pour the wine from a sparkling decanter a servant had brought out on a silver tray and placed on a small table. As he sipped, he gazed over its rim at her. It was unbelievable that this man could enjoy his drink without the slightest qualms of conscience, here in this eating chamber where his victims, her mother and father, had entertained and dined with eminent guests!

'I hope you and old Uma find your quarters comfortable,' Markham said, breaking the silence that stretched uneasily.

She jumped a little, and cursed herself for displaying her nervousness. 'Yes—yes, thank you, Colonel. But Uma is not well. She coughs too much and has refused her meals. I fear it may be the wasting disease.'

'I will send a *hakim* to tend her.'

'There's no need for a doctor at present. She's asleep, and a woman servant is with her. Lieutenant Pullen kindly arranged it.'

When Markham's face hardened with anger, she wondered whether he objected to her asking his men for help. Did he imagine he owned everybody?

'Tomorrow then, send word to me if she's no better and I'll send a doctor.'

She nodded her thanks.

'I see that you found some good clothes in that chest I had conveyed to your room.' His eyes lingered on the fitted bodice.

'Where did you find it? It belonged to my mother. This sari she wore on state occasions.' She hoped he caught the innuendo in her last sentence, implying that she too had donned the sari to treat this dinner as a formal event and not some illicit tryst.

'In one of the godowns.' He tossed back the wine and refilled his glass.

Her mother must have packed away her clothes until after her confinement. Tara remembered that she had taken to wearing embroidered kaftans a few weeks before her death. Oh, Mama, the pain! This man must have offered the clothes to his paramour and that wench probably refused them, dubbing them outmoded.

'Colonel.' She lifted her eyes to meet his steady gaze. 'I didn't come here for polite conversation, but to discuss something of importance with you.' Her voice now held the hardness of resolution.

'I know. You said so in your letter. Perhaps we could detain it till after dinner, lady,' he said quickly. 'Meanwhile, I want you to enjoy whatever meagre hospitality I can offer.' He stood up, bowed and indicated the cushions on the floor round the low table. 'Highness, after you.' His hypocritical courtesy sickened her. She yearned to tell him to go to the devil.

The army cook had excelled himself in the Indian dishes brought out on large platters and placed in the centre of the circular table. Servants, immaculate in white cotton and blue cummerbunds, hovered dutifully behind the two diners.

Tara noticed none of the Chiriabagh gold plate; crockery of European design was set out in its stead. She supposed that Markham had converted the gold and treasure to money. She helped herself to saffron rice and mince-balls in spiced sauce, but waited until he began eating before she started; she could not rule out the possibility that he might poison her and eliminate the last claimant to the rich prize of the Chiriabagh throne. Since the water in the tumbler was for her alone, she decided against drinking it.

He frowned at her. 'I can promise, lady, that none of this food or drink has been...er...tampered with.'

Although she felt justified in her wariness, she could not prevent her face from turning scarlet with guilt, but refused to be drawn into an argument and remained silent.

When the dessert of almond pastry and a basket of fruit arrived, she decided to speak. 'Colonel, tell me, what brought you to India?'

His green eyes narrowed and his lips curved in cynicism. 'I was beginning to wonder whether you observed silence at meals. Why did I come to India? I fear it had to do with a killing.'

She was not surprised, but why had his betrothed, Mademoiselle Dupont, not mentioned it? Perhaps she was too ashamed to do so.

'Perfectly legal, I might add.'

Tara cast him a cutting glance. 'Is there such a thing as legal killing, Colonel?'

'I assure you, ma'am, that killing in warfare and duels is lawful.'

'And you killed someone in a duel, so you decided to run here to avoid retaliation from your victim's allies?'

'No, my stepbrother François did.'

She raised her eyebrows in disbelief. 'Indeed?'

'Yes, indeed. His opponent was the son of a wealthy and influential Virginian planter. It was just as well I was due to sail on my father's merchant ship carrying tobacco for France. I smuggled François aboard.'

'But why come to India?'

'A matter of chance.' He went on to repeat what Céline Dupont had told her.

Markham selected a mango from the fruit basket, cut off a side and scooped up spoonfuls of the sweet orange flesh. 'Unfortunately, a few months after our arrival in Pondicherry, François died of an unknown fever.'

'And you founded a mercenary contingent?'

'Yes. All European armies are mercenary in this country, ma'am. The French, British and Dutch hire out their battalions to various rulers. I just happen to have an independent corps of my own.'

'And you will be returning to America?' *With all the booty from my realm!*

'No. I like India.'

'You mean you like the wealth you can rob from it?'

He did not answer her question, but repeated, 'I like this country and its people.' He finished his mango, and a servant brought in fingerbowls of water, and napkins.

As soon as the retainers had cleared the table and left the chamber, Tara and Roger resumed their seats on the divan.

'Colonel, it's time I . . .'

'I think, Tara,' he let her name roll out softly, 'we should enjoy the night air on the roof. It's private there.'

At first she stiffened, eyeing him with suspicion; she had no wish to experience a repetition of the kiss he had forced on her that night at the tower, but observing his bland expression, she gave a nod of consent.

On the flat roof, they viewed the semicircle of silver moon that sliced the indigo sky coruscating with large stars. Tara could feel his stare boring into her, and shifted her gaze from the sky to his face. It looked pale and taut, the eyes smouldering with passion. He frightened and enraged her. Could this wretch not sense her abhorrence of him? She backed to the waist-high parapet edging the square roof, and slowly, deliberately, he followed. She came up short against the wall, its intricate design digging into her back.

As he caught her shoulders and drew her to him, Tara cried in alarm, 'Don't dare to touch me, Colonel! I shall not tolerate your advances. What do you take me for? Have I not plainly shown how much I hate you, a vile mercenary who makes a fortune from spilling blood?' While she struggled to free herself, he tightened his hold, squeezing her shoulders until she cried out, 'Let me alone! I saw it all from there!' She nodded to the adjoining roof.

Slowly he released her and she slumped against the parapet, staring at him in terror. He looked fierce and stunned. Had he guessed that she suspected him?

'You saw what?'

She could not answer his sharp question because of the tears clogging her throat as she recalled the whole ghastly slaughter.

He persisted, 'You saw the massacre?'

Abruptly she turned her back on him so that he would not see the tears gathering in her eyes. 'Y-yes.'

'And you were able to identify the assassins?' He spun her round to face him, and the tears trickling down her cheeks sparkled in the moonlight.

'No, they were masked. I saw my mother and father and all the inhabitants of the palace—murdered.' She could not look at him, her glance settling on the nearby roof. She pointed to it. 'From that pavilion in the corner.' Tara heard his sharp indrawn breath. 'I saw it all, Colonel. And I shall not forget. Night after night I hear the screams, see the blood, the headless bodies. I—I could not get out of the pavilion because the door had jammed, or I might not be up here to tell you about it.' She added in her mind: slaughtered by your evil hand. Losing control, she sobbed bitterly, overwhelmed with grief, scarcely aware he had gathered her into his arms.

'Then what happened, Tara?'

She hardly noticed the huskiness of his voice. 'I—I lost consciousness,' she gulped against his strong shoulder. 'But—but when I revived I—I heard jackals. I managed to unlock the door and make my escape.' She thought she felt his chest heaving. 'You discovered the bodies. What happened to them, Colonel?'

'We cremated them on a common pyre. Hindu priests performed a ceremony, and our army chaplain said a Requiem Mass.'

She buried her face in her hands, her body racked with harsh sobs. 'Oh, the screams, the blood!'

'Tara!' he whispered. His arm circling her waist drew her closer against him. Then he slowly lifted her chin, but she could see his face only as a blur through her tears. The next moment, his mouth covered hers.

Too stunned to move, she did not resist at first. When she felt his hand move up towards her breast, her senses sprang alert, making her fully aware. Apart from his bold handling of her, she found he had partly bent her over the parapet as though he were about to toss her down. No doubt he would, after he had amused himself.

With a sudden twist, she swung out of his embrace away from the parapet and backed away from him. 'Don't touch me, Colonel! I will not tolerate such insolence from you,' she said in a stinging voice. 'I came here to ask if I might leave Chiriabagh.'

He dropped his hands, his mouth lifting in a derisive smile, eyes black with savage fury. 'Arrogant bitch!' he hissed through clenched teeth. 'Who the devil do you think you are? Some goddess to be worshipped and not touched? You have suffered a terrible tragedy, but when I try to offer you help and kindness, what do I get? I have it all hurled back at me!'

'Touching me...in—in that way is not offering me help and kindness, Colonel. I'm not a naïve innocent, neither am I arrogant. But I'll not bandy words with a worthless mercenary. I wish to leave Chiriabagh.'

He gave a short bitter laugh. 'It doesn't make sense. Chiriabagh is your home...'

'It *was* my home, Colonel. *You* have usurped it. *You* have made yourself master here.'

He said impatiently, 'Only as a temporary measure...'

'And you have a mind to beguile me with your advances! That's what that lustful kiss meant—to treat me as a concubine!' She drew herself up, throwing back her head, glaring up at him.

'Certainly I'm not dallying with you, and have no intention whatsoever of treating you as my concubine.'

'Ah, you don't know that Mademoiselle Dupont has informed me that she is to be your wife. Congratulations, Colonel!'

Stunned silence reigned for a few thundering beats of her heart.

'Indeed?' He raised an eyebrow, an ironic smile curled his lips, but anger blazed from his eyes.

'And I, Colonel, am betrothed to his Highness Raja Todar Ram of Motipur. I wish to be conducted to his palace.'

He stared at her moving away from him, her clothes susurrating with her quick steps until she disappeared down the stairs. Then he turned, and thumped the parapet. His head rang like the clanging of a temple gong.

'Bitch! Goddamned bitch!'

CHAPTER EIGHT

TARA FLED towards the zenana, her heart pounding from her encounter and Colonel Markham's lecherous kiss. The dinner had turned into a fiasco. After the rage he had been in when she left, she wondered whether he would permit her to leave for Motipur. Moreover, had he invited her to dine solely to hurl her over the parapet to crash below in the ill-fated courtyard after he had violated her? She felt shaken at her close brush with death. He had shown his crude nature when he had called her an arrogant bitch, she thought wrathfully, and wished she could have voiced her resentment. How dared he!

At the archway entrance to the zenana she groaned as she met Céline Dupont coming out. 'Ah, mademoiselle, you have left the colonel already?'

'I have already told you it was but a formal dinner, mademoiselle. I asked Colonel Markham if I could leave Chiriabagh. Perhaps you can be more persuasive? I also congratulated him on his betrothal to you.'

She could see Céline plainly in the flare from the torches her suwar escorts carried. The French girl's eyes widened in alarm. 'But it—it is not official yet . . .'

Tara felt complacent at having caught the woman out in a lie. 'I think, mademoiselle, you should not waste time in talking to me, but join your fiancé. I dare say he is in an amenable mood and will welcome you.' Céline looked pleased. 'But hurry, mademoiselle,' Tara swept on, 'lest he change his mind. *Bonne nuit!*' With a slight nod she took her leave, but not before she saw Céline frown. So at last the silly creature had detected a trace of sarcasm!

Her two guards came to a halt when she stepped into the bare reception hall. Inhaling the smell of fresh whitewash, she flopped on to a divan to regain her breath. Once her breathing returned to normal, she stood up and crept to the side chamber Uma occupied.

The old woman lay in peaceful slumber on a comfortable divan. Beside her, stretched out on a rug on the floor, slept a woman servant. Tara tiptoed over and gazed lovingly at Uma, hoping that she would be well on the morrow, for they must not linger in Chiriabagh. To remain here in dangerous proximity to Colonel Markham and his detestable paramour Mademoiselle Dupont was unthinkable. Nor could she leave the old woman behind, or the colonel might throw her out on the streets to beg. She would have to resort to bribery yet again; she still had valuable pieces of jewellery in her possession.

Closing the door of Uma's chamber, Tara walked down a short corridor to her own room: large, bleak, with a single divan near the fretted window and the chest in which was stored an assortment of her mother's apparel. She removed her clothes and slipped into a night robe, trembling at her actions and not from cold; the apartment was hot despite the open window. Turning down the lamp, she lay on her back in bed, unable to compose her shivering body as she relived the dinner in Markham's company and the earlier confrontation with his mistress. She cursed herself for being immersed in her own grief and dull-witted enough to allow Markham to kiss her: a traitor's kiss, and she a traitor to the memory of her parents. They had met their deaths at the hands or orders of the man who had succeeded in touching her so intimately.

'No!' she moaned aloud at the ugly thought that she had allowed him to go so far. She raised her hand as if to ward off the guilt like a knife about to plunge into her brain. Why had he looked so astounded when she had informed him of her betrothal to Todar Ram? Could it have upset his plans? Had he intended to seduce her, to make her his temporary mistress and consolidate his hold over Chiriabagh? Yes! It made sense. Once he had accomplished his purpose, he could toss her aside, if not over the parapet, and marry Mademoiselle Dupont—just as her father had discarded his Hindu wife and concubines to marry her mother. She felt discomfited by the direction of her thoughts. Why am I brooding over my father's Hindu wife? Has fate decreed that I should suffer in the self-same manner to answer for my father's sin? It seemed uncannily so.

Her own plans could prove successful now! With her announcement of her own betrothal to Todar Ram, she had avoided humiliation and made it possible for Markham to marry Céline Dupont, and hence to gain possession of Chiriabagh without involving her. But would the people accept an alien ruler and his alien wife? It was difficult to say.

She smiled in triumph. He had no idea what *she* planned for him! With Todar Ram's help, she would regain her realm and effect Markham's downfall. The smile deepened, not with humour but with artfulness. He thinks I am a half-wit, easily hoodwinked by his lascivious kisses. How wrong you are, Colonel!

'*Hazrat*, Tara Bai!' A voice penetrated Tara's sleep-enshrouded head. 'Princess, wake up!'

Tara mumbled, yawned, turned over and snuggled down for further sleep.

'Please wake, Highness.'

The beseeching wail of the female voice brought her out of her slumber, and she made disgruntled noises, rubbed her eyes and frowned at the woman-servant employed to tend Uma. 'Yes?'

'Umaji has left her bed, Highness. She will not lie down and has locked herself in the bathroom. She is telling me in proud voice, "Go!"' the woman elaborated, wringing her hands in distress. 'I am thinking, what am I to do?'

Tara's frowning disapproval, changed to one of anxiety. She leapt out of bed and raced to Uma's room, where she came to a surprised halt.

Uma was standing upright, twisting a gold-bordered yellow sari round her. No longer did she stoop, and with astonishing deftness and swiftness completed dressing herself.

'Uma?' Was it the same woman? Tara stretched her head forward, and edged tentatively towards the old lady. 'Uma, are you... Are you well?'

'Can you not see, Tara Bai, that I am quite well? The servant is troubled because I refused to let her into the bathroom. Is one to have no privacy?'

The croak had vanished, the crone had vanished. In her stead stood a tall woman, still blind, still thin. A woman who held herself with a dignity Tara had not glimpsed before. Such an awesome, unbelievable change left her aghast, bereft of speech.

'The *hakim* tended me at dawn. He gave me a potion which worked well,' Uma said casually as if she were unaware of the shock she created, her speech and tones cultured, and from what Tara suspected, enjoying herself hugely.

Tara lifted her shoulders in a helpless shrug. 'But—But yesterday you ... you ...'

Uma laughed, and it was no longer the cackle of the very old woman that Tara had known. 'I was dying?'

'No, not dying. I meant to say you were so ill.'

'Nothing more than a cough, Tara Bai,' she said dismissively. 'Sleep is healing, and it helped to cure my cough, along with the learned *hakim*'s effective mixture.'

'It seems to have done a great deal more than cure your cough,' Tara said, partly drily and partly awestruck.

Uma addressed the servant, who stared, mouth agape. 'Rumi, are you still there?'

'*Ji*, Umaji.'

'Then leave us, good woman.'

The servant backed out of the room and bowed low as she went.

Tara's amazement increased, marvelling at this miraculous transformation in Uma. 'Crone' seemed an inappropriate word now. She watched Uma move regally, arms outstretched, feeling for the fretted window. 'You think I am gifted with magical powers, Tara?'

'N-no, Uma, but I believe you are an adept at masquerade.'

'Hmm. Are you dressed, Tara Bai?'

'No, I'm still in my night robe.'

'Then get dressed quickly and return here. We must talk.'

Without ado Tara obeyed the old lady's authoritative command. Somewhere at the back of her mind lay a hazy recollection of Uma's cultured voice. Of course, in the tower! So, although the old one had slipped up on a couple of occasions, she was to be lauded for her clever deception.

Outside the apartment the servant crouched on her haunches and stared at Tara as she went by, her eyes rounded with superstitious fear. In a daze Tara completed her toilet and rushed back to Uma. The sight that met her eyes left her thunderstruck.

Uma sat cross-legged on a high cushion, her clean hair now coiled neatly on her nape, and a silk blindfold hid her disfigured eyes. She was smoking a hookah. She sucked in smoke through a silkbound pipe attached to a flat-bottomed glass bowl filled with water that gurgled every time she drew on the mouthpiece fixed to the pipe.

Removing the hookah from her mouth, she asked, 'Is that you, Tara?'

'Y-yes,' she replied in a dazed whisper. The old lady must either be possessed or rejuvenated from the brink of senility, a result of the *hakim*'s amazing potion!

'Come, child, be seated. You are wondering what has become of the village hag. Eh?'

Tara moved to do Uma's bidding and sat down. 'Naturally. I—I mean, you *have* changed. And I—I cannot understand this needless deception. Why pretend to be what you are not?'

'Why does one practise deceit, Tara? You yourself have tried to do so, have you not? You attempted to hide your identity from Sikandar Sahib out of fear. So it is with me. But I have fooled you both.'

'You have indeed. But why? I do not understand.'

'It is fear that makes us deceive. But I comprehend that you who lived with me are wondering who I really am.' Uma pulled on the hookah, and it chuckled as if enjoying the enigma. 'I shall tell you when the right moment comes. I had intended to dissemble for a while longer, but I am weary of acting the ignorant crone.'

Tara's forehead puckered in perplexity; she felt disconcerted by this serene old...stranger, for that was how Uma appeared to her. 'I dare say you are playing a mischievous game.'

'*Ji*, yet a carefully thought out game, Tara, not for sport, and well performed, although I say this myself. Be patient, my child. In time you will know all. Not yet. Not yet.' She dragged on the hookah and puffed out a stream of smoke. 'I hear we leave for Motipur today, so the servant said. I heard much disturbance in the pigeoncote last night, so I am thinking Sikandar Sahib was busy sending messages.'

'You say "we leave for Motipur". You, too, wish to travel there?' Tara waved away the smoke that drifted towards her, resenting that she was the last to know of the journey, and indirectly too. And she was the main reason they were leaving! Or was this Colonel Markham's way of showing petty revenge on her for her rejection of his advances last night?

'*Ji*.' Uma paused thoughtfully. 'I must go for a reason. You have been kind to me, Tara Bai, so now it is my turn to repay you. And it shall be done in Motipur. I have thought long on that.' She angled her head, concentrating on listening. 'I hear someone approaching.'

After a while Tara too heard booted footfalls. She wondered if Markham had decided to deliver details of the journey himself. Her heart began a rapid dance of panic; she did not want to meet him ever again; did not want to be reminded of that shameful kiss!

A knock sounded on the door. 'May I come in?'

'Enter!' Uma commanded, well into her role of—Tara knew not whom.

To her relief, Lieutenant Pullen stepped in. He almost stumbled backwards when he spotted the old lady, elegantly garbed, smoking a hookah.

'Ye gods! What have we here?' He squeezed his dark eyes shut, then opened them wide. For an instant he stared. Then he threw back his head and roared out laughing.

He alerted Tara to the humour of the situation. Uma smoking a hookah, a male preserve, was indeed a novel and hilarious sight. Tara hid her eyes behind her hand and joined Pullen in his mirth, her shoulders heaving helplessly.

The old lady smoked on with cool impassivity, heedless of the hilarity she created. She drew on the hookah, gurgling away, until Pullen's laughter petered out.

'You have a message for us, Pullen Sahib?' Uma's stern question sobered him.

'Er... yes.' He cleared his throat self-consciously, dipped into the pocket of his waistcoat and withdrew a slip of paper, which he handed to Tara with a brief bow. 'For you, Highness, compliments of Colonel Markham.'

'Thank you, Mr Pullen.'

Tara read the note written in a large flourishing hand. Colonel Markham informed her that he had despatched a message last night by carrier pigeon to Raja Todar Ram to tell him that Tara wished to join him at Motipur Palace. If he agreed, arrangements would be made for the journey. By the same method, the raja had replied early this morning that Tara was welcome at any time.

The missive conveyed a terseness that Tara welcomed. She folded the note and handed it back to the lieutenant. 'I don't need this any more.' She wanted no reminders of Markham! 'Will you be coming with us, Mr Pullen?'

'Alas, no, Highness.' The young officer sighed his regret. 'Captain Dupont and a few of his suwars will escort you.'

His words filled her with alarm; she was aware of the Frenchman's dislike of her. Perhaps Markham was, too, and this was his way of punishing her. As if she cared.

Pullen continued, 'However, Colonel Markham advises that the old lady be left behind until she recovers from her illness. He says he understands your haste to reach Motipur and fears she might hamper your progress.'

Tara was filled with qualms. She recognised the sting in the words so innocently relayed. She glanced at Uma puffing serenely. The old woman's thoughts seemed far away.

'As you can see, Uma is fully recovered and will now travel with me. It is her wish to do so. Please tell Colonel Markham so, Mr Pullen.' She saw the pained expression in the officer's eyes, and regretted her sharpness.

Soon after breakfast, they left, and Tara's heart ached with nostalgia as her gaze roamed the zenana courtyard where she had spent a happy childhood playing with the children of the palace ministers. She raised her eyes and looked up at the marble domes on the flat roof of the main palace. I'll be back, she promised silently. I'll throw that usurper out when Todar Ram gives me his assistance!

Tara found Dupont's brusque orders for Uma and herself to climb into the tonga distasteful, and despite her enmity to Colonel Markham, she wished she had raised objections to travelling with this rude man. She did not relish being in the Frenchman's unwelcome company for the next few days or as long as it took to reach Motipur.

On its way to the northern gate, the small column with baggage train of foodstuffs, fodder and luggage loaded on mules passed the palace *maidan*, the field where Tara's father had taught her to ride and to play polo. What happy hours those had been!

She parted the curtain, and her body tensed with outrage when she espied Colonel Markham and his officers playing at tent-pegging. The effrontery! The desecration! But the change in the weather prevented her from acting on any foolish impulse of ordering him off her land. The hot blue sky was suddenly invaded with billowing dark clouds, and the distant growl of thunder could be heard. Rapidly the storm approached; a strong wind sprang up and gusts swirled spirals of dust on the road.

Her attention fastened on Markham, dressed in tan breeches and white shirt, sleeves rolled up to display his muscular arms. He had made himself completely at home, she thought acidly. She watched as he streaked along on Galaxy, his hair tied back with a broad black riband, a copper-gold forelock blown forward in the wind. Lance in hand, he bent low in the saddle, then riding at full gallop on a roped-off track, he speared up one of the tent-pegs hammered in the ground parallel to the track. He laughed aloud with pure enjoyment while his men applauded. Not once did he glance at the travellers riding by, although he must have seen them and been aware that she was watching him from the tonga.

Her gaze slid away from him to a spreading tree under which sat his paramour, Céline Dupont. She was garbed in pale pink muslin and satin, a matching wide-brimmed hat gracing her blonde curls. She dropped her fan and clapped enthusiastically as Markham scored his victory. He rode up to her, said something, and they both looked across at Tara and laughed. They were mocking her, and she knew a burning humiliation and rage. The next moment lightning flashed, thunder crashed and rolled and the rain came sheeting down. Markham swooped, caught Céline round her waist, swept her in front of him on the saddle and galloped away. For an instant he twisted round and gave Tara a parody of a salute.

Seething with fury, Tara drew the side curtains and stared ahead through the open front of the tonga at the wall of rain. They deserved each other, those two—the bitch and the bastard! She wished them every unhappiness in their betrothal.

The French woman had been correct: Markham had indeed been dallying with her, Tara, last night. Her face felt scorched with angry mortification. Tears of painful frustration and helplessness gathered in her eyes and flowed in unrestrained streams. She made no move to stem the flow, since Uma could not see and had no idea of her distress.

In the monsoon-drenched days that followed, Tara experienced the extent of Dupont's dislike. He did not venture near the women's tent when the group camped for the night. Once a day they were fed with coarse stale chappatis and a thick unsalted lentil gruel filled with grit. When Tara complained to the two suwars guarding their tent, they said it was captain sahib's orders. Out of sympathy they cooked appetising food and shared it with the two women. But after a couple of days the kind suwars, Hanif and Wazim, were replaced by two insolent troopers who angered and frightened Tara. She suspected that Dupont employed them as spies.

Uma's odd behaviour added to Tara's uneasiness. She made no complaints, ate little and smoked her hookah far too much. She would wake in the night and call out for 'Sharmali'.

'Who is Sharmali?' Tara asked.

'My daughter. She may be dead.'

But Tara sensed that other things troubled the old woman. 'Tell me, Uma, what else distresses you?'

'You will find out soon, Tara Bai. Soon—in Motipur,' she said, dragging in smoke, and the hookah plopped and gurgled as if involved in some sinister conspiracy with its owner.

Monsoon rains increased their discomfort. The torrential downpour and intermittent hot sun produced humidity, and sweat poured down Tara's body, inducing prickly heat. They were allowed only half a bucket of water to wash with daily.

Her mind swirled in turmoil as they neared their destination. So engrossed had she been in her hatred of Colonel Markham that she had given the future little or no thought. What would be her fate in Motipur? It hit her with unprecedented force that she would have to marry the gross Todar Ram in order to accomplish her revenge. She felt sick as she visualised giving her body to so repulsive a being. She hardly noticed the villagers chanting and toiling in the flooded paddy and cane fields, so immersed was she in the hell of her thoughts. Uma did not improve matters. She surrounded herself with a wall of silence, discouraging conversation.

At last, on a dismal humid afternoon, they entered the city of Motipur. Tara stared in horror at the army of ragged beggars swarming in the bazaars. An atmosphere of fear reigned. It was visible in the dark eyes of the citizens who slunk about, making themselves inconspicuous to the richly garbed armed men patrolling the streets which were filled with darkened shops with

4 BOOKS PLUS A CLOCK AND MYSTERY GIFT

Here's a sweetheart of an offer that will put a smile on your lips . . . and **4 FREE** Mills & Boon Romances in your hands. **Plus** you'll get a digital quartz clock and a mystery gift as well.

At the same time, we'll reserve a Reader Service subscription for you. Every month you could receive 6 brand new Mills & Boon Romances by leading romantic fiction authors, delivered direct to your door. And they cost just the same as the books in the shops — postage and packing is always completely FREE. There is no obligation or commitment — you can cancel your subscription at any time. So you've nothing to lose! Simply fill in the coupon below and send this card off today.

Please send me 4 FREE Mills & Boon Romances and my FREE clock and mystery gift.

Please also reserve a Reader Service subscription for me. If I decide to subscribe, I shall receive 6 brand new Romances each month for £7.50, post and packing free. If I decide not to subscribe I shall write to you within 10 days. The free books and gifts will be mine to keep in any case.

I understand that I may cancel my subscription at any time by simply writing to you. I am over 18 years of age.

9A8T

NAME＿＿＿＿＿＿＿＿＿＿＿＿＿＿＿＿＿＿＿＿＿＿＿＿＿＿＿＿＿＿＿

ADDRESS＿＿＿＿＿＿＿＿＿＿＿＿＿＿＿＿＿＿＿＿＿＿＿＿＿＿＿＿

＿＿＿＿＿＿＿＿＿＿＿＿＿＿＿＿＿＿＿＿＿＿＿＿＿＿＿＿＿＿＿＿

＿＿＿＿＿＿＿＿＿＿＿＿＿＿＿＿＿POST CODE＿＿＿＿＿＿＿

AS A READER SERVICE SUBSCRIBER, YOU'LL ENJOY A WHOLE RANGE OF BENEFITS. . .

This attractive digital quartz clock — Yours Free!

★ Free monthly newsletter packed with competitions, recipes, author news and much, much more.

★ Special offers created just for Reader Service subscribers.

★ Helpful friendly advice from the ladies at Reader Service. You can call us any time on 01-684-2141.

So kiss and tell us you'll give your heart to Mills & Boon.

✂ -

Reader Service
FREEPOST
P.O. Box 236
Croydon, Surrey
CR9 9EL

POST THIS CARD TODAY!

NO STAMP NEEDED

no wares on display. Cows and bulls, however, ambled about unmolested, and pariah dogs, their ribs showing through mange-covered coats, scavenged in the gutters. The stench of open sewers polluted the air.

All of a sudden a band of armed men surrounded the travellers. With trepidation Tara moved the curtains wider apart and peered out. She spotted Dupont, his skin gone pale, approach the commander of the band. He saluted while still mounted and said in an authoritative voice, 'We are from Chiriabagh. Lead us to the palace. His Highness Raja Todar Ram expects us.'

'Who are you? What are you doing in the street of the potters?' barked the man Dupont had addressed. And Tara observed with soaring consternation that he whipped out a pistol and levelled it at the captain. 'We treat all strangers to Motipur with distrust.'

Behind the commander—she presumed he was an officer of the Motipur state army—troops in bright yellow uniforms of surcoats and pyjamas slowly raised long-barrelled Indian flintlocks, and covered the surprised suwars.

'Put your guns away. I am Captain Dupont. Now take me to his Highness. He knows me well.' He spoke with fearless arrogance.

'He knows me well.' Those words rang in Tara's brain. What connection did Dupont have with Todar Ram? The situation grew more complex as time advanced. Unless, of course, Dupont was using bluff to gain admittance to the palace. But the Motipur officer's reaction soon disproved Tara's misgivings.

He holstered his pistol and respectfully performed a *namasta* to Dupont.

'*Ji,* Captain Sahib, his Highness awaits you. Come.'

Tara's suspicions mounted. She sensed the mistake she had made in her insistence on being brought to Motipur. She should have asked Colonel Markham to have her escorted to Fort William, Calcutta. In British hands she could be sure of protection. Thomas Orme, her god-father and her mother's cousin, would have ensured that she and Uma came to no harm. Uncle Thomas, she had called him. She fretted that she had not thought of him before, but now it was too late.

Escorted by Motipur troops, they rode through more bazaars and finally arrived at the palace gates, which were of solid timber bristling with jutting iron spikes, flanked by thick walls with iron shafts on top. The Motipur officer barked commands, and the gates creaked open to allow them access to the palace *via* a drawbridge across a moat. As they rode on, Tara glimpsed expanses of gardens, marble pavilions, fountains inlaid with precious stones. They emerged into an arcaded courtyard, where they came to a halt.

Dupont dismounted, flung back the tonga curtains and rudely beckoned to the women. 'Out, and quickly!'

Tara's sapphire gaze speared him with anger and con-tempt. No one had dared to speak to her in so uncouth a manner except Markham. But now she was a nobody. 'I beg your pardon, Captain!'

'You heard, woman! Your hauteur is wasted on me. *Mon Dieu*, must I drag you both out?'

'We shall get out. Do not shout, you foreign bar-barian!' It was Uma who spoke, her voice ringing with bewildering fearlessness and command. 'Come, Tara my child, give me your hand. Heed not that uncivilised savage.'

Tara alighted with dignity and helped Uma down. She dared not chance a look at Dupont who, she could sense, radiated fury.

'What will you do with the grain you saved on us, *feringhi* Captain? Sell it in the Motipur bazaars?' Uma sneered. 'Tell us.'

Dupont's face turned scarlet, and he took a step, lifting his hand to strike Uma. 'You old cobra!'

'Beware, Captain Sahib!' the Motipur commander grabbed Dupont's wrist. 'This old woman might be valuable to his Highness the raja. He has commanded that no one be injured till he has seen and spoken with them.'

Dupont struggled in vain to release his wrist. 'Let go of me, fool! Who are you anyway? What is your rank?'

The commander calmly loosened his hold on Dupont, again took out his pistol and placed the barrel at the captain's head.

'Call me Subadar. We waste time. Let us hasten.' He smiled menacingly, the tips of his upward-curving moustache reaching for the outer corners of his eyes, and motioned to the suwars. 'Surrender your arms.' Promptly they laid their guns on the flagstones of the courtyard, and the subadar's men collected them up. Holstering his pistol, he beckoned to the travellers.

Tara saw with some satisfaction that Dupont resented being treated as a prisoner, and his bravado vanished. With a sullen face he followed the subadar. Guards ushered them into a perfumed hall of scalloped arches, supported on wide piers decorated with bas-relief images of gods and dancing girls studded in precious stones of every colour. Musicians strummed sitars, while nubile girls in transparent silk bespattered with gems and bordered in gold braid, and wearing heavy jewellery, danced in front of a high podium. On this, against silk cushions strewn over an ivory couch upholstered in red satin, lolled an obese man. Tara recognised him as Raja Todar Ram.

He clapped, and the music stopped. Spitting into a jewelled spittoon, he allowed his black eyes, bulging and bloodshot at the corners, to range over the party until his contemptuous gaze came to rest on Tara.

It filled her with abhorrence and fear. Despite his garb of gold-shot muslin and turban afire with emeralds, diamonds and rubies, he did not possess the regal bearing that distinguished a prince from the common people. His gross body, flabby face, weak chin disappearing into the loose folds of his neck and thick mouth were reminiscent of a eunuch. A cruel one.

Tara's dread increased. She moved closer to Uma, who concealed her face by drawing the headpiece of her sari right down to cover her chin. She could not imagine why the old lady had decided to stick to convention and cover her face. But then Uma had become unpredictable.

In a high voice, Todar Ram commanded, 'You, Dupont Sahib, and your suwars must join the Motipur army. I cannot let you return to Sikandar Sahib. Those who resist will be imprisoned. Go with the subadar, who will take you to your countryman Captain Delacroix, who commands the mercenary division of my European troops. I will speak with you later.' He brooked no refusal, waving his hand in pompous dismissal.

The subadar bowed low. 'Always as the great and noble *Hazrat* desires.' He turned to the group. 'Bow down!'

Tara derived a glow of amusement from seeing Dupont bowing low, his face puce with indignation. When he straightened, he hesitated for a moment as if he meant to address the raja, but appeared to change his mind.

He nodded stiffly and followed the subadar, Markham's suwars and the Motipur troops bringing up the rear.

Then Todar Ram swept a beringed hand at the dancers and musicians. 'Go!' The guards in livery of green and yellow silk hustled them out. Except for the palace guards dotted round the podium and the attendants waving fly-whisks and fans over Todar Ram, Tara and Uma were alone with him.

'You are Tara Bai?' He shot the question at her, simultaneously examining his hennaed nails. Tension and hostility pervaded the room.

She swallowed an angry retort. Although she was aware that he knew who she was, it would be unwise to antagonise him; he had a reputation for cruelty. Blandly she said, 'I thought that Colonel Markham—that is, Sikandar Sahib—had already informed you, your Highness.'

'Mm, that is true. But I have never seen you.' He continued the idle inspection of his nails. 'Why did you want to come here? Why did you not go to the *Angrezis*? Your mother was English, was she not?'

I wish I had! Tara silently screamed. Since I have made such a foolish mistake, I must do the best I can to rectify it. His scornful tone made her temper rise, but to lose it would bring on disastrous consequences. 'Your Highness, you know about the terrible massacre of my people?'

He nodded coolly. 'I heard about it.'

She thought she discerned a flash of surprise or perhaps guilt in his eyes. So fleeting was the look that she dismissed it as a trick of her imagination.

Todar Ram stopped staring at his nails, sat up and tucked his legs under him in a Buddha pose. 'It is sur-

prising, Tara Bai, that you escaped the slaughter by unknown barbarians. How was this?'

This time she was not deceived by the blatant curiosity in the bulging eyes staring at her. Since she could
not meet that evil look, she stared at the red line drawn
down his shallow forehead and the horizontal lines across
it. She recognised it as the Shaivite emblem worn by
worshippers of the god Shiva. All the markings were red,
which denoted that he was of the second-highest caste.

Briefly she answered him and caught the fleeting
expression of annoyance that shadowed his face, which
she found puzzling.

When she had finished, he drummed his fat fingers
on his knees. 'I see. You want my help?' A sly look
came into his eyes. 'I shall give it to you. But I do not
grant aid without rewards. How do you propose to pay
me?'

'I—I have only myself to offer, because you once told
my father you were anxious to marry me. But now I
have no dowry.'

His laughter started in soft chuckles, then grew into
high jarring hoots that resonated in the chamber. He
rocked back and forth, body heaving, tears of mer-
riment coursing down his fat cheeks.

Tara cowered against Uma, and felt the old woman
trembling. This man's laughter was that of the insane.

Todar Ram dried his eyes with a gaudy kerchief
drenched in strong Indian perfume. 'You are ... asking
me to—to marry you? And you ... have ... nothing in
the way of a dowry?' He laughed in between the words,
stabbing a finger at her. Abruptly his laughter died, and
a sinister pause ensued. He snatched a fly-whisk from
an attendant and pointed it at Tara. 'You want me, a
high-caste Hindu, to marry you, the daughter of the man

who divorced my sister, his true wife a princess of royal blood, for marriage with an English outcaste?' His voice rose shrilly. 'I, who am a kshatriya, of the caste of princes and warriors, would not defile myself by marrying you, a half-caste lower than an untouchable! You are an outcaste. You know what I am thinking?'

Tara could only stare dumbfounded, her brain and tongue frozen.

'I am thinking that you are an English spy.'

Her legs threatened to collapse, and she would have fallen had Uma not steadied her. Half-caste? A Eurasian like Lieutenant Pullen? Is that how those of mixed blood were regarded by high-caste Indians and perhaps Europeans? As pariahs of society? Is that what Todar Ram meant: that she was a pariah? Never had she experienced the humiliation of prejudice, and it wounded her deeply. She belonged nowhere in society. She wanted to run away from here, from everyone, to hide herself in a deep hole—to die.

'Are you?'

'What?' She looked up startled at Todar Ram.

'What you are thinking of? I ask if you are spy for the *Angrezis*, and you behave like an imbecile!'

Spy for the English! It was bizarre. 'I am not a spy for anyone, your Highness! Why should I wish to spy on you?'

'The English want power over Hindustan. They are sending spies into our realms to see how much revenue they can take for themselves.'

'I'm no spy for the English, your Highness. I might add that the British respect the Indian nobility and have no intentions of taking over their states unless there is misrule. But, believe me, I did not come here to spy on you but to ask for your help.'

'And I have no wish to help you. Your father not only disposed of my sister; he also had my beloved mother killed in his forest.'

'You lie!' Uma set Tara aside and stepped forward, drawing herself up and pushing back the sari headpiece. Her blindfolded face hardened like a sculpture in brown stone. The raja gasped and shrank against his cushions.

'Look well, Todar Ram!' Uma said. 'Do you deny that I am the rajmati, the Dowager Ranee of Motipur— your mother?'

CHAPTER NINE

'MY MOTHER? You?' Todar Ram shrieked, struggling to his feet. But Tara perceived beneath his rage and bluster an undercurrent of fear. This man had something to hide.

Straightening his arm, he shook a finger at Uma. 'Miserable wretch, low-born servant of this outcaste!' A spray of saliva flew from his mouth. 'You dare to say you are my mother? She was never blind! She became a martyr, killed in the forest by that—that,' he pointed his finger at Tara, 'that half-caste's father. The rajmati's body was discovered and brought back. I saw to the burning myself.

'You! You! You!' He heaved his bulk round and grabbed at the guards one at a time by their clothing or arms. 'The rajmati was not blind, was she? Is this woman my mother? I defy you scum to say that she is!'

None answered. All stared at their feet.

Uma broke the silence. 'Stop your childish tantrums, Todar Ram! These people are aware of who I am. They know full well that I would not roam the forest or hunt. The guards are afraid of you, but I am not!' Her voice rang with fierce defiance. 'You saw to it that some other body was cremated to pretend to all that it was mine. I refused to die on your worthless father's pyre and you feared my curse; thus you were afraid to have me burned. But you had me blinded to appease your hatred and left me in Chandra's forest, so that he would be blamed. Alas for you, I survived, and it was due to his kindness.' The old lady paused for breath and took a couple of

steps forward, while Todar Ram retreated to the podium.
She went on, 'Beware! I am not finished yet. If you have
Tara or me put to death, I will use my curse. You all
know the effects of a *sati*'s curse!'

Uma's words and threats succeeded in fuelling Todar
Ram's rage. 'But you will not be a *sati*, for you will not
be burning on your husband's pyre, therefore your curse
will be useless. But I'll not bandy words with you, hag!'
He waved to the guards. 'Throw these women into the
dungeons, to await my pleasure.' When the guards hesitated, glancing at each other with terror-filled eyes, he
screeched, 'Do as I say, idle fools!'

'They will do no such thing, Todar Ram!' a woman's
voice shrilled. From a curtained antechamber stepped a
small figure entirely concealed in the wrappings of a dark
sari.

Uma gasped, and whispered, 'Sharmali!'

The woman's entrance generated a sense of awe. It
stirred the guards, who shuffled their feet and mumbled
among themselves. Tara observed with surprise that
Todar Ram looked shaken, his face ashen, eyes bulging
with fright. He returned to his divan, where he perched
with guilty uneasiness.

'Sharmali, my good sister, what are you doing here?'
he addressed the moving bundle, his voice fawning and
gentle.

Tara wondered with growing consternation whether
this sister was her father's exiled Hindu wife. Certainly
she appeared to exercise power over Todar Ram. Between them they could make life unbearable for her. Then
she recalled that Uma had mentioned this Sharmali in
her dreams. Would the old lady turn against her? Her
heart drummed; she had walked into a trap of her own
making.

'You will not have our mother—*I* can see she is the rajmati—thrown into your stinking dungeons!' the bundle said. 'You will place her and her young companion in my care. You pretended to me that *maji*, our mother, immolated herself on our father's pyre. It is now clear why you prevented me from attending the burning.'

'But, Sharmali...'

'I know what you are thinking, Todar Ram. You are thinking that Sharmali does not interfere with your decisions. Perhaps it is time I did! Our *maji* was kind to me. She did not treat me like some leper god, as everyone else here does.'

Tara's relief on knowing that Sharmali meant her no harm was short-lived. Leper! She took an involuntary step back and her skin tightened. A moment later, logic dispelled her incipient horror. A leper would not be permitted to roam freely, of that she felt certain. Even so, there must be something odd about the woman to create a climate of awe. Not a sign of her flesh was visible, so Tara was unable to see what afflicted this Sharmali.

'*Ji*, very well.' Todar Ram succumbed to Sharmali's wishes, gave her a sheepish half-smile and turned to the guards. 'Take these women to Princess Sharmali Bai's *tehkhana*.' He sounded eager to be rid of the women.

Guards marched the three women to the *tehkhana*, the cool underground quarters of the palace, built for use during the hot months of the year. They arrived at Sharmali's apartments beneath the *bibighur*, the women's house, the Hindu version of the Muslim zenana.

Tara groped her way down the gloomy steps, following Uma, who clung to Sharmali. The steps led to a corridor, and eventually the women entered a large cool chamber with skylights in the ceiling. Oddly enough, these were shaded with dark paint. An oil lamp burned in a niche, shedding sufficient illumination for Tara to notice that all the furnishings were in dull greys and dark shades. Nothing gleamed, unusual for a royal household. She knew how Indians, rich and poor, favoured glitter and opulence. Sharmali left them, to order a meal.

'Come, Tara Bai, sit beside me, while Sharmali sees about our food. Are you not hungry, little one? Assuredly *I* am, now that I have unburdened my secret and eased part of my worry.' Uma felt for Tara. 'Where is the couch?' Tara guided her to a drab but comfortable divan. 'You tremble, my young friend. I know you have had a sudden surprise today, but try to keep calm.'

'In truth, I am astonished, your Highness.' It seemed ridiculous to address Uma as 'Highness', and she felt a pang of regret that their easy rapport of the past might cease forthwith. 'I—I had thought you...' Tara shrugged. But realising that Uma could not see the gesture, she added, 'Why didn't you tell me who you were? I see no reason for secrecy.'

'You once mentioned, Tara, that you hated Todar Ram and all his family. I did not want you to know I am connected with so vile a person. But now you must see how much I despise him, although he is my own son. This I do believe: he has inherited his evil from his father.'

Tara gave the old lady's arm an affectionate squeeze. 'It wouldn't have made the slightest difference, except that I would have treated you with the respect you deserve.'

'Ah, Tara Bai, but I have no idea how your mind works. It was better that I remained silent. Also, you might have insisted that I stayed behind at Chiriabagh and not risked danger in coming here. Assuredly I would have been safe with Sikandar Sahib, but I have a great fondness for you and had an inkling that Todar Ram meant to harm you. I know I am old and frail, but I thought I might be of help.' She gave a mischievous chuckle. 'I also wanted to astound that fool!'

'Thank you for your offer of help. I'm sorry if at times I've shown impatience.'

'Do not be. I know you have enough troubles, Tara Bai.'

'No, please don't use my title. Your son says I'm a despicable half-caste, lower than an untouchable. I shouldn't be in your presence, Highness.' Unshed tears glittered in Tara's eyes, and slowly she rose. 'I wish I had perished with my parents!'

'Sit down!' Uma clucked her annoyance, waving her arms about. 'Self-pity will not help you at all. You live for a purpose.' The old lady dropped her voice. 'Now listen. Todar Ram may think you are a half-caste, but mark you, it is *something*, no? He dismisses me as dead and *nothing*.' And Tara joined Uma in a low chuckle. 'To me, you will always be the good and compassionate Tara Bai. Ah, here is Sharmali, I know her step well. You have brought us food, my child?'

'*Ji, Maji.*' Sharmali placed a tray of metal bowls filled with various curries, *dal*, vegetable dishes, rice and fried pancakes of wholemeal flour stuffed with vegetables on a low table in front of the divan where her mother and Tara sat. The appetising aroma brought saliva into Tara's mouth.

But all thought of food and drink vanished from Tara's mind when Sharmali seated herself, pushing back the headpiece of her sari to reveal her face. Her eyes widened, riveted on Sharmali in utter astonishment as though she were a being from another world. Sharmali was an albino.

Tara had heard of them, but had never seen one before. She realised why this girl lived underground, why she could not tolerate light, since albinos' eyes cannot withstand much brightness, and why she was treated with superstitious fear.

'I do not hear you eating, Tara.' Uma's voice startled Tara out of her rude scrutiny of Sharmali.

'Yes, yes...I...er...' She trailed off, too embarrassed to explain her behaviour. She tore off clumsily a piece of pancake and popped it in her mouth.

'Ah! I know why it is that you are surprised. It is my Sharmali. She astounds you, no? You are wondering how one as dark as I can produce offspring with pink skin, white hair and pink eyes. It is so, is it not?'

'I confess it is true that Sharmali amazes me, Highness...'

'What is this calling me "Highness"? Have I not told that I am now a nobody whose former powers have been stolen by her evil son?' Uma growled her petulance. 'You must call me Uma as you did before. Understand?'

'Yes, Uma Bai. Permit me to add "Bai" at least as a mark of respect?' Tara said, and at Uma's resigned nod, glanced apologetically at Sharmali. 'I'm sorry, Sharmali, for staring at you in so ill-bred a manner and hope I have not given offence? You see, I've never seen anyone like you before. But I do know that you are no supernatural being.'

'That may be,' Uma answered for Sharmali, feeling for the cup of lime-juice and sipping from it. 'But thankfully much superstition surrounds her. She is treated with respect and fear in the same way as the white elephant, the white peacock, the white cobra are treated as sacred. It is as well, or her life might be in danger. Even that fool Todar Ram is afraid of her. Is it not so, Sharmali?'

'*Ji,*' Sharmali agreed in an offhand manner. She appeared to take little interest in what Uma was saying; her strange pink eyes with deep red pupils glared at Tara. 'You are Raja Chandra's daughter?'

She found the eyes, framed with white lashes, unnerving and could understand why people reacted with mild terror to Sharmali. 'Yes.'

'Why have you come here?' Sharmali asked gently enough, but Tara detected a trace of disapproval in her voice.

'Were you my father's Hindu wife, Sharmali?' Tara countered. If the albino had been that woman, her resentment of me is understandable, she mused. And that adds another enemy to my growing list.

Sharmali laughed. '*Nahin.* My half-sister was. She was the daughter of my father's favourite concubine. Both mother and daughter perished on his pyre.'

Uma's face hardened with cruel satisfaction. 'And so they should. He treated them and Todar Ram well; whereas he beat me and ignored my Sharmali and Nagandra, my first son and rightful heir, because they shielded me from his lash. Todar Ram plotted to put Nagandra to death, but Sharmali overheard the plan and persuaded him to flee. He founded a small state in the Himalayas.'

'Shush, *Maji*, you make too much noise. The guards might hear,' Sharmali cautioned her mother in a low tone.

'Did you not lock the door, my daughter?'

'Assuredly, but it is still possible for the guards to overhear. I am listening at such doors every day. But I have a better thought. To drown our voices, why do you not smoke the hookah?'

'By the gods, why not?' Uma said jubilantly. 'But first let us finish our meal.'

After the guards had carried out the dinner dishes, installed a hookah beside Uma and departed, closing the door behind them, Sharmali spoke in an undertone. 'Draw hard on the pipe, let the water bubble well, *Maji*.'

Although Sharmali spoke just above a whisper, she mouthed her words so that Tara could assimilate what she said. 'Now tell me, Tara Bai, why have you come here? Why did you not remain with Sikandar Sahib? As his guest, you would have been safe. Forgive me if I remark that you have indeed been foolish to desert your protector.'

'Safe with him? Protector? What talk is this?' Tara bristled, affronted by Sharmali. 'Do you not know that this colonel massacred my people—my beloved parents? And you ask why I come here! I came to honour my father's desire for me to marry Todar Ram. As my husband, he could help me to wrest my kingdom from the American usurper, I had hoped. But your brother is hostile, and now I wish I had sought assistance from the British, perhaps.'

Sharmali gave Tara a look that frightened her, and with incredulity asked, 'You think Sikandar Sahib massacred your people?'

'In truth I do. I have good reason to believe that this obnoxious mercenary did. But he doesn't know I suspect him. I had to leave Chiriabagh before he did, or I might be languishing in some dungeon, perhaps put to death.'

The albino shook her head. 'You are wrong, Tara Bai. Oh, how wrong you are! Your life is in grave danger. The killer of your people lives—here.'

'I'm sorry, but I don't understand.' Tara felt a chill of foreboding. 'What are you trying to tell me?'

'Can you not comprehend that my evil brother, Todar Ram, ordered the massacre? He is the killer of your people.'

'What!' Uma dropped the hookah pipe, and Tara stared at it in a daze. With her keen sense of hearing, the old lady had no doubt heard every word of the whispered conversation. 'How do you know this, my daughter? Tell us.' And turning to Tara, 'Did I not foretell that Sikandar Sahib is no ruthless killer?'

Rendered dumb with astonishment and dismay, Tara was conscious of the extent of her blunder: she had walked straight into the clutches of Todar Ram's executioner! She must take pains not to reveal to him what she suspected. The whole situation was becoming a paradox that was leading her deeper into peril.

Sharmali grabbed up the hookah mouthpiece and dragged on it until the contraption hubbled and bubbled loudly. With a grimace she blew out smoke, which had formed a blue haze in the room and gave off a mildly acrid odour. Handing the pipe to her mother, she went on, 'Because I am considered a sacred freak, people do not harm me; on the other hand they don't believe I possess any brains. Like a pet, I am allowed to roam the palace at will and listen to gossip. Once I heard Todar Ram say that even if I did hear what was said, I would not remember; a white brain holds little blood and therefore lacks intelligence and memory. He is wrong, the imbecile! I learn much, Tara.' She paused to give Uma a rest from puffing the hookah.

In this way, bit by bit, Sharmali revealed a horrendous tale.

'Todar Ram had been incensed with your father's re-
solve to divorce my half-sister Veda, and to marry an
English outcaste. I do not mean to offend you, Tara
Bai, I am but repeating Todar Ram's words.'

'You do not offend me, Sharmali. Pray continue.'

'Todar Ram was fond of Veda, a foul woman.'
Sharmali shivered as if in horror. 'She bore Chandra an
infant daughter, and strangled her before he could see
her,' Sharmali said in an enraged whisper, and Tara gave
a horrified gasp. 'She wanted a son, but could not bear
any more children. Rumour has it that your father hated
Veda for destroying his child and refused her his bed.
When he met your mother, he divorced Veda, and my
brother was furious. After your father and mother were
married, Todar Ram showed no malice, for Chandra
paid his ex-wife handsomely. But before she committed
herself to my father's pyre, Veda extracted a promise
from Todar to have Chandra and his family slaughtered.
She used her *sati*'s curse.'

'The massacre,' Tara whispered. 'The curse proved
effective.'

Sharmali nodded. 'It was. Now do you know why
many fear it?'

Indeed Tara knew, and understood why Uma uttered
the malediction whenever danger threatened. 'But why
didn't you send word to my father, warning him of the
peril?' Tara asked, angry that Sharmali had made no
effort to save so many lives.

'I comprehend your distress, Tara, but in truth, I did
not think my brother would honour so evil a request. If
I had but known... Forgive me.' Sharmali sighed her
remorse.

'It's all right, Sharmali. You were not to know the
extent of your brother's evil.'

'And I would have you know, Tara Bai, that at the time, I was grief-stricken over my mother's supposed burning,' Sharmali pointed out defensively.

Tara felt ashamed of her intolerance. 'I'm sorry, Sharmali.'

The albino gave a pale smile. 'All right, let us proceed with the tale. Todar Ram persuaded Chandra that an alliance by marriage with you, Tara, would ensure a strong opposition to a Maratha invasion. This was a screen Todar Ram used to deflect suspicion from himself. Greed played a major part in the purpose of the massacre. My brother knew of the wealth amassed in the Chiriabagh Palace treasury. He visited your father often on the pretext of asking for your hand. But in reality he bribed your father's ministers to find out about his wealth. Then he ordered his *feringhi* mercenaries to plunder it. He knows you have no money. Why would he marry you?'

This recital made sense, Tara reflected, and all the creases were being smoothed out.

Sharmali cleared her throat and drank some water from a carafe on a nearby stand. 'What he had not thought of was that Chandra had appealed to Sikandar Sahib for assistance,' she said, turning her pink eyes on Tara. 'But, through spies, Todar Ram found out in time, intercepted the courier and believed he had been left for dead. Therefore it was a blow to my brother when he learned of Sikandar's arrival at Chiriabagh the morning after the raid. I dare say the courier survived and passed on Chandra's message to the good Sikandar, may the gods preserve him.'

'But—but...Colonel Markham removed the state rings from my parents' fingers. How could Todar Ram's raiders have been so remiss?' Tara enquired, feeling a little regret for her disgraceful treatment of the colonel. Even so, he was still guilty of ousting her from her rightful inheritance!

'The mercenaries were in a hurry,' Sharmali went on to explain. 'Before he died, Chandra warned that help was on the way. Whether this was true or false, the raiders thought it wiser not to remain and find out. They must have mistaken your servant-girl for you.'

'Yes. She was of a similar build and as tall as I,' Tara said. 'But pray carry on.'

'When Todar Ram heard that the rings had been left behind, he raged like a rabid tiger. Then the *feringhi* mercenaries persuaded him to believe that all in your palace had died, even though they had not removed all the heads. The slaughterers were in a great hurry to be gone.'

'But don't you understand, Sharmali and Uma,' Tara said looking worriedly from one woman to the other, 'when Colonel Markham informed Todar Ram that I wished to marry him, he snatched at the chance to have me brought here, and now—now he'll arrange for my death.' Fear bathed Tara in chilling sweat.

Sharmali shook her head. 'He will not kill you, Tara Bai; he fears to offend me, and is terrified since my mother has returned, and terrified, too, of her curse. But, Tara, I am thinking he will not spare you.'

'Then what will he do, Sharmali?'

'He might try to profit from you, Tara.'

'How will he do that?'

'He might try to sell you.'

'Like a common slave?'

'*Nahin*, Tara Bai. Not like a common slave—like a very costly one!'

Tara looked stricken, her eyes wide and dark. 'No! What have I done by coming here?'

Uma relinquished the hookah to speak. 'You must prevent her from being sold, Sharmali.'

'I said he *might* sell Tara, *Maji*. Assuredly I will do all in my power to save her. But, as you know, Todar Ram is gifted with great cunning.'

'How will you do that, Sharmali?' Tara asked in desperation, marvelling at her courage, and wishing she could emulate her.

'I shall write a message to Sikandar to tell him you are imprisoned here and need his help. But he will have to know the reason why you left Chiriabagh, understand? Then one of my friendly servants will carry the message to him. This courier is one of my brother Nagandra's followers. Several live here and spy for him. They want to see him on the throne, as mother and I do. He has appealed to Sikandar for help, but as yet there has been no response.' Sharmali sighed. 'What we lack is money.'

'I can help!' Tara exclaimed at once, happy to be of assistance. She untied the purse of jewels and handed it to Sharmali. 'These are worth a fortune. In fact, they are part of my dowry. You are welcome to them.'

'May the gods favour you, Tara Bai. I know I should refuse...'

'I shall be exceedingly angry if you do! It's a joy for me to help in any way I can to bring about Todar Ram's downfall and thus avenge my people.'

Little out of the ordinary happened in the next two weeks except that Tara worried about whether Colonel Markham would come to her rescue. He had not hidden the fact that he found her attractive, and for this alone she hoped....

She and Uma remained confined in the *tehkhana*, while Sharmali continued to collect snippets of gossip around the palace. As she had predicted, no one took the least notice of her. She told them, 'Although feared, I am famed as the palace half-wit. I took advantage of this enforced reputation and despatched the message to Sikandar Sahib to apprise him of Todar Ram's crime and your imprisonment, Tara. I also besought him to assist my brother, Prince Nagandra, to capture his rightful kingdom.'

Sharmali's blind faith in Colonel Markham's agreeing to help her warranted Tara's sympathy. Did the girl not realise that he was just as grasping as Todar Ram? Would he not oust Nagandra and claim Motipur for his own, as he had done at Chiriabagh? But she hesitated to warn Sharmali in the event of her reasoning being wrong; it had proved so before. She appreciated that it took time for messages to be exchanged between Motipur and Chiriabagh, and decisions to be arrived at. Using a courier, it would take at least a fortnight. Carrier pigeons, Sharmali had stated, were too risky. The birds were trained to return to their keeper and trainer, and any messages he received were forwarded directly to Todar Ram.

That night the raja sent for Tara. She was full of apprehension, aware of the man's reputation for depravity and cruelty.

Uma seemed to sense Tara's fear, and comforted her. 'He will not harm you, Tara. Be not afraid. Go, there must be something of import he wishes to speak with you about.'

So, escorted by guards, she arrived at the private palace of Todar Ram. As a way of acknowledging her presence, he lifted a corner of his loose mouth in what passed for a smile of greeting, but which to her resembled a sneer.

'I have been corresponding with the mercenary Sikandar Sahib by carrier pigeon, daughter of Rao Chandra.'

Tara bit back an angry retort. I am too lowly for him to address me as Tara Bai, she deliberated acidly; too lowly for him to offer me a seat. Here I stand in the centre of the hall, far from him, like a reviled untouchable. The only way she could hide her humiliation and indignation was to adopt a haughty stance and feign indifference; most human beings hated to be treated with unconcern, especially if they were people of position and power! She stared beyond him at a patterned silk curtain draping the back wall, and said nothing.

'You, wench, you are listening to what I am saying, hey?'

Tara obtained some satisfaction from knowing that her attitude riled him. 'I'm listening.' Aloof was her tone, disdainful her raised eyebrows, withering her glance.

'You will address me as "Your Highness"!' Todar Ram hissed through his large yellow teeth.

Tara treated him to a sidelong glance of pure boredom, and said in a dry voice, 'Highness,' with a sigh, as though she were dealing with a spoilt and dull child.

He snorted, and spat into the jewelled spittoon at the side of his silk-adorned couch, on which he lounged like a comic Roman emperor. 'Sikandar Sahib wishes to know when I am to marry you. You told him this?'

She started, surprised that she had once cherished the idea of marriage with the obese repulsiveness confronting her. Perspiration beaded his oily face and gleamed in the lamplight. Trying to recover some of her aplomb, she said with mock patience, 'Yes...Highness.'

'Indeed, you are brazen and rash to make such false statements. I have denied my betrothal to you. I have told him you are my prisoner.'

She did not speak, anxious for him to continue; she yearned to know Colonel Markham's answer.

'He desires your return. Therefore I have invited him to collect you—at a price.' So Sharmali was right! Todar Ram wiped his face with the loose end of his green gauze turban. 'A ransom.' He smacked his fleshy lips with satisfied malice. 'How does it feel being returned to your parents' killer, hmm?'

Tara broke her silence. 'I don't think Colonel Markham...' A pause. It was her turn to be spiteful and watch Todar Ram suffer. 'I...'

'You what? Tell!'

'I do not believe he is the killer of my people.'

She glimpsed terror in his eyes, rapidly masked. 'You said he was,' he whined, and she assumed he was afraid of being found out.

'I think differently now...Highness.'

Todar Ram's eyes narrowed. He snapped his fingers. A servant rushed forward, opened a silver-chased box and offered it to him.

Todar Ram helped himself to a triangle of *pān* and chewed fast, glaring at Tara. 'Oh? Why is that?'

She could not, of course, tell him the truth and endanger Sharmali, so she compromised with a fatuous, 'It's just a feeling I have. There's no evidence to show whether he's guilty or not.'

He stopped chewing to ask with some trepidation, 'Then who do you think did it?'

She would have to lie, because to accuse himself would result in some horrifying punishment for her. 'I do not know.' She observed a subtle relaxing of his body, and added, 'I—I don't believe Colonel Markham is prepared to pay a ransom for me.' She decided it would be safer now to channel his thoughts away from the massacre. 'He might do so for Captain Dupont, but not for me.'

'The French soldier is now my man. He has deserted Sikandar Sahib.' He dismissed his mention of the mercenary with a flick of a podgy hand scintillating with gems of dazzling colours. 'Sikandar Sahib has specified that it is you he is wanting, and he has agreed to pay a ransom.' His high-pitched laughter made her nerves jar. 'He will make you his favourite whore!'

CHAPTER TEN

TARA DREADED meeting Colonel Markham, whose sensual desire she was aware of, but it left her unmoved. He might be absolved of the massacre, but he still remained her enemy. An enemy she paradoxically needed, not only to deliver her from the clutches of Todar Ram, but also to vanquish him. Neither had she any intention of allowing the mercenary to rule her Chiriabagh. In truth she faced a dilemma, and the only way she could think of to solve it was to speak to him.

A further anxiety tormented her; she felt reluctant to leave Uma and Sharmali in the hands of their ruthless kin. She would miss them, especially the brave old lady, whom she had grown to love. Moreover, she experienced an uneasiness as to what fate the monster Todar Ram planned for the mother he hated. Perhaps Sharmali would use her influence to save Uma. Meanwhile, if she could persuade Colonel Markham to do battle with Todar Ram, both women would be saved—that is, if the Blue Cloaks won, but...

'You have nothing to say?' Todar Ram startled Tara out of her musings and bestowed on her a glance filled with scorn.

'I cannot imagine why Colonel Markham wishes to pay a high ransom for *me*. He can acquire the services of a—a courtesan to provide the pleasures I'm not prepared to give him.' She wanted to add that she knew for a fact he already had a fiancée, but decided it would sound as though she wished to amuse Todar Ram with cosy gossip.

He shrugged. 'You are comely enough,' he unwillingly confessed. Then, with a gesture of contempt, he remarked, 'Pah! Foreigners bed with anything. They do not observe the pride of caste that we Hindus do.' Then he quickly added, 'Ah, I forgot your father.'

Tara could no longer bear being in this creature's company, and said, 'Is that all . . . Highness?' She hoped that her tone of irony would affect him enough to dismiss her.

'You are an insolent wench, daughter of Chandra, and I shall be happy to be rid of you. Go!'

And I you, fat ape, she averred silently. A brief nod was all she allowed him before she turned and departed swiftly, escorted by two rows of guards.

Three weeks later, on a wet, steamy day, Todar Ram sent for Tara again. Next to him on the podium lounged Colonel Markham in full military dress of blue tunic, gold epaulets, tight breeches and knee-length boots.

When Tara sighted him, her heart gave an odd flip that she found difficult to define. She had a struggle to maintain her equilibrium with him watching her closely, his green eyes cold and calculating. His coolness did not surprise her, after the trouble she had put him to.

All her cosseted life, she recalled, she had had little opportunities to meet men, except people close to her such as her father and Uncle Thomas, or elderly ministers and occasionally European traders, all of whom treated her with respect. Having to stand and converse while these two lounged on elaborate divans humiliated, embarrassed and infuriated her. Their ill-mannered behaviour she attributed to ignorance, yet her freedom depended on these individuals. The paradox was that she would use that freedom to eliminate them.

'Here she is, Sikandar Sahib.' Todar Ram grinned affably, treating Tara as though she were a slave on the block. 'You can see that she is well, hmm?'

Colonel Markham handed Todar Ram a casket, and stood up. 'I'll not tarry and waste your valuable time, Highness. Perhaps we'll meet again. Good day.' He brought his right hand up to his high-crowned turban in a smart salute, no doubt to offset the sting of sarcasm in his words, Tara presumed.

Todar Ram remained seated with the heavy casket on his lap, but performed a polite *namasta*. The flash in his black eyes told her that the sarcasm had not gone unnoticed.

'Allow me, ma'am.' Markham caught her elbow, and her arm vibrated mysteriously. It must be my nerves, she thought.

Outside in the courtyard, blue-cloaked suwars dashed forward to shelter Tara and Markham from the rain with huge umbrellas made from straw and rattan.

Once comfortably seated inside a *ghari*, a vehicle drawn by two restless ponies, Tara said, 'Is it possible, Colonel, for me to wish her Highness goodbye?'

'You mean old Uma? Hoodwinked us, she did,' he said on a soft laugh filled with admiration. 'I'm sorry, ma'am, but it wouldn't be expedient. We must be away from here with all possible haste. Motipur is too dangerous for you in particular to tarry in. If Todar Ram suspects that you and I know he slaughtered your people, I fear for our lives. Certainly you may send a message by carrier pigeon, once we reach Chiriabagh.'

After the contingent of Blue Cloaks and the *ghari* clattered and rattled out of the palace at great speed,

Tara said with a lift of her fine brows, 'Considering the animosity at our last meeting, I'm surprised that you troubled to come, Colonel.'

He sat stiffly on the seat opposite, gazing out of the window, but when she spoke, his head jerked sideways and his green eyes narrowed on her. 'Would you like to go back?'

Heat swept into her face. 'No—no, of course not. But at our last meeting, I received the impression that you were happy to be rid of me.'

'I was?' A short incredulous laugh issued from his throat. 'Lady, it was you who were eager to rush to your betrothed, and now I know why.'

'I misjudged you, Colonel.' She betrayed a hint of remorse.

His mouth lifted in faint irony. 'Indeed, in what way?'

To her surprise she felt a little piqued by his aloof attitude. She hesitated, conscious of the calumny she was about to voice, and tried to summon appropriate words to soften the delivery of her next sentence. She failed, and blurted out, 'I—I thought you were responsible for my parents' deaths and the massacre.'

No astonishment registered on his face, but she observed the ridging of his clean-cut jaws and the flaring nostrils of his slightly aquiline nose.

'I have already stated that I know why you were so keen to leave Chiriabagh. Princess Sharmali Bai informed me in her message.' Although quiet, his voice was icy. 'What convinced you that I was the killer?'

Her cheeks grew hotter with shame. 'The—the rings, Colonel. In my overwrought state I was apt to condemn anyone who aroused my suspicion, and on the least pretext.'

'And you chose me as your whipping-boy? Why, lady?'

'You were the first on the scene the next morning, and I heard your men call out in French...' Briefly Tara related why she had suspected him of the slaughter, and finished with a shrug. Why should I apologise to him? she cogitated. In my eyes, he is still very much in the wrong!

'You have come to your opinion on flimsy evidence! A judgment about a major atrocity such as murder should be based on concrete proof.'

Her lower lip quivered, but she said nothing.

'Perhaps you should know that I'm as guilty as you are.' He half laughed and half sighed. 'We humans seem to labour under the shadow of doubt. Mistrust of our fellow men far outweighs trust. And I predict that it will always be so.'

Tara's sapphire eyes stared at him, a question in them. 'I'm afraid I don't grasp what you mean, Colonel. You say you're as guilty as I am? Please explain.'

He looked squarely at her. 'To be candid, ma'am, I suspected you.'

She frowned, and then, as the meaning of his words penetrated her brain, her eyes widened in angry disbelief. 'You suspected *me*?' She drew in a sharp breath. 'You suspected *me* of—of... No!'

'I fear so.' His voice was flippant. 'It's happening all the time, the world over, I do believe. History tells us that here in India family feuds abound. The nobility slaughter their relatives with impunity to acquire power and riches: witness the Mogul emperors of bygone ages who slaughtered their brothers to mount the throne. It's feasible that you could have been similarly affected.'

'Your reasoning is logical, I dare say, Colonel, but why should I wish to commit such a crime? I have no rivals, no brothers, sisters, cousins. I am sole heiress to the throne of Chiriabagh,' she choked. The colour went out of her face, and she stared at him in horror. Holy Mother of God, did he really believe her capable of parricide?

He leaned forward, resting an elbow on his knee, his gaze one of speculation. 'Why? Because your mother was with child. If she had borne a son, you would no longer inherit Chiriabagh. Right?' He straightened back in his seat.

'That's not true!' she cried, almost choking with outrage. 'How dare you suggest anything so abominable, so evil!'

Coolly his green eyes scanned her flushed face, her eyes glittering with enraged tears and hands clenched in her lap. Quietly he said, 'Indeed, now you know how *I* feel at being labelled a killer in a crime I didn't commit.'

She bowed her head and began absently fiddling with the embroidered sash that gathered in her voluminous blue kaftan. She controlled her wrath and decided it was time to use some tact; she hoped to ask him a favour presently. 'I'm sorry, Colonel.'

'I'm sorry too, ma'am. I know you're innocent. Let it rest at that. We owe each other nothing.'

He was right up to a point, she reflected, but doubted whether her ransom equalled the value of Chiriabagh.

Colonel Markham let the silence in the *ghari* hang for a while, then he said, 'It is of no importance now, Tara. We must look to the future, not back to the past.'

'Colonel, how much was the ransom?' she could not resist asking.

He stared at her. 'What? How did you know about the ransom?'

'Todar Ram told me. How much did he ask?'

He shrugged and looked out of the window, clearly demonstrating that he had no desire to pursue the subject.

Tara mustered her courage, breathed deeply, and said, 'Colonel Markham, I—I need your help.'

He swung his head to stare at her. In those dark green eyes she saw a glint of suspicion. 'I'd wager half my life that you'd never ask for *my* help! From me, someone you loathe? You must be desperate.'

She did not deny the fact. 'You owe me your help.'

His laugh was brittle and incredulous. 'You are demanding my help?'

'That's right. You have installed yourself, your so-called fiancée and your army at Chiriabagh, and you are all living off my land. You might have saved me from Todar Ram, but I feel it's the very least you could have done to compensate for your usurpation of my realm. No doubt your conscience prompted you to act accordingly.'

He smiled with genuine humour, and she was struck by how handsome he was. 'Your reasoning, lady, lacks logic. I'd scarcely possess a conscience if I had deliberately commandeered your throne!'

'Oh, I'm fully aware you have no conscience,' she said tetchily, 'but you have certainly schemed astutely in order to impress others that you have.'

'Let me clarify the situation, ma'am. If you would exert yourself to think a little...'

'I beg your pardon?'

'Wait! Let me finish. If you tried, you'd discover that the Chiriabagh treasury was plundered, along with most of the items of value in the palace. Therefore, to prevent the people from starving, those of them who depended on the raja for their livelihood, I have had to use my own resources.'

'Really, Colonel? You've forgotten the revenue that's collected from the villages. What have you done with that?'

He inhaled wearily, took out a large handkerchief and wiped the perspiration trickling down his brow, then said with mock patience, 'Lady, we are in the midst of the monsoons. You are fully aware that no harvesting can be done until the rains stop. And then, only after the produce is sold, can revenue be collected.'

Incensed by his capacity to make her feel foolish, she could do little but scream in her mind, Damn you to the devil, Markham!

'What is this favour you require from me, ma'am?'

Tara started. She had been so busy hurling accusations at him and arguing that she had clean forgotten the most important factor of asking for his help. 'You'll probably refuse.' After the recent clash of words, she could expect little else.

'Try me.'

Glancing at him warily, she wondered if she could risk his rebuff, or remain quiet. She could try to contact her godfather, but that meant money. She had none. All her jewels she had given to Sharmali. Markham was her only option.

'I made a pledge that I would seek out and kill all those responsible for my parents' deaths. I need your help, Colonel. You have a strong army, and the power to march on Motipur and conquer it. Todar Ram must not live!'

For a long time he said nothing, but just gazed at Tara thoughtfully.

Outside noises penetrated the silence in the carriage: the driver shouting to his ponies, the thudding of their hooves, the rattle and sway of the *ghari* and the rain drumming on the roof. Something else seemed to be happening, in that she sensed a subtle change taking place in her, an awareness of being in the company of an extremely attractive man. Slowly her gaze locked with his. Did she imagine it, or had the expression in those heavily fringed green eyes taken on more than an expression of thoughtfulness? Was it desire and admiration, or surprise at her lust for revenge?

'Do I shock you, sir?'

He smiled wryly and shook his head. 'Not at all. I admire your loyalty and your determination to carry out retribution. I'd do the same. But it's a relief to know I'm no longer the butt of your vengeance.'

She leaned forward, and asked eagerly, 'You'll help me, sir?'

'I might—on certain conditions.'

Deeply disappointed, Tara flopped back. She might have guessed that Markham, like Todar Ram, did not grant any favours without payment.

'And what are the conditions, Colonel?'

'The conditions are, ma'am, that I'll storm Motipur, provided you give me your hand in marriage.'

Tara gaped at him in numb disbelief.

'What's the matter, Tara?' he asked softly. 'Am I so repulsive to you?'

She gave herself a mental shake to say in a shocked voice, 'No, I don't think you're repulsive. But why do you want to marry me?'

'You're a beautiful woman. It is as simple as that.'

She glanced at him dubiously from the corner of her eyes. Men like him did not marry women simply because they were beautiful. They married them to improve their station in life, to acquire more wealth, more power, such as controlling a fertile state like Chiriabagh and gaining the approval of the people by marrying the heir. Her realm might be impoverished now, but once it settled down to normal life and the revenue from the rich land poured in, he would live like a raja! Then, with his immense wealth, he would elope with Mademoiselle...

'Colonel Markham, I think you've forgotten that you are affianced to Mademoiselle Dupont.'

'Lady, I assure you that I'm affianced to no one.' With an agile movement, he left his seat and sat beside her.

Tara slid away from him. 'Then tell me what she is doing, a lone woman, among all those soldiers? Is she your mistress, Colonel?'

'She was—but not now.'

'Oh? I fear, sir, that I am unable to marry you. Do you really expect me to tolerate a mistress in my palace? I'd be a laughing-stock!'

'Do you want to see Todar Ram's downfall?'

'Yes, of course I do, but...'

'Then marry me, Tara.'

She thought about that. This man would probably arrange for one of his officers to perform a brief civil ceremony, but according to the precepts of the Catholic Church, such a union would not be recognised. It was for this reason that her mother was able to marry her father within the laws of the Church, as his previous marriage in the Hindu faith was considered null and void. She would agree to wed Markham, and once he had taken Motipur, she would divorce him without fear of excommunication. And then she would appeal to Uncle

Thomas to ask for British assistance to expel the Colonel and his army *and* his mistress from her domain!

'Very well, Colonel,' she said, stiffening her body as he moved nearer to her.

The next few moments were a confusing blur of movement, as Tara suddenly found herself draped across Markham's lap. 'Good! Now kiss me.'

She struggled to free herself. 'I beg your...'

'Still the arrogant bitch? This is a challenge for me, my beauty, and a change from the predictableness of females!'

She continued to wriggle, but his iron hold convinced her that she was unequal to his physical strength. 'How dare you call me an arrogant...er...she-dog!' she panted. 'Ruffian, uncouth...'

'Bastard?'

He was laughing at her, and Tara could have howled in frustration at her inability to lash out at him. 'I wouldn't lower myself by uttering such obscenities,' she sneered, glaring venomously up at him. 'Let me go this instant, sir!'

She watched the resolute tightening of his sculpted jaw and the determined set of his lips. Seeing with trepidation the rage and raw desire in his eyes, she fought to break free, but gasped in pain as he crushed her against his wide chest.

'Stop struggling. You'll get badly hurt, and I don't want to hurt you, my darling,' he taunted her. 'Now for that kiss!'

And even as she began to protest, his mouth came down on hers, forcing it wider. The impact of the kiss affected her as nothing sensual had done in her life. Jolt upon jolt jarred through her body as if she had been struck by lightning again and again. But instead of burning her to cinders, the sensation brought her body alive. She could not understand it, could not prevent it. The disgust she had experienced when he had kissed her all those weeks ago outside the tower no longer existed, perhaps because at that time she saw him as her parents' killer. Now the stigma had been removed and, with it, her revulsion. Even so, she had not expected to react so strongly. Her mind became dazed, but her senses blossomed in tune with her body. The thud of her heart responded to the pounding of his, which vibrated through her.

His hand gently stroked her throat, and then he deepened his kiss. His fingers moved lower over her breast, and wave upon wave of feeling swept through her in liquid heat starting up a dance of her nerve-ends.

Then suddenly he eased the pressure of his lips to whisper ardently against her mouth, 'I want you in my bed, not here on this damned hard seat! I want your naked body next to mine, Tara, not just this.' His breath was ragged.

His voice jerked her back to sanity. This man was using all his charm to seduce her and induce her to marry him, his whole plan being to rob her of Chiriabagh. Oh no, he was not going to succeed!

'You forget yourself, Colonel! Do you mean to force yourself upon me? Release me, now!'

The stunned look in his dark green eyes gave her malicious satisfaction, and the moment he loosened his hold she moved rapidly to sit on the opposite seat.

'You deceive yourself, lady. Your body responded to my caresses. Remember, you are to be my wife.'

He thought her arrogant, so she would live up to the part. Staring haughtily at him, she said, 'We are not wed yet.'

'When we are, I'll claim full conjugal rights.'

'You'll take me against my will?'

'Don't look so appalled. You'll give me your body willingly. I want you, Tara, and I mean to have you.'

'But, sir, I'll give myself to you only after Todar Ram has been delivered up to justice. He'll be tried by British law, since Bihar is British territory.' She returned his gaze of angry admiration with one of triumph.

'I'll grant that you are a clever woman, but you'll not thwart me. I have every intention of consummating the marriage. I'll...'

His words ceased when the *ghari* rocked and weaved from one side of the muddy road to the other. The ponies reared and whinnied. The rain had stopped and everything vibrated with a muted roar.

Markham lunged and dragged Tara to him, and yelled, 'What the hell...?'

'Sikandar Sahib, *heela deela*!' the driver screamed from his canopied perch, his voice riven with panic.

'Good God, an earthquake?'

CHAPTER ELEVEN

As ABRUPTLY AS it had started, the shaking of the earth stopped, and in the sultry aftermath the *ghari*-driver was having difficulty in controlling his panic-crazed animals. He spoke soothingly to them, he bawled abuse at them—to little avail.

Colonel Markham shot Tara a look of consternation, gathered her up and, to her utter surprise, sprang out of the moving carriage, which fortunately, had slowed sufficiently for him to land like a cat on his feet. His stiff turban rolled off into the mire but he made no effort to retrieve it.

Carefully he stood Tara on a rock beside the slushy mud track and gingerly tested the ground with his booted foot as if expecting the earth to give. 'Earthquake?' he muttered in confused tones, passing a hand through his copper-gold hair. 'Incredible!'

'There's no necessity for alarm, Colonel.' She spoke calmly, now that the danger was over and she had recovered her equilibrium. With cynical amusement she observed the dazed expression on his face; pleased to perceive he was capable of fear, and that for once she had an advantage over him. She added, casually, 'This is but a slight tremor. I've known worse.'

His eyes widened as he continued to stare at the ground. 'It's the first time I've witnessed one. How does one deal with natural phenomena?' He frowned, turning his gaze on her. 'Is this common hereabouts?'

'These past months, there have been frequent tremors. On a single day we have felt three,' Tara said, faintly scornful of his ruffled demeanour. 'We tolerate them now, and accept that the country round is subject to quakes. Some seers foretell of a major calamity. It could happen tomorrow, it could happen ten years hence, or it might not happen at all.' Slanting him a withering look, she asked, 'Surely an adventurer like yourself, Colonel, is not afraid of a mere tremor?'

He ignored her sarcasm. 'Major calamity? Do you mean such as a volcanic eruption? I've heard of that.'

'Yes, it's the same sort of event,' Tara said, feeling piqued that her acerbity had had no effect on him. 'Five years past, the earth cracked open and swallowed a whole village on the outskirts of Chiriabagh, and the River Ghauri changed its course, creating havoc.'

After helping the driver of the *ghari* to bring his ponies under control, Colonel Markham ordered his mount and rode beside the carriage in preference to sharing it with Tara. She felt greatly relieved to be free of his company and sensual overtures, which she could not seem to cope with effectively.

There remained the delicate issue of marriage to him. This small respite would, she hoped, give her time to think of excuses to avoid becoming his wife, even if only through a civil ceremony. He would nevertheless consider it valid, and demand his 'rights'. Alas, no ingenious ideas emerged in Tara's mind except to refuse to wed him and abandon her pledge of vengeance on her parents' deaths. This last, to renege on her vow, she could never do. Never! Therefore she would have to sacrifice herself in a mock marriage.

At dusk, they encamped in an abandoned village near a temple shaped like a beehive, with statues of gods and goddesses in niches. The only inhabitant of the village, seated outside the temple, was a Brahman priest, a devotee of the feared god Shiva, as Tara noticed from the three horizontal white lines marked on his forehead. Draped across his bare chest was the sacred black cord, the symbol of the twiceborn worn by the three highest castes.

'Are you alone here? Have you no family?' Colonel Markham asked the man.

'Two monsoons past, Sahib,' the Hindu began to explain, 'a scourge of disease wiped out all the people of this village. I lost my family and I too became ill, but the gods decreed that I should live. In thankfulness for my life, I spend my days in prayer. I work on my small plot to produce vegetables and grain for my own use; I am too old for hard labour. Devout wayfarers give me oil to burn in the temple and dung cakes to cook my food.'

'Have no fear, you'll not be harmed, and we'll pay you for any shelter you can provide for the night,' Markham said.

'Come, follow me, Sahib.'

The mud huts comprising the village had partly disintegrated, but the hard mud-packed ground, bare of vegetation, which at one time had been the village centre where meetings and entertainment took place around the central well, afforded an ideal site for pitching tents. A nearby field, perhaps once under cultivation, supplied waist-high grass, excellent feed for the horses.

Her tent satisfied Tara. A *charpoy* occupied one side and a large *durrie* covered the tamped floor. She observed that under an awning extending from the tent a round wicker table had been laid, and two chairs placed opposite each other on either side of it. So we shall enjoy

an intimate meal, shall we? she assumed drily, watching
a suwar place a lit candle in the centre of the table. Not
far off, food was being cooked over a charcoal brazier,
and the savoury smell wafting to her nostrils sharpened
her hunger.

For some unfathomable reason she sensed a dis-
quietude that she was unable to shake off, as though
some unpleasant incident would shortly occur. The
foreboding persisted, as she tried to sweep it aside by
the act of brushing her hip-length dark tresses shining
in the amber light of a lamp filled with sandalwood oil
which perfumed the air in the tent. She reasoned that
perhaps the stillness, sultriness and blackness beyond the
circle of light cast by the candle flame and the brazier
affected her with a disturbing, unknown fear; an eerie
uncanniness prevailed—as if...as if she were being
watched! Deciding to investigate, she lifted the lantern
and peered into the corners of the tent. Then she heard
rustling from behind the canvas screen that divided the
bathing area. As she prepared to move behind the partition, a figure stepped out and hissed, 'Shush!'

Tara froze, and stared at the intruder, whom she could
see was a suwar. He wrenched off his turban to reveal
flowing locks, pale gold in the light. And she gasped as
she recognised Mademoiselle Dupont.

'What are you...?'

'Quiet, fool! I am come to warn you that you must
not marry the colonel, understand? You must extract
from him enough gold, say 2,000 gold mohurs, for me
to get my brother back from that toad of a raja, or else
you will know much pain, even death. This I vow! If
you whisper one word of what I've said to anyone, or
if you mention I'm here, you'll not live. Beware!' Céline

lifted the back flap of the tent and vanished into the cricket-chirring night.

Tara blinked and shook her head in an attempt to assure herself that she had not imagined the French girl's brief appearance and her spiteful words. That she had meant what she had said, there could be no doubt.

If I had only waited, Tara reflected, I would have convinced her that she could have had her beloved Markham as soon as he had helped in bringing Todar Ram to justice. As for extracting gold from the colonel, that was preposterous! Céline's threats failed to daunt her, and she refused to dwell on them. She felt confused when Markham appeared in the open entrance of the tent.

He wore a clean muslin shirt with full sleeves, and cotton breeches that hugged his long shapely legs. A lock of hair fell forward on his broad forehead, and the remainder of his wavy hair swept down and was secured with a black riband.

Slowly, deliberately, he came forward, his green eyes grown dark, gazing at her through his lashes. A half-smile curved his mouth, and she was forced to admit that he was indeed attractive. Her skin shivered as she felt his quickened breath when he raised her hand to bestow a kiss on each finger. All his gallantry, she told herself, was lost on her!

'Good evening, ma'am.' The timbre of his voice was deep and alluring. 'You look like a madonna in that blue kaftan, the exact colour of your eyes. Eyes created to bewitch a man...'

'I assure you, Colonel, that I have no desire to bewitch any man, least of all you. I put on this kaftan after my bath because it is clean and the material cool.'

He continued as if she had not interrupted. 'I am surprised that Todar Ram was so eager to be rid of you.

Indian princes, I hear, rarely part with beautiful women, no matter what price they are offered. There must be an exceptional reason for him to have allowed you to leave the palace so easily.'

Gently he drew her hand through his arm and led her out to the table under the awning. With European courtesy he held out her chair and with light touches settled her in. Each delicate stroke of his hands on her shoulders, back or waist, she was surprised to note, felt quite pleasant and gave her a feeling of being cherished. Absurd, of course! Rapidly she tossed the idea aside.

She waited for him to be seated before she spoke. 'Todar Ram considers me too lowly for him, Colonel. That's why he was so eager to get rid of me.'

Markham lowered the wine glass he was about to sip from. 'Too lowly for *him*? This is too much to believe!'

'You forget, Colonel...'

'Roger.'

Tara felt her face grow hot, and wished she could control these childish flushes and summon a degree of sophistication. She disliked the intimacy of using his first name, but it seemed petty to object, since she had agreed to marry him. 'Er...Roger.'

'I forget what, Tara?'

'You forget that caste plays an important role in the lives of orthodox Hindus. Todar Ram is of the kshatriya caste of warrior princes, the next highest to the Brahmans.'

'But was your father not of the princely caste? You are a raja's daughter, therefore you must share his caste.'

'You see, Col—Roger,' Tara said, peering down at the flakes floating in her glass of lime-juice. 'You see, my mother being English makes me a mixed breed, a Eurasian.'

'Like Pullen?'

'Yes.' She thought she heard him say, 'Like me, as well.' It was such a low whisper that she believed she had been mistaken, and went on, 'Hence, in the eyes of Indians—and a goodly number of Europeans too—I am considered a half-caste and thus an outcaste. With Hindus, prejudice comes into play only when marriage is considered. There are exceptions, of course, for a large dowry can banish caste distinction. My father found no shortage of suitors for my hand, and they included European merchants.'

'Why then have you not married, Tara?'

'My mother wanted me to marry for love, and I agreed with her.'

'I take it that you've never been in love?' His eyes held hers.

She returned his gaze without flinching. 'No, and I have no intention of being so! All I want is to avenge my parents' deaths and take possession of my state.'

He swallowed his wine and poured out more from the cut glass carafe, saying nothing.

After all the talk of mixed blood, Tara saw no reason to be ashamed, and decided to make her point clear. 'I wish to stress, though, that I do not consider myself of low birth because of my mixed blood, Colonel. In my veins flows good blood; blood that I am proud of, you understand? If my parents and I had behaved wrongly— that is, committed acts of felony, oppression, cruelty and murder—I would be ashamed. To me, it's not blood but actions that count.'

She thought she detected a flash of anger in his eyes and a ruddy glow in his cheeks, but it could have been a trick of the candle flame or her imagination. The expression passed so swiftly that she wondered if it had occurred at all. 'I quite agree, Tara. You're a human being, a very beautiful one. And had you been a Christian...'

'I am a Christian, of the Church of Rome. You'd no doubt call me a papist. My maternal grandmother was an Irish Catholic, and she taught my mother. I learned Christian doctrine from a gentle Portuguese priest. He—he too perished in the massacre.'

Markham stretched out and squeezed her hand, and his touch, warm and protective, made her want to weep. 'I'm sorry, I didn't mean you to grieve, lady.'

She smiled ruefully. 'You were saying?'

'As you are a Christian, you must have been brought up to believe that you are as good as anyone else.'

'I do believe it. But through painful experience I'm aware that we live in a world rife with prejudices of class and caste divisions. If we are to survive, we must accept them, or, if powerful enough, fight them. I'm not sure where I belong.' Then her face brightened. 'Ah! But I have just come to the conclusion that being of mixed blood has proved a blessing, God be praised. I might well have suffered violation at the hands of that murderer, Todar Ram. I—I shudder to think...' She drained her glass.

'In truth, let's not dwell on so gloomy a matter. Here comes the good cook with our meal.' Addressing him, he asked, 'What have you prepared for us, Mudassar?'

Mudassar saluted. He looked smart in his suwar uniform of the Blue Cloaks. 'Sikandar Sahib, I have made teal curry, pilau, katti kebab and parathas, and for dessert, carrot halva filled with nuts.'

'You've done well,' Markham said. He fumbled in his cummerbund and drew out a rupee, which he placed in the delighted cook's outstretched hand. He salaamed profusely and with buoyant steps set about serving his appetising dishes.

Much of the conversation during dinner centred on the excellence of the food, and the servants were accorded lavish but worthy praise. No sooner had the table been cleared, the servants departed and Markham had led Tara inside, than the scene changed.

He dropped the tent-flap. Tara experienced an aura of intimacy, a sensual awareness of him, hovering in the perfumed confines, and she was afraid of the hitherto unknown sensation.

He came straight to the point. 'You know what I want, Tara.' It was a statement, not a question, and his frankness took her aback. There was a subtle warning in his voice, implying that he did not expect any resistance. Tall, handsome, face flushed, eyes shining, he looked magnificent.

Her uneasiness grew, and she tried to still the rapid slamming of her heart. She stepped back and glared up at him. 'Yes, I know. I congratulate you on your cleverness, Colonel—forgive me if I address you formally, as your forename does not come easily. I admit you caught me in a vulnerable moment, encouraged me to speak my mind. But I fear I'm not naïve enough to succumb to your lustful charm. May I remind you that we made a pact, sir?'

He sighed in boredom. 'Ah yes, you'll give yourself to me in exchange for my troops storming Motipur, etc. Tara, why don't you try to relax? Forget about war and vengeance for a while.'

She laughed scornfully. 'I dare say that, by relax, you mean allow you to seduce me. I am sorry, Colonel, but I'm not cast in the mould of a whore.'

'But you will soon be cast in the mould of my wife, for God's sake, and therefore I'm entitled to this.'

His action was so sudden that Tara was too confused to protest. He seemed to rejoice in taking her by surprise, in the same way as he had done in the *ghari*. In a single stride he reached her, caught her in his arms in hard passion, lifting her on to her toes, arching her back beyond her balance, forcing her to cling to him. He crushed her closer, and as she made to cry out, his mouth came down on hers in savage possession. And, as in the vehicle, a small flame ignited in the lower centre of her body. Again she felt the heat growing, arousing a desire that fired her blood, drummed in her heart. She knew an instinctive urge to respond to his kiss, but before she could do that, he lifted his head.

Slowly, almost reverently, he raised her until she stood erect, and loosened his hold but did not altogether release her. Tara caught her breath as she observed the splintered brilliance of his mango-green eyes, and felt drawn into their magical orbs.

'This is a hint of what to expect after we are wed. I'll expect a lot more when you share my bed, Tara.' Then he dropped his arms.

His voice broke the spell, startled her back to reality. Collecting herself, she said, 'I'll refuse to bed with you until you've fulfilled your pledge.'

His face hardened into obduracy, his eyes opaque. 'If you refuse, then there'll be no raid on Motipur. Which is it to be?'

Tara's eyes wavered and flickered away from his. 'You are forcing me to sin, Colonel?'

The hardness disappeared from his face, and he grinned disarmingly. 'There'll be no sin; we'll be married, my Tara. Think on it. Goodnight, fair one.' He sketched her a bow and abruptly left the tent.

She fell asleep while contemplating her starry-eyed reaction to Roger Markham. Amazing! She, who had never been given to frivolity.

The sound of torrential rain drumming on the canvas and the refreshing smell of wet earth and grass woke her. Disorientated for a few moments, wondering where she was, Tara remained lying down, staring up at the canvas ceiling. She started up when she heard the water-carrier shouting from the bathing cubicle that he had poured out her bath water. She waited until she heard him drop the back flap, and then swung out of bed.

The bathing area reminded Tara of her meeting with Céline Dupont. So preoccupied had she been with Markham that she had obliterated her from her thoughts. Now, as she poured the chilled well water over herself, she wondered what Céline was doing, masquerading as a suwar. Did Markham know she was here, or had he ordered her to disguise herself? He probably was not aware that his mistress had visited Tara, hence her secretiveness. Or was Céline pandering to Markham's lust while he wooed her, Tara? Once he had married her and gained absolute power over Chiriabagh and exhausted his desire for her, he would abandon her in order to wed Mademoiselle Dupont. Except, Tara vowed, she would not give him the chance to possess her. And if he did conquer Motipur, he would keep that realm too for himself.

Tara put on a yellow kaftan, and closed her eyes in distress. Dear God, if she could only send word to Uncle Thomas, or, better still, go to him. A suwar brought in her breakfast of ripe mango, chappatis spread with *ghee* and preserves, and a container of lime-juice. She was relieved to see that the fruit had been skinned and cubed and that there was a spoon; peeling a mango was a messy task.

The trooper who came to collect the half-empty tray turned out to be the well-disguised Céline. Ferocious amber eyes glared at Tara from an artfully darkened face, and it caused her to shiver inwardly with apprehension. 'Did you ask him for the money?' Céline asked.

Tara hid her fear behind a cold façade and replied, 'If you care so much about your brother, mademoiselle, why don't *you* ask Colonel Markham for the money?'

'Fool! Did you think I had not? He refused. He also forbade me to travel with him, hence my disguise. But at present he is infatuated with you and will listen to you.'

What a puzzle! Tara thought. It defeated her supposition that Céline and Markham were in league with each other, conspiring for the Chiriabagh throne. 'I can't understand why he has refused to help your brother.'

'It is none of your business. I must have the money for Antoine, and I'll need no less than 2,000 gold mohurs. That is the price that fat toad of Motipur demands.'

'I'm sorry, mademoiselle, you'll have to find help from some other source. I've never asked anyone for money; I consider it unethical.'

'*Mon Dieu!* Ethics! Who cares for ethics. *Bien!* Suffer the consequences then!' Tossing her turbanned head, Céline marched out, forgetting the tray.

While Tara sat brooding about what Céline planned for her, a sudden idea surfaced. Uncle Thomas! Her mind harked back to her godfather. Why had she not thought of him before? Of course he would promptly and without quibbling give the 2,000 mohurs Céline demanded. Moreover, he was a powerful Company servant and rich merchant who could persuade the Governor to attack Motipur. Then she could reject Markham's proposal of marriage and relegate both him and Céline Dupont to the devil! She sighed. The drawbacks to her idea were enormous.

If she could cajole the Dupont woman into taking her to Calcutta, all her worries would be over, but distance could prove her worst enemy. Calcutta lay 400 miles away, a two-month journey at the fastest pace. Would Mademoiselle Dupont be prepared to wait so long? And how could she contact her? Why did I not think of this when she was here? Tara groaned.

Agitatedly she was pacing the confines of the tent like a caged prisoner when Colonel Markham arrived. He kissed her hands dutifully, and said, 'As soon as your tent has been dismantled and packed on mules, we'll continue the journey to Chiriabagh.' He caught her elbow and steered her out. Under the awning he picked up a canvas umbrella. 'Come, wait in the *ghari*.' He hugged her to his side as they both ran out into the teeming downpour. Once he had helped her into the vehicle, he shouted above the crashing of rain, 'I'll be riding beside you to keep an eye on the route and the possibility of being attacked.'

'Attacked? By whom?' she shouted back.

'Bandits or marauding armies.'

She paid scant attention, her gaze scanning every suwar who came into her sight, looking for the tell-tale amber eyes of Céline Dupont. Even when they moved off, she leaned her head out of the window, oblivious of the rain, to see as far back and forward as she could.

Markham's sharp voice startled her out of her inspection. 'Who are you looking for? Your head is wringing wet. Who's so important to you?'

She hastily withdrew her head, and flushed deeply with guilt. 'It's so hot in here,' she improvised. 'I—I thought I'd cool my head.'

Wrapped in the blue cloak, Markham sat astride Galaxy, who sidled impatiently beside the *ghari*. He gave a sharp order to the suwar trotting alongside, and the man wheeled his horse and rode back to the baggage train. In a few moments he returned and handed Markham a stiff hand-fan woven from palm fronds, and a leather bag.

'Here you are, lady. A towel in that bag to dry your hair and a fan to keep you cool.'

She took the articles from him and began mopping up the drops on her face and carefully coiled hair. Mademoiselle Dupont, where are you? her brain screeched. She had to know whether Céline would be agreeable to her plan before they reached Chiriabagh. Rapidly she fanned herself. She felt too afraid to marry Markham in either a civil ceremony or a Church one, and also afraid of sharing his bed. How could she give herself to a renegade?

At sunset, they encamped in a large paved area surrounding a well. At several stalls, people sold foodstuffs and other goods. Men, women and children ran up to the newcomers, offering their services as attendants. Markham chose an elderly woman, whom he paid in advance to wait on Tara. He brushed aside her protests that she could see to herself, but the trying journey had wearied her too much to oppose him further.

After her cool bath, she was surprised to see that the old woman had spread a beautiful kaftan on her *charpoy*. The gown and wide sash were of white silk spangled with silver. Beside them were satin slippers and a long spangled muslin scarf.

'What's this for?' Tara asked the woman.

'Sikandar Sahib ordered me to put them out.'

'Well, I don't wish to wear such finery. Where is my trunk with my own clothes?'

'Sikandar Sahib has it, Sahiba.'

Tara had never vented her rage on servants; her mother had forbidden her to do so. Since she possessed only the dusty robe she had travelled in, which she could not bear to wear again, she put on the white garment. It felt pleasant against her clean skin and smelt pleasantly of attar of roses. Perhaps today was a Hindu festival, and Markham had arranged for entertainment for his men. Naturally he did not wish her to disgrace him by wearing dirty clothes.

Some minutes later, he entered the tent. He looked so handsome that she felt a little dazed. His hair, still damp from his recent bath, shone with copper glints in the lamplight. He wore a white satin waistcoat embroidered in silver over a full-sleeved muslin shirt, and white breeches tucked into tall black boots. His hair had been taken back into a broad satin bow. Dismissing the old woman, he appraised Tara, a slight smile of approval curving his mouth.

'Colonel Markham, I'm in no mood for this finery. I would be happy, sir, if you would return my trunk. My cotton kaftans are cooler than this silk.'

'Ah, Tara,' he drawled, sauntering towards her, 'this is a special night.'

She backed away from the glint in his eyes. 'I don't understand, sir.'

'I thought you might have guessed, my darling. We are shortly to be wed.'

CHAPTER TWELVE

MARKHAM'S ANNOUNCEMENT could not have stunned her more had he thrown ice in her face.

'You look stricken, lady,' he said with a mocking lilt. 'I thought by now you'd have accustomed yourself to the idea of marrying me.'

She recovered some of her poise, which was now spiced with anger, her blue eyes flashing. 'You, sir, have broken your word! You assured me that the marriage would take place after our arrival at Chiriabagh.'

'Sorry, I've changed my mind. Afraid of losing so beautiful a bride.'

'You don't deceive me with your flattery, Colonel. I dare say you have a reason for this sudden change?'

'You're right. I've a gnawing suspicion that you are plotting to evade marriage with me.' He spread his hands airily. 'Oh, I haven't proof, but I observed from your restless behaviour that you've thought of an alternative. But I don't intend to be outwitted, so I have brought the ceremony forward.'

Tara did her best to control the flush threatening to betray her guilt, and nearly succeeded. She laughed without humour. 'Your imagination is singularly vivid, I do declare, Colonel. What chance have I of escaping from here?'

'None, lady. Even so, we'll be wed shortly. All arrangements have been made, and Abbé Étienne will be here soon.'

Tara swallowed. All colour went out of her face. 'You—you have asked a—a priest to marry us?'

He breathed out an incredulous laugh. 'Of course! Who else has the authority to perform a marriage service?'

'I thought perhaps you had arranged for an officer...'

'Oh no, not a civil ceremony, Tara. You're a Catholic, and your Church does not consider any but a Roman Catholic service to be valid. Why do you think I asked you what your religion was?'

Faith! How she had underestimated him. But she had no time for thought as a priest and two of Markham's officers entered.

Abbé Étienne's skin, sunbrowned and leathery, bespoke his spiritual ministration to French soldiers on the march under a pitiless sun, and braving the burning winds. Scanty grey locks surrounded his tonsure, and his pale bloodshot eyes twinkled with delight while he placed necessities for the wedding service on a table covered with a snowy cloth. He donned a white surplice over his black cassock, then kissed a brocaded and fringed stole and placed it round his neck.

'It is not often that I perform the rites of Holy Matrimony in this country, *mon enfant. Comprenez-vous?* Alas, few baptized within the fold of Holy Mother Church wish to be joined in the sacrament of marriage. They prefer to fornicate with the heathen.' He clicked his tongue in distress, lifted his eyes to the roof of the tent and made a pious sign of the cross. 'Come, *mes enfants*, stand together. You have brought a ring, Colonel Markham?'

'Yes. This.' He removed the Chiriabagh state ring from his finger and handed it to the priest.

She stared at the jewel, dazed at Roger Markham's effrontery, dazed at what was happening.

'In nomine Patris et Filii et Sancti Spiritus...'

The ceremony was short and impressive. Tara barely assimilated the fact that she was wed to this man for the rest of her life. The two French officers did duty as witnesses, and Markham pledged them and the priest to silence until they reached Chiriabagh, where he promised there would be day-long celebrations throughout the palace in honour of the wedding.

He served the men and the priest with brandy, and when they had drained their glasses, the priest took his leave after blessing them all. The French officers, however, lingered, eyeing the decanter in the hope of another drop, but Markham summoned the servant to remove the tray.

'We must make an early start on the morrow, gentlemen. Goodnight.' Since he dismissed them so peremptorily, the men had no option but to leave, and did so looking dejected.

With a mixture of incredulity and fear, Tara stood in the centre of the rug, watching Roger Markham despatch his men and drop the tent-flap with a muttered, 'Insensitive fools!' Slowly he turned to her. 'Alone at last.' His smile was relaxed, alluring, his eyes half-closed, glistening with passion. 'Come, let us to bed, my lovely bride.' He held out a hand to her.

With faltering steps, she backed away. 'No!'

'I won't hurt you, Tara. Not you,' he murmured, advancing on her.

'Wait, Colonel. You have forgotten something. I recall vowing to refuse to consummate the marriage until you have conquered Motipur and brought Todar Ram to justice.'

A frown appeared on his broad forehead and anger hardened his face. 'You would deny me yourself?'

'Until you have honoured your pledge to take Motipur, sir.'

To her astonishment he threw back his head and roared with laughter, and she wondered if the brandy had addled his brain.

'This is no laughing matter, Colonel.'

He became serious. 'Is it not? You talk of honouring a pledge, yet you have broken the most sacred pledge of all; to be my wife.' He put his arm round her waist and hauled her against him. 'You are a cheat, woman, and I'll not be denied!' he snarled. His mouth crushed down on hers in fury and rampant hunger.

Tara bit him. Then, appalled by her savagery, she relented and let go of his tongue without drawing blood.

His head reared up, rage afire in his green eyes. He still held her to him, but he moved one hand to clasp her throat loosely. Softly, menacingly, he said, 'Do that again, and I'll break your neck, my darling.' For a long time he gazed at her, the flames of wrath in his eyes dying down to be replaced by a subtle darkening that suspended her thoughts and threw an invisible net of magic over her. His kiss when it came was gently arousing. The awakening of her latent passion was like a shoot pushing up from the darkness of the earth. And like the plant responding to the sun, her sensual need for fulfilment grew and she kissed him back, felt his shudder of pleasure.

Between kisses he undressed her and himself, then carried her to the bed. Now he stared down at her nakedness: the proud tilt of her breasts, narrow waist, the rounded swell of her hips and her long, long legs. He did not have to tell her how desirable he found her;

it was there openly expressed in the gleam of his eyes. He was superb, she thought languidly, and he had her completely in his spell.

Lowering his mouth, he trailed burning lips along the length of her throat. Tara moaned and arched her neck, and moved her hands over the crisp hairs of his chest and caressed him, marvelling at her audacity, but unable to resist it. When his hands stroked downwards, held and fondled her full breasts, and his warm mouth nibbled their swollen peaks, Tara released a loud sigh of pleasure.

He laughed softly against her fullness. 'I've dreamed of this, darling. Night after night. To kiss these.' He pressed his open mouth over each breast. 'And this.' He trailed a path to her navel.

Tara caught his face between her hands and drew him up to her mouth. She kissed him with an ardour she had not been aware of. She gazed in hypnotic wonder into the depths of his eyes, like green pools casting enthralling spells of magic over her.

'Kiss me—hard,' he groaned.

Tara did so with a fiery abandonment that came naturally to her, encouraged by the arousing movements of his hands. His hot response to her kiss sent fire throbbing in her veins; his hand moved lower to fondle her hips, and then lower still. She groaned, and invited his pulsing desire.

'Relax, darling,' he whispered, and although his invasion was gentle, she whimpered in pain. The moment was brief, and then she was responding to his movements. She clung to him while he held her tightly, his mouth ravishing hers as their bodies rocked in bliss.

In the languorous aftermath of passion, Roger gathered Tara to him, and with sighs of pleasure and satisfaction, they both drifted into deep sleep.

* * *

'Sikandar Sahib, *huzoor*.' A male voice calling softly woke Tara.

'What is it?' Roger asked, removing his arms from her.

'Sahib, there is one messenger who comes from Chiriabagh. He would have urgent speech with you.'

'Very well, I'll come out in a moment.' He pulled on his clothes and then left the tent.

Tara's skin tingled with fear when she heard an obscene oath from him. A thud. Then silence.

She became aware that someone other than Roger had entered the tent. Even as she tried to rise, something pressed against her mouth. She could not scream, could not move. She was being dragged from the bed, heaved over a burly shoulder. Blackness descended.

When she came to, it took her some time to realise that her arms and legs were bound, and her mouth gagged. Her dazed brain refused to function. She could see nothing, and after a while became aware that a robe had been thrown over her naked body and a hood over her head. Gradually it occurred to her that she might be a victim of abduction, and could not imagine why. The man carrying her was fleet-footed and none too gentle. She was bumped along in agony, in complete blackness, so breathless, so terrifying. Panic and terror combined to cast her brain into oblivion.

Rocking...rocking. Tara opened her eyes, but a black wall met her gaze. Where was she? From the sounds, she gathered that she lay in some vehicle pulled by swift horses. Where to? And why? She lay on something hard, a plank or a bench, and although bound, gagged, hooded and stifling, she attempted to raise herself into a sitting position.

'She's regained her senses. Give her the potion,' a woman commanded, and with her mouth grown dry, she recognised the voice as that of Céline Dupont.

I might have known! Tara reflected. This woman will never let me rest until she has obtained her objective.

'Take off the hood, imbecile! Point the knife at her throat. Force her to drink.'

The chilling order petrified Tara.

A man responded in servile tones, and roughly dragged off the hood, untied the gag and held the drink to Tara's mouth. She blinked to accustom her eyes to the sudden, though feeble light from a candle inside a lantern. The vehicle, a *ghari*, raced as if in fear of being pursued. She swallowed when she saw the masked man holding a dagger: curved, sharp and flashing with menace.

'Drink that!' Céline snapped. Draped in black, she reminded Tara of the witches her mother had once told her about. A beautiful witch with golden curls and tiger eyes, but minus broom and steepled hat.

'Where are you taking me? What is this mixture, mademoiselle? What...?'

'Ah, now she plays the innocent! I warned you, wench, not to marry the colonel and to get the 2,000 gold mohurs from him. But you heeded me not. Now you must suffer.'

'Mademoiselle, please wait. I had no choice but to marry Colonel Markham; he promised to help me to avenge my parents' deaths. However, I had another plan, which would have saved me from marrying him and helped you with the 2,000 gold mohurs. Alas, I had no idea where in the camp you were, so how could I contact you?'

Céline flashed Tara a grin of malicious triumph. 'I fear that whatever plan you had is of no use to me now. You see, I have received word from Todar Ram that *he*'ll

give me 5,000 gold mohurs if I deliver you up to him.
Enough of idle talk. Drink, I say. Or, *ma petite*, you'll
see what will happen.'

Tara felt the sharp edge of the dagger at her throat,
and swallowed. She yelped when the servant pressed the
metal goblet to her lips still sore from Roger Markham's
kisses. Roger! What had they done to him? She remembered his curse, the thud of his fall. He could be dead!
'I will not drink this potion until you assure me that
Colonel Markham is alive.' Pursing her lips, she refused
to drink.

'Oh, stop whining! He is alive, little fool. What reason
have I to lie?'

'Why am I being forced to swallow this liquid? Are
you trying to poison me?' Tara asked, attempting to
sound calm.

'I'm not trying to poison you, woman. Todar Ram
will not pay me for your dead body. He wants you alive.
This drug is to keep you quiet. But if you do not do as
I bid, the alternative is...' She drew her finger across
her throat.

The liquid tasted sweet; Tara assumed it was *bhang*
brewed from hemp-leaves, mixed with sherbet. Or—
Or...the hair on her nape rose. It could well be poison.
Céline's word was not to be trusted. Tara's skin chilled,
seemed to shrink.

'Finish every drop!' Céline rapped out when she
hesitated.

No, it was not poison, she rationalised. If this woman
intended to kill me, how much easier to have this wretch
slit my throat and toss me out. 'Where are you taking
me?' she gasped, after draining the goblet. She might
as well talk, and keep herself from going berserk.

'Back to Motipur. This time you'll be in my charge, *ma petite*. And I can be a cruel jailer!' From Céline's smug expression, Tara knew she meant every word.

In spite of the threat, she experienced some relief. At least she was to remain alive. 'Why should you be my jailer?'

'Ah, you are curious? I shall tell you. Raja Todar Ram sent word to me by one of his spies that my brother is his ally and not his prisoner. Both wish the downfall of the mighty colonel, as I do.' Céline's lip curled in malice. 'Todar Ram wishes to add Chiriabagh to his domain, but first he will extract a higher ransom for you from Markham. And I shall have a part of it, *mon amie*. I need money to return to France. And through you, *mon amie*, the colonel will supply the gold. So I must keep you under my eye, must I not?'

Tara felt the drug taking effect, her limbs and body growing heavy, and tried to fight it. 'If you'd asked Colonel Markham for your fare home, he would have given it, mademoiselle.'

'But he has, madame; he has. Alas, my fare is all he will give. Am I to live on nothing when I reach France? No, madame, I want more, much more. The colonel, he is rich. He owns much land in Oudh, he has much money collected from hiring out his army in successful campaigns.' She laughed shrilly. 'You fool, do you think the colonel married you for love? He jests, madame. He married you for Chiriabagh, for power. He is not known as Raja Markham for nothing!'

Céline's words confirmed the ever-present niggle of suspicion in Tara's mind. She was forced to concede that the woman's ranting was not motivated simply by jealousy. And she, poor idiot, had allowed herself to be manipulated into marriage and seduction by that lecher!

What value did he place on the sacred vows of matrimony? None.

Mademoiselle Dupont continued her tirade. 'The colonel, he has spurned me for a half-caste like you. *Mon Dieu!* For that he shall pay!'

Spiteful though the French girl's words were, they brought some consolation to Tara. She knew that Roger had married her of his own free will. He had no need to take the serious step of marriage to establish power over Chiriabagh; he already possessed it. Why had that not occurred to her before?

'What went wrong, mademoiselle? Could you not persuade him to marry you?' Tara asked with mock concern.

'He calls my brother a traitor. He calls me a whore!' Céline spat with bitter spite. 'Bastard! He shall suffer!'

'Then—then,' Tara's voice thickened from the effects of the drug, 'why did you not kill him? You had the chance.'

Céline's voice began to fade. 'He is alive because he must pay a ransom again for you, you dolt! But when I have finished with him, the colonel will wish he were dead.'

Tara's eyes grew heavy, her brain churned, the *ghari* seemed to spin, and Céline's bright angry eyes grew distant and dim. He is free and alive, her confused brain echoed. There is hope for both of us. What hope, she could not determine.

She fought to resist the potency of the *bhang*: she sat up straighter and widened her eyes, but her lids refused to remain open. She found herself slipping…slipping….

CHAPTER THIRTEEN

SOUNDS OF confusion and turmoil coming from above brought Tara out of oblivion. Voices bawled, 'Fire! Put out the fire! Quick, bring water!' She sat up and grabbed her aching head, closed her eyes, choked and coughed on the foul-smelling air. Panic struck her when in the next instant she discovered she sat on a pile of dirty straw placed beside a wall that oozed slime. A ray of sunshine shafted through a grating high above, whence the noise of the commotion penetrated.

Running to the solid, wooden door banded with iron, she thumped on it, sobbing out, 'Get me out of here! Open, I say! L-let me out! P-please!' Even as she wailed, she knew that her commands and pleas went unheard or ignored. In a flash she recollected her ordeal with Céline Dupont. The woman had said she would be her jailer. 'Mademoiselle Dupont, where are you?'

Tara let out a despairing sob, dropping her hands to her sides, staring impotently at the door. I have been brought here to die. Please, God, don't let me be entombed in this stinking cavern!

'Tara Bai, do not waste your breath, child. Come and join me.'

Tara staggered and whirled round, peering through the gloom whence the voice came. It sounded like old Uma's. 'Is it you, Uma Bai?' Hope brightened her voice. 'Where are you?'

'*Ji*, it is I. Come, Tara, give me some help. This dungeon is fearful, is it not?' The old voice shook with weariness.

An immense relief flooded Tara. Thank the good Lord she had not been left to perish alone in this forbidding place! But when she had absorbed Uma's words, renewed fear gripped her. 'Dungeon? Is that where we are?'

Uma remained silent; the answer was obvious, and Tara groaned. Picking her way with care over the damp, slippery floor of uneven bricks covered in moss and slime, she reached the pallets of straw stacked against the opposite wall.

The old lady looked fragile and thinner, her sari grimy, her oiled hair loose and untidy. Tara helped her to sit up more comfortably. Uma exhaled a ragged breath and held out her hands to the girl. 'My darling child, I heard someone being dragged in last night. From the whimpering, it seemed that some tortured woman had been thrown in. I did not think it would be you. I thought that you were safe in Chiriabagh with the good Sikandar Sahib. By what misfortune are you now a prisoner?'

Tara lowered herself beside her old friend, taking the elegant fingers in her hand. 'But you, Uma Bai, what . . . ?'

'What am I doing here?' She gave a long, quivering, sigh. 'Tell me first of yourself, Tara.'

The noise penetrating through the grille grew louder. 'What is happening up there?' Momentarily distracted, she glanced up and then returned her enquiring gaze to Uma.

'I do not know for certain.' She shrugged. 'Sharmali, here,' she pointed to another pallet, where what looked like a dark bundle lay, 'believes the commotion is caused by troubled people from the villages. They are rioting because an earthquake has destroyed their homes and crops, and Todar Ram refused to open the granaries. So the people started a fire, and the palace guards are trying to put it out. My evil son wants payment for the grain, and these people have lost all their money. The granaries are next to the jails so that the police can protect them.'

'Earthquake! Yes, we felt it.' Tara's heart jerked when she recalled how Roger had kissed her just before they felt the tremor. She swept the thought aside; now was not the time for frivolous reminiscences. 'What are you and Sharmali doing here?'

Uma gave a despairing shake of her head. 'It is bad for us, I fear, Tara. When you left, Todar discovered that the ransom Sikandar had given him was imitation jewellery made from glass, such as the common people buy in the bazaars.'

So Roger Markham, for all his wealth, believes that I am worth no more than glass! Tara thought angrily.

'This enraged my son to the point of madness,' Uma was saying, 'and he thinks that, since we befriended you, we are somehow involved in the deception. Then he set one of his spies on us, a guard, and this devil found out that Sharmali was sending messages to Nagandra, her brother, my eldest son whom Todar Ram ousted. He accused us of inciting the riot up there.'

'He accused us rightly, *Maji*,' Sharmali confessed without remorse and much pride. She sat up. 'I incited them to fight for their rights. The grain harvest last year was plentiful, the granaries full. It is the custom to distribute free grain when disaster strikes the villages or when the monsoon fails. Now, after centuries, Todar Ram revokes the rule and demands payment. The people will starve; they lost all their possessions in the earthquake. I told Todar Ram so. He called me a traitor for conspiring with Nagandra. I did not deny it.'

Uma took up the tale. 'And for that we were thrown in here. Todar Ram still fears our curses, but believes that we must be punished.' Uma clicked her tongue. 'But we talk too much of our worries. What of yours, Tara?'

Her headache had eased, the heaviness was lifting. She was able to provide a lucid account of her abduction arranged by Céline Dupont and how she was forced to drink the *bhang*. 'Why she sweetened it with sherbet is a mystery to me.'

'Not to me,' Sharmali said. 'She wanted you to swallow the draught without being sick; not out of kindness! The Dupont woman is the sister of the *feringhi* traitor, the captain in Sikandar's army, is she not?' Her red pupils gleamed in the dimness.

Through the grille the sun's rays, opaque with dust-motes, cast a pool of light in the centre of the dungeon, but left the areas near the wall in gloom, which suited Sharmali's eyes.

Tara nodded, releasing Uma's parchment-textured hands and brushing away hovering flies. 'She says I am to remain alive, because another ransom—or should I say a genuine ransom—is to be extracted from Colonel Markham, and this time she'll get part of it. Her desire is to return to France, her homeland, and to live there in luxury.' Tara added with vehemence, 'Such avarice I have yet to meet!'

'You have yet to meet? Huh! You forget the avarice of Todar Ram, Tara,' Uma said drily, and reached for her hookah. 'Avarice is a fault that afflicts most of mankind.' She dragged on the pipe, and the water in the bowl chuckled merrily and incongruously in the grim surroundings.

'Tell me, Uma,' Tara said, still plagued with curiosity, 'tell me, how long have you been here in this dungeon?'

The old woman puffed out a stream of smoke before replying. 'We have been here since Todar Ram discovered Sharmali talking to a man recognised as one of Nagandra's spies. That was last evening. This morning, we heard he was tortured to death, poor man. May he know *samadhi*, union with God. To his great credit and bravery, he revealed none of Nagandra's plans. Hence we remain here by Todar Ram's orders till we disclose all.'

'We were dragged into this stinking hole,' Sharmali now spoke with the heat of indignation, 'like common felons! It is baffling why Todar Ram in his fury did not have us put to death. I am thinking he still fears us. Soon, soon, Nagandra, with Sikandar Sahib's help, will strike!'

Tara admired Sharmali for her faith and fearlessness. 'I'm sorry to hear about the painful death of Prince Nagandra's agent,' she said, her lips curving in sympathy. A small silence followed as if in honour of the unfortunate man.

'Did Sikandar Sahib mention anything to you about launching an attack on Motipur, Tara?' Sharmali asked, leaving her pallet and crouching down in front of them. She looked unearthly with her white hair, pink skin and red eyes. At home in the gloom, she had thrown off the sari from her head.

Tara jerked guiltily and reflected, He and I were otherwise engaged! War, politics, the world, all forgotten in the demonstrations of love. She had no time to analyse her true feelings for Sikandar Sahib. What she was sure of was that she still didn't trust him. Aloud she said, 'No, but I'm surprised he's not been taken prisoner also. We were...er...together at the time. He was knocked senseless, and could easily have been abducted along with me.'

Uma offered an explanation that appeared logical. 'He, I feel, has been given another chance to collect a ransom for you. He's rich, you say?'

'According to Mademoiselle Dupont. Now I recall, she did tell me more or less what you have,' Tara said. 'You seem to know your son well.'

'Assuredly! As I said, Sikandar has been left to collect ransom money for you. That is one reason. The other is that Todar Ram knows his forces are not powerful or disciplined, as Sikandar's are. My son is afraid that the Blue Cloaks will attack the palace if their commander is taken prisoner. Dead or imprisoned, Sikandar is useless to Todar. Alive and free, he is worth a fortune if he produces the price for you. And, this time, there is no tricking my son.'

'Will the colonel yield to Todar Ram's demands again?' Tara wondered aloud, the ever-present misgivings creeping into her brain.

'He will yield,' Uma said with complete confidence. 'He might have deceived my son with false jewellery, but Todar Ram is no fool, Tara. He knows the good commander is besotted with you. He'll do anything to have you with him, and I do not doubt that he will marry you.'

Tara said nothing about her marriage. How could she bear the two women's congratulations in this horrific den?

As the days passed, no summons arrived from Todar Ram to tell Tara that she was free to join Roger Markham. The irrepressible doubts rose to torture her.

Why should Roger pay out for her? He did not think she was worth even a few pieces of glass! Perhaps he and Céline Dupont were still in league with each other and had conspired to effect her abduction. She rejected that. It did not make sense; why would he have taken the risk to rescue her in the first place? Unless he only wished to gratify his lust—which he had done, and now had her sent back to Motipur jail. But why all the furtiveness? He could have acted openly.

Then it struck her. Perhaps Céline was right. He had taken care to make the marriage legal, performed by a priest and signed by witnesses. He could now truthfully say that he had wed the heir of Chiriabagh. When he returned there, he would put it about that unfortunately she had run from him, but the marriage entitled him to become the legitimate ruler. Oh, how she hated this devious man who had stolen her virtue! But not her heart— never her heart. And how, she moaned, could she get rid of both him and Todar Ram?

The riot had long since been quelled, but something else appeared to be amiss. In spite of her anxiety, Tara sensed more disturbances, and so did Uma and Sharmali, from their talk. Much toing and froing went on above the grating, as though an army were being mustered. French, English and Urdu voices bellowed commands. There came the tramp, tramp of marching feet. Turn! About turn! Run! Halt! Forward march! Again and again.

Eventually Sharmali asked the turnkey what was afoot. Instead of passing the midday gruel through the hatch at the bottom of the door, he came in. A superstitious character, Tara judged him to be from the fear apparent on his face as he eyed Sharmali. His expression seemed to say: She might be from the gods or the devil, but either way, she must be pacified. With alacrity he imparted the news that indeed his Highness was preparing for war.

'With whom?' Sharmali demanded.

'It is rumoured, *Hazrat*, that Sikandar Sahib and Rajkumar Nagandra have formed alliance and are marching to assault Motipur. There is also talk that the *Angrezis* have sent battalion of sepoys, but it is believed to be hearsay.' Enormous though he was, the turnkey avoided tiny Sharmali's red glare and peered at his grimy toes exposed in well-worn sandals. '*Hazrat* Todar Ram's foreign army, it is said, will slaughter Sikandar Sahib and his men.'

Sharmali's shrill laugh echoed with disbelief. 'Who said?'

The turnkey jumped back a pace, startled by the laughter. 'The Chief of Police tells of how it will be, *Hazrat*.'

She and her mother laughed, and the turnkey looked discomfited. 'An idle boast!' Uma exclaimed with a derisive twist of her dark lips. 'You do not know that Sikandar Sahib has yet to be defeated in battle. The English and the Marathas, the two main powers, try to coax him to join their armies, offering much money and promises. He prefers to be his own master, and abides by his self-made rules. Todar Ram has become a madman.'

'Why tell me this, Rajmati?' The turnkey shuffled his feet and sounded uneasy, impatient to be gone, and Tara felt a twinge of sympathy. Turnkeys, she knew, were inured to suffering and the torture they witnessed being inflicted on their prisoners, but this man seemed possessed of a human soul.

'Because, foolish one,' Uma replied without remorse, 'do you wish to be slaughtered? Sikandar's cannon will reduce the palace to rubble before long. Let us out and take us to Sikandar Sahib's camp. He will reward you well. I swear by the gods.'

'Let you out?' He jerked his head back, eyes protuberant with fear. 'Never! The prison guards would cut us down well before we reach the gate. I pray you to forgive me, Rajmati. But is there anything else I can do to ease your discomfort?'

Instantly Sharmali shot back, '*Ji*, assuredly you can, good man. You can fetch us wholesome food in future. And when Sikandar captures Motipur, we shall remember you.'

The turnkey was only too eager to oblige. He kept his promise and passed edible food through the hatch. Even so, he did not enter the dungeon, perhaps fearing another confrontation, Tara assumed. Immediately after he thrust the tray in, he dashed away.

Sharmali often called out to him on these occasions, trying to cajole him with extravagant promises at least to forward messages to Sikandar or her brother Nagandra, who by now must have joined up with each other. 'While everyone is busy preparing for battle, you can leave the palace undetected, perhaps as a villager.' But her efforts were in vain.

Apathy took hold of the women. Tara's hope began to slide into despair and her doubts about Roger Markham increased. Each day she woke expecting Todar Ram's summons, but now a couple of days had passed with no word. Was she to rot in this bug-ridden and stinking place with these two dear women? She resorted to prayer, said every one she knew, and invented a few. The next day an ominous change came over the weather.

Down in the usually cool atmosphere of the dungeon it became stifling, and the heat seemed to be rising from the earth. An unnatural, eerie stillness oppressed the air. And then, in the hush of evening, the women were startled by the boom of a cannonade.

'What goes on?' Sharmali sidled up to the door and bawled.

No one answered. Outside, it seemed that chaos reigned. For the first time since her incarceration, Tara heard the shouts and screams of panic from other prisoners. Guards and turnkeys spoke agitatedly among themselves, or yelled abuse and threats at the screeching captives. Another boom from the cannon. This time the floor vibrated, and Tara heard a distant explosion. Gunfire sounded closer. Running feet raced back and forth; voices rose in panic and alarm, and to Tara's stricken ears they were an incomprehensible babble. All three women, affected by the commotion, pressed against the door, hoping to glean what went on.

Then a voice yelled that Sikandar Sahib's army was attacking the palace, and that Todar Ram stood on the battlements ranting at his European officers. They were threatening to mutiny if he did not keep quiet.

Finally the prisoners were quelled with threats of no food, and a sullen silence hung, broken intermittently by sounds of gunfire and cannon. Foreboding crept into the fear-racked prison. Something of significance, of danger, was about to occur; Tara could feel it in her jangling nerves, her sweating body. She got to her feet and began pacing the rapidly darkening cell. Every now and again she sighed heavily to relieve her tension.

Uma sat cross-legged on the straw beside Sharmali smoking the hookah, and from the fast gurgle, Tara assumed that she was much perturbed. 'I hear the earth growl,' she murmured once.

When Tara lit an oil-lamp just after the evening meal, she heard a rumbling, and attributed it to the cannon. Throughout the night the battle raged, and Tara found difficulty in falling asleep, her mind swimming with frightened prayers. Her rambling pleas were brought to a halt when the floor of the dungeon began a light tremble and gradually built up to a vibration accompanied by a roar. She leapt up, weaving and rocking her way to Uma and Sharmali, crouching with them against the warm wetness of the wall. In dumbfounded terror she watched the centre of the floor cracking open. Wider. And wider.

The uproar started again. Prisoners yelled and chanted, 'Let us out! Earthquake! We'll be buried alive! Child of Satan, let us out!' Voices demanded, pleaded, swore. The guards, it seemed, had vanished to save their own skins, because none could be heard. Débris began to fall from the ceiling as the crack in the violently shaking floor continued to widen. Tara pressed closer to the wall, convinced that the dungeon would cave in.

Then a stillness, sharp and sudden. Heat rose from the fissure and scorched the atmosphere.

For a few moments none of them moved. Tara stared at the other two faces, which trickled with sweat and looked gaunt, horrific; their jutting bones and hollows were accentuated in the flickering light from the lamp, like emaciated corpses risen from graves. She shuddered. The dungeon had become a tomb of the living!

Taking a grip on herself, Tara crushed her ghoulish imagination. She rose, tentatively testing the strength of her quaking legs. Picking up the lamp, she moved away from her companions and, drawing in a deep breath, approached the crack in the floor. It was about a foot wide, dividing the dungeon in half and running in almost a straight line. Crash! She jumped. Something had toppled beyond their cell. Jubilant cheers erupted. 'God sent the quake to save us, brothers. See, it felled the door for us! Come, we shall join Sikandar's army and slaughter these dogs. May their souls rot!'

Colonel Markham's army! These prisoners must be his Blue Cloaks, his suwars, those who came here with Dupont as her escorts.

'Help!' she shouted, pounding on the door to attract the men's attention before their rapid departure. 'I'm Rajkumari Tara Bai; do you remember me? I think it was you who brought me here to Motipur. I'm also a prisoner. Help me!'

A surprised pause, then, 'Rajkumari Tara Bai?' hesitantly.

Tara recognised the voice as that of Hanif, who had been kind to her and Uma on their journey here.

'That's right. Is that you, Hanif?'

'*Ji, Hazrat.* Assuredly we shall do our best to free you! After we brought you here, we wanted to return to our Sikandar Sahib, but Dupont Sahib, the traitor,' here Hanif spat his contempt, 'he had us imprisoned. He said we were mutineers. Stand back, Highness! We shall see if we can break the door down.'

'How many of you are there?' Tara asked in growing excitement triggered by hope.

'Five. Move away from the door, *Hazrat.*'

Tara's eyes shone with expectancy when she joined Uma and Sharmali and asked, 'You heard?'

They nodded, but neither seemed to share Tara's hope.

'May the god Vishnu help them,' Uma prayed in a fervent whisper.

But Sharmali in her forthright and practical assessment of the situation soon disillusioned Tara. 'That door is banded with iron,' she pointed out. 'If an earthquake couldn't move it, nothing will, except a key.'

And she was right. The suwars' efforts were in vain. Despite the shaking, the door held firm. Moreover, the poor men must be half-starved, Tara thought, and so lacked sufficient strength. 'I can see it's useless, good people,' she called dejectedly. 'Don't waste what little strength you possess. Try and reach colonel sahib's lines and tell him that Uma Bai, Sharmali Bai and I are imprisoned here.'

The suwars apologised profusely, but promised to relay her message to Markham. 'Do not despair, *Hazrat*. Believe in us. Believe in Allah.'

With the padding of their feet dying away, Tara's last hope vanished. Heaviness settled in her heart, tears scoured her face.

The next day at dusk, a hush fell, as though a truce had been called. Indeed, Uma said as much. They had eaten nothing all day, since the guards and the turnkey had bolted, and their stomachs growled in protest. Even so, Tara tried to cheer them all by assuring them that someone would soon come.

'I do not mind starving down here, Tara Bai. I am old, I do not worry for myself.' Uma dragged on her hookah. 'I had hoped to live long enough to see my son Nagandra restored to the throne and the oppression of our people eased. But fate decrees otherwise. It is for you and my Sharmali that I fear. You are both young and do not deserve to rot here.'

'Nagandra will not forget you and me, *Maji*. He will come. Have faith.' Sharmali put a comforting arm round her mother.

But no one came.

The door was thrust open at some time in the night, but the joyful, expectant smile on Tara's face died, and fear replaced it. Brahman priests and Motipur guards and, behind them, the tall turnkey stood on the threshold. The three women rose and clung close together.

'Who are they?' Uma asked, slanting her head to listen.

'Brahman priests, *Maji*.' Though Sharmali spoke reverently, Tara detected a hint of rebellion in her voice.

'We have come to inform you, noble ladies,' said one of the Brahmans, a devotee of the god Shiva, Tara saw, from the lines chalked across his forehead. 'Todar Ram, the gods save his soul, is—dead.'

Tara rejoiced. Her parents had been avenged through the hand of the Almighty. Thanks be to God!

'He was shot on the battlements by the enemy.'

'And why are we, ignoble prisoners in this stinking hovel, honoured by the presence of high caste priests, the twiceborn, who would not deign to defile themselves here?' Uma asked with mock esteem. 'Why did you not send untouchables with your message? Are we not sunk to their level?'

The Brahman showed no rancour. 'We are come to bestow upon you a great honour, requested by his Highness in the few moments he lived after the musket-ball struck him.' The priest smirked. 'It is his last wish, and it must be obeyed.'

Now Uma was less bold. 'And—and his request?'

The brief moment of joy she had experienced deserted Tara. She shivered on noticing a macabre enjoyment on the priest's face as he looked at each woman in turn.

Then, taking his time, he said, in a soft voice rife with deadliness, 'His Highness Todar Ram, late of Motipur, commanded that all of you——' there was a pause, while he gloated '—must burn on his pyre.'

CHAPTER FOURTEEN

HER STOMACH churning in fear, Tara observed the sinister enjoyment etched on the Brahman priest's face as his black eyes ranged over the women.

He continued to speak, his voice impassive. 'His late Highness requested that all the women in the palace, be they wives, mothers, sisters, servants, slaves or prisoners, be sacrificed for the purification of his soul and theirs in preparation for the entry into paradise.'

Uma swayed, and Tara and Sharmali hastily supported her.

Horror knotted like ropes in Tara's body. 'You—you mean the rite of *jauhar*?'

'*Ji, Hazrat*, that is what I mean,' he said. So respectful, so mocking. He even brought his palms together in a *namasta* and bowed low.

'It must not be allowed!'

The priest straightened abruptly. He looked shocked by Tara's commanding tones. 'Not be allowed? By what authority do you speak? The last request of his Highness Raja Todar Ram must be fulfilled. I am entrusted to see that *jauhar* is celebrated. I do not understand you, *Hazrat*.'

'Then I shall explain. Bihar province is under British jurisdiction.' Although her control was deteriorating, she tried to impress him by maintaining the haughtiness in her voice and a proud stance. 'Suttee, the burning of single widows, and *jauhar*, the mass burning of women during times of war to save them from defilement by the enemy, have been outlawed by the British. They have decreed that these rites are illegal, and the British are powerful. They'll annex this state if you defy their rules. Your powers will be curtailed. Worse, you might face execution, because burning people alive against their will is murder!'

Tara's heart slumped as the priest appeared to be un-daunted. 'You speak like a true *Angrezi*; some of the blood flows in your veins, does it not? I would have you know, Tara Bai, that for centuries we defied the Musulman conquerors. Their persecutions did not crush Hinduism. We shall defy the *Angrezis* likewise. No one shall abolish our rites unless we choose to do so. And at this time, *Hazrat*, we do not choose to do so!' He was almost shouting now with vehemence and scorn. 'The dead ruler has authorised *jauhar*, and *jauhar* there shall be,' he added, and thrust out his chin and waved his arms to confirm his doggedness.

'You underestimate the power of the British. When they receive word of what you have done, you'll suffer. Pray, reconsider.'

'How will they find out?'

'How...?' Tara looked stricken, and trembled as she realised that all women witnesses would be burned. For a certainty, the priests and their male followers would say nothing!'

'I see you know nothing of our rites.' He gave Tara a withering glance and motioned to another Brahman, who held a tray on which stood a metal jug and matching handleless cups. 'Come, good martyrs, drink the opiate, and you will not feel anything. When all is done, you shall enjoy eternal bliss.'

'How do you know how we'll feel?' Tara asked with desperate boldness. 'Did *you* burn in a previous incarnation?'

Tightening his mouth, the Brahman ignored her.

Uma shrugged off the supporting hands and drew herself up proudly, chin high. 'If you spare the young ones, I shall become a *sati* willingly, without the opiate, and you shall have my blessings. This I pledge. But if you burn them as well, then not only I but they will curse you.'

The priest looked nonplussed, his eyes shifting in uncertainty from one colleague to another, silently inviting their opinions. Puzzled glances were exchanged, then the black gaze swung to Uma. 'We shall discuss what you've said, Rajmati.' He accorded her the noble address, and hands steepled together, he touched his forehead, and withdrew with his retinue. The door slammed shut, a key grated and the slip-slap of sandals faded.

Tara was thunderstruck by Uma's startling words. Recovering, when the men departed, she said, 'You *cannot* sacrifice yourself on our account, Uma Bai! We must devise a plan to escape from here.' Her eyes darted about the dungeon, and came to rest on the grating on the ceiling.

'How, my brave Tara Bai? There is no way in which we can contact Nagandra and Sikandar Sahib. Our only hope lies with the suwars who escaped, and they might have been killed before they reached their lines.' The old lady sighed heavily. 'Therefore, to preserve your young lives, it is best that I perish in the flames; I am old and blind, of no use to anyone. But, before I die, I shall use the one thing in my power: the *sati*'s curse, that all fear; or the *sati*'s blessing, that all yearn for.'

Tara's sceptical mind could not believe that curses or blessings would save them. She appealed to Sharmali. 'You know the plan of the palace. Surely you can remember a way out for us? What about that grating? If we could only climb up there.' She refused to dwell on the forthcoming ordeal, or she would go insane. Escape! They must escape.

Sharmali shook her white head in resigned despair. 'There is no way out from here. All the gates will be guarded by troops defending the stronghold, and they'll cut us down if we are able to get out through the grating, and that is impossible without a ladder.'

'Oh Jesus,' Tara prayed fervently. 'Spare us, save us!'

'Prayer is all you have left, Tara, my child. I have myself to give, if you and Sharmali are to escape the flames. An old blind woman will not take long to die.'

'As I asked the priest, I ask you—how do *you* know?' Tara cried. 'The dead do not return to tell us.'

'Does it matter, Tara?'

Tara stared. No, it did not matter, because there was nothing she or Sharmali could do to make it matter. Uma's terrible plight could only be relieved by the intervention of the supernatural.

The door creaked open and the head priest and his colleagues stepped in, followed by armed guards and the tall turnkey. Tara tried to catch the latter's eye in a plea for help, but he as usual was staring at his sandals.

'We have agreed to do your bidding, Rajmati,' the Brahman again addressed Uma by her title of queen mother. 'But we have decided that Sharmali Bai and Tara Bai must witness the burning. You, Rajmati, will be privileged to burn with the raja and his wives. Separate pyres are being built for the other women.'

'No! No!' Tara stepped in front of Uma to protect her, arms outstretched, tears of grief streaming down her face. 'Please spare her! Spare us helpless women; we have done no wrong.' Again her eyes sought the turnkey's. He had shown a little kindness previously, he might... But his feet held his fascination.

'This is not a case of right or wrong, *Hazrat*, it is a sacred rite,' the priest said, unmoved. His colleagues regarded Tara with stone-hard eyes, and in desperation she resorted to threats.

'Why do women have to suffer? We bear your children in pain, we cook and care for you. Now we must die in agony to save you from hell. Why don't you men burn as well? I tell you that this rite is outlawed! You will all hang!'

'Hush, Tara.' Cool, commanding, Uma's voice, her face tranquil. 'I know you are trying to save me, but you are not improving matters. I am not afraid, my child.'

Tara recognised the old lady's resoluteness; and slowly, weeping quietly, she dropped her hands in defeat and stood aside. Uma caught her, felt for her face and kissed her cheek. 'The gods care for you, Tara.'

Sharmali stepped in front of her mother, fell to her knees and rested her head on Uma's feet. '*Materji*, my revered and beloved mother, give me your blessing. Honour me with your wisdom and courage. May you enjoy the fruits of paradise. Oh, *Maji*, the pain, the terrible pain!'

Uma bent and raised Sharmali and hugged her. 'My beloved daughter.' Her iron control broke a little as her voice shook. 'Your brother prepared me well for pain when he had me blinded. Dry your tears. All will go well with you and Tara. May the gods bless you both.' And, sharply, to the priest, 'I do not need drugs, venerable one.' She released Sharmali and held out her hand imperiously. 'Take me to Todar Ram's pyre.'

A gleam of admiration sparkled in the priest's eyes. He placed his palms together and bowed low to Uma. Taking her hand, he placed it on his shoulder and said, 'I shall lead you to the raja's pyre.'

Three priests in white *dhotis*, their chests bare except for the sacred thread, started up the funereal chant: *'Ram, Ram...Ram nam sat hai...Ram, Ram'* ('The name of God is truth'). The priests and musicians slipped behind the old lady.

As Tara and Sharmali began to follow, the guards and the big turnkey stepped in the women's path. The screeching of conch-shells and the rapid beating of hand-drums drowned out the shouts and struggles of protest. Cloths were bound round their mouths, and both girls found themselves thrust back in the dungeon, the door quietly but firmly locked in their bewildered faces.

They helped to untie each other's gags. 'What new ruse is this?' Tara asked, more to herself. She felt shaken and confused. Pressing her ear to the door, she listened until the last of the chanting and music had dwindled away.

'We shall burn as well. That is their plan,' Sharmali said in answer to Tara's question.

'What? How do you know?'

'Did you not hear the priests say that Todar Ram wants *every* woman in the palace to burn, Tara?'

'No!'

'I fear so. They are taking advantage of my mother's blindness. She will have no idea whether we are in attendance at the burning. She will go to her death thinking that we are free, and instead of curses, she will shower blessings on the priests. But remember, Tara, they are doing what they believe to be their duty. You must not blame them.'

'Oh, Holy Mother of God!' Tara cried, her heart bounding with terror. 'Is there nothing we can do to save Uma and ourselves? There *must* be something. Perhaps you could use your curse to frighten them, Sharmali?' She lifted her head and her stricken blue eyes stared hopefully at her. 'Sharmali?'

Sharmali ambled to her pallet, where she sat cross-legged, gazing at her hands. *'Nahin.'* Tara's heart sank. 'They are no longer afraid of me,' she went on in a monotonous voice. 'They believe my mother's blessings will overpower my curses. But be consoled, Tara, I shall exercise as much power as the gods have granted me to free us all—if it is not too late. These ceremonies take time. Let us be silent, think and pray.' She lay down, then turned on her side, face to the wall.

Slumping on Uma's pallet, Tara watched the last of the light fade from the grille. What were they doing to poor Uma? With macabre clarity she imagined the old lady stretched out beside her son on the pyre, the priests intoning, a torch applied to the four corners of the bier... No! She must think of something else to quell the scream rising in her throat.

Unwittingly her thoughts strayed to her husband, and soon he permeated not only her mind but her body. She relived the passion he had aroused in her on their wedding night. No other man, she felt convinced, could have given her so much pleasure. Because he attracted her sensually, powerfully, how could she have responded other than with complete abandonment to his love-making? Yet she shrank from admitting to any deep feelings for him; certainly not in the present circumstances, when she would shortly face the horror of an excruciating death....

Voices in French curtailed any further thoughts. Tara sat up and was about to wake Sharmali, when a key scraped in the lock and the door creaked open. As she rose to her feet, a flaming torch dazzled her for a few moments until her eyes grew accustomed to the sudden brightness. Then, with a gasp of alarm, she recognised Céline Dupont still dressed in the black gown. A European in army uniform stood beside her, and behind them hovered the turnkey, holding aloft the light.

'Mademoiselle, you are being foolish!' the French officer said. '*Mon Dieu!* Why waste time on revenge, when this woman is to burn soon? Let us be gone.'

Tara recoiled. She recognised the man's voice; it was the one she had heard on the roof of Chiriabagh Palace on the night of the massacre. This man had slain her parents, and there was nothing she could do but feel her skin crawl and stare helplessly at him.

Céline held a horsewhip, which she cracked, and moved in a crouch towards Tara, a snarl of cruel triumph lifting her upper lip, her amber eyes bright with evil anticipation. 'Then be gone, Captain Delacroix,' she flung at the Frenchman without taking her eyes from Tara. 'The turnkey will see me safely out of here when I've finished with this bitch!'

Even as she spoke, Delacroix retreated out of the cell, tossing back, 'My men and I shall be waiting at the east gate for you. But don't tarry too long!'

'Shut that door, *canaille*!' Céline yelled at the huge turnkey after Delacroix's departure. He obeyed, and socketed the torch in a rusty sconce on the wall.

'Now, bitch! Because of you, I've lost everything. My brother lies dead in a pool of his own blood. That toad

of a raja also died before he could pay me the 5,000 gold
mohurs, if he ever intended to. But at least I'll have the
pleasure of whipping the skin off your back.' She laughed
harshly as she saw the colour leave Tara's face. 'Tie her
up,' she ordered the turnkey, 'and quickly. I do not have
much time.'

'I think not, mademoiselle.' Cool as winter rain, deadly
as venom, the male voice came.

Tara froze; the voice belonged to Colonel Markham.
Where . . . ?

She would have thought her hearing had become im-
paired through shock had Céline not whirled round to
face the turnkey. 'You!' She raised the whip to lash out
at him, but with ease he twisted it from her grasp.

'Mademoiselle, I give you the choice of getting out of
here as best you can, or being locked in the next cell.'

Céline lunged at Markham, trying to claw his face.
Then suddenly she stopped, and started screaming. Tara
followed the direction of her stare. Stark with terror,
Céline's eyes were locked on Sharmali. The albino stood
to one side behind Markham and, from the frightening
grin she displayed, Tara knew she meant to terrorise the
French girl.

In a flash Markham had Céline by the mouth, tugged
open the door, and lifted her out. By the time Tara and
no doubt Sharmali had gathered their wits, Markham
returned. He locked the door and came to stand in front
of Tara.

Still dazed from the unforeseen sequence of events,
she gazed at him. He was totally unrecognisable in the
turnkey's disguise of dirty turban, ragged shirt and
pyjamas. He had darkened his face, and in the light of
the flaming torch, his eyes looked black.

'My God,' he breathed in a shocked whisper. 'What have they done to you?' He swept Tara into his arms. 'I thought this moment would never come!'

Guided by instinct alone, she clung to him and burst into tears.

He kissed her closed eyelids, licked away her tears, and gently kissed her mouth. 'I'll get us out of here,' he said, rubbing his bristly cheek against hers.

'Sikandar Sahib, what did you do with the foreign she-devil? She is very quiet.' Sharmali alerted them both to her presence.

Reluctantly Markham released Tara, and replied, 'I've locked her in the next cell. She's quiet because she swooned. Any moment now she'll recover, screaming, and rouse the guards waiting on the floor above. Soon they and priests will be coming down to collect you for the burning.'

'But, Colonel, if there are guards waiting, how can we get past them?' Tara asked with a worried frown. From the flicker of annoyance on his face, she guessed he disliked her using his title.

He did not comment, perhaps because of the exigency of the circumstances, but looked up at the gaping hole in the ceiling where the grating had been. A dark rope-ladder dangled from it to the floor. 'That's our escape route. My men await us. Come.'

Barely had he spoken, when they heard Céline screaming abuse in French from the next cell.

'Quick!' Markham lifted Tara as high as he could on to the ladder. She swayed precariously, but Céline's screams propelled her up. Then hands grasped her wrists and hauled her out into the black overcast night. Next came a grunting Sharmali. And as Markham heaved himself out of the hole, shots were fired.

She assumed that the guards were aiming for the lock, since Markham, as supposed warder, would have the keys to the cells and he had used them to lock them in to gain enough respite for their escape.

The men who had hauled them out dropped the heavy grating back in place and shot the bolts just as the cell door crashed open.

'Follow me,' Markham commanded softly, taking Tara's hand and pulling her along in a swift run.

They had scarcely crossed the courtyard when a row of armed men with flaring torches confronted them, and soon they were surrounded.

'Ah! What have we here, André, *mon ami*?'

Tara's heart missed several beats. The man who had spoken was none other than her parents' killer—the hated Captain Delacroix!

CHAPTER FIFTEEN

'THIS TURNKEY must have misunderstood you, *mon capitaine.*' With chilling clarity Tara recognised the second voice she had heard in the pavilion. Her body shaking with hatred, she observed the man whom Delacroix had called André, his lanky frame clothed in a dirty grey uniform, his pale eyes cruelly cold.

'So it would seem,' Delacroix commented, nodding and fingering a raised scar like a caterpillar frozen on his right cheek. Unlike his companion, he was of medium height, sturdily built, his small eyes hard, denoting an innate brutality. 'You were supposed to bring Mademoiselle Dupont, *canaille*, not these prisoners! They're destined for the pyre. Where is she?'

Tara scarcely heard Delacroix, nor his henchman who interpreted the words in Urdu. The blood pounded in her head as she recalled in bitter rage that these two monsters had destroyed for ever the good people of Chiriabagh, who, under her father's just rule, had made the state prosperous. Her fury bubbling over, she screamed, 'Monsters! Misbegotten murderers! The blood of my people be upon you!' With enraged recklessness, she hit out at Delacroix, her open palm connecting in a ringing slap with his cheek.

In swift retaliation he knocked her sprawling to the flagstones with a backhand blow that stunned her with pain. Through a haze she heard him ordering the turnkey to take the women up to the battlement, where the priests were preparing the pyres. 'Let the bitches burn!'

Tara raised her head a little to stare at Markham. He had made no effort to defend her or to reveal his identity, but was continuing in his role of sycophant turnkey, bowing to Delacroix and mumbling, '*Ji*, Sahib.'

This man had proved himself a coward and a renegade, and the most galling truth she faced was that he was her husband. Why did his suwars not denounce him? Of course, they were saving their own skins! Even Sharmali, whom she admired so much, was as cowardly as the others. Well, she would betray them, but found her jaw too painful to move. Markham, the wretch, had the temerity to help her up, and as soon as she had steadied herself, she snatched her elbow out of his grip, only to feel her head spinning. So when he caught her arm again, she did not resist. Yet she felt furious at him for not saving her from that French monster's blow. She ignored the frequent pressure of his fingers on her arm, which she knew conveyed a message of conciliation.

'Hey, warder!' André called, and Markham paused. 'Where is Dupont Memsahib?'

Markham turned, bringing Tara with him. 'The memsahib thought the albino woman was a ghost, *Huzoor*, and she fled. Although I and the other guards,' he jerked his head to indicate his suwars, 'searched, we could not find her. I thought instead to bring these women to you.'

Tara begrudgingly marvelled at his fluency in Urdu and impromptu explanation. They did not, however, mitigate her poor opinion of his cowardice.

Before the Frenchman could speak, a man came running into the courtyard and pushed his way to the French officers. He raised his hand to his forehead and bowed low in a salaam to Delacroix. 'Captain Sahib,' he said breathlessly, 'the enemy have fled.'

Delacroix left the talking to André, while Tara tried to listen intently despite the throbbing of her swollen cheek. Was this man telling the truth, or was it a ruse? She glanced questioningly at Markham: his darkened features looked like carvings in granite and he stared ahead. A question and answer discourse followed between André and the courier. Tara gathered that the messenger, dressed in filthy clothes, his face streaming with perspiration, was one of Captain Dupont's suwars employed to spy on the enemy. He lamented the captain's death on learning that the latter had been shot along with Todar Ram.

The spy apparently convinced André, who relayed the conversation to Delacroix, and he laughed in triumph. 'Well, let us all go to the battlements and fire the victory rocket. Now that Todar Ram is dead, Motipur will be ours!' He waved to Markham to go ahead with the prisoners and the French-trained sepoys, and added with cruel glee, 'Let us witness those heathens burning the women. That should be an . . . er . . . experience, eh, *mon ami*?'

'*Oui, mon Capitaine.*'

Her terror brought a rolling queasiness to Tara's stomach. These fiends actually looked on the atrocity—the burning of women alive—as an entertainment. More painful than her aching cheek rose the thought that her husband was hustling her to a cruel death. She glanced at Sharmali, who had not spoken since their emergence from the dungeon and now walked straight, unsupported, her face shaded from the flaming torches by the *chuddah* drawn forward.

Tara knew she had no strength to mount the steep steps that she assumed led to the battlements, but the firm grip on her arm held her up and propelled her

forward. A great listlessness afflicted her, a kind of res-
ignation to accept her fate. Let it be over quickly, she
prayed. At last, exhausted, she was helped on to the
battlements and half carried by Markham to the back
wall against which other women crouched. Their faces
had vacant expressions and she presumed that the poor
creatures had been drugged. He propped her to lean
against the wall, and she thought he had said, 'Trust
me', before he left her. Vaguely she realised that Sharmali
stood next to her, and that armed soldiers were positioned in embrazures overlooking the moat. Then she
felt a searing wind spring up as though to prepare the
victims for cremation. She had tried to divert her mind
from the actual *jauhar* to prevent being engulfed by
panic, but now her eyes alighted on the raised platforms.

Priests, clothed in white *dhotis*, the sacred cords
draped across their chests and backs, and horizontal lines
marked across their foreheads symbolising devotion to
the violent god Shiva, sprinkled oil on the platforms, all
the while intoning the funereal chant: *'Ram, Ram...Ram
nam sat hai...Ram, Ram.'* She watched the as yet un-
occupied pyres and the ceremony with an enveloping
sense of horror; her mouth grew parched and bile rose
in her throat. The burning winds blew stronger, swirled
high with dust. She could feel a slight vibration of the
floor, but ascribed it to the quivering of her limbs.

'Aaaah!' A woman's scream pierced her brain. 'Let
me go, *diable*!' She could not mistake Céline Dupont's
voice. She followed the direction of the sound and saw
her trying to tear herself out of a guard's grip.

He was cursing her, 'This troublesome foreign bitch!'

'Captain!' Céline screeched. 'Tell these guards who I
am!'

Delacroix, Tara noticed, stood a short distance away with a group of his men who were about to light firework rockets. He spun round and hurried to Céline, removed his hat and bowed. '*Mon Dieu*, mademoiselle, I thought you had left the palace!'

'Left? What tales have you been listening to? I was locked in the dungeon like a dangerous criminal, monsieur. Those guards in the jail thought I had let those women escape!' she raged, pointing at Tara and Sharmali. 'They assumed I had bribed the turnkey to lock me in, safe in the knowledge that you would come to my assistance.'

Tara had forgotten about the guards who had burst into the dungeon immediately after she, Markham and Sharmali had passed through the grille, pulled up the rope ladder and shot the bolt. Obviously the men had not considered the grating as a means of escape, and disbelieved Céline's explanation.

'Leave the lady alone!' Delacroix snapped, pushing the guard away. 'Your quarry is there!' He pointed to Tara and Sharmali.

The guard was all contrition and obsequiousness. Delacroix booted the man out of the way and said to Céline, 'Ah! But I have good news for you, *chérie*! Markham and his allies have fled!' At that moment, rockets were fired into the air and a great cheer rose from the soldiers crowding the battlements.

'Markham has fled? I vow, Captain, *you* have been made the dupe!'

Delacroix frowned. 'How so, mademoiselle?'

Céline gave a bitter laugh. 'He was masquerading as the turnkey. It was he who helped those wretches out and locked me in. Where is the man? If you found those women, you must have found him.'

Delacroix glanced around nervously and fingered the hilt of his sword. 'He could be anywhere.'

'And they? What are you going to do with them?' Céline pointed to the women, her eyes glittering with hatred.

Delacroix brightened, showing his teeth in a vulpine grin. 'I think you'll rejoice to know that they are going to the pyre. It is windy enough for a good blaze. I intend to watch.'

'So do I, monsieur! What a pity the colonel is not here to see his wife burn.' She sauntered up to Tara and shook her head with mocking sadness. 'Poor madame, you do look hideous with your swollen face. Did your craven husband beat you and leave you?'

Tara did not reply, but shook her head and glanced away; she had enough agony to bear without having to put up with Céline Dupont's taunts.

Delacroix gave Céline his arm and said, 'Come, mademoiselle, let us go to the parapet. It should be cooler there.'

She gave him a charming grin and placed her hand in the crook of his arm. 'And we'll watch your departure from life, madame.' She gave Tara a sweet smile.

Guards dragged more women up to the battlements and hustled them towards Tara. A young girl began screaming and a guard hit her, bringing her to her knees.

'Stop hitting the women!' a Brahman priest cautioned the guard. 'Fool, do you not know that they are to be *satis*? That they must be revered? Beware of their curses!'

Tara felt dazed, unable to move, unable to make sense of the situation. This bizarre absurdity was beyond human comprehension, unless her teetering brain had slid over the rim into the realms of madness and she was imagining all this.

Helping the sobbing girl to her feet and bowing in apology to her, the priest ordered the guard, 'Go and bring a tray of the sleeping-water.'

'She bit me!' he snarled, but did as he was bidden.

'You will feel nothing,' the priest assured the girl.

Hairs rose on Tara's nape, terror hammered in her breast and head. They were going to administer opium-water. It was a Rajput custom, she had learnt. The opiate fogged the brain and brought on apathy, or sometimes an elation so powerful that the victims went to the pyre without any signs of resistance. She remembered from her history lessons that when the emperor Akbar the Great captured the fort of Chittor he found that all the women had broken their iron wedding bangles and immolated themselves in the rite of *jauhar*. Their menfolk had donned yellow robes and, high on opium, rode out proudly to meet their deaths in a battle they could not win. Tara knew she was not as courageous as her Rajput ancestors; she would not be able to endure the agony of being burned to death. Willingly she swallowed the contents of the cup, hoping to deaden the despondency and terror oppressing her. There was no sign of her husband coming again to her rescue. She must try to forgive him. That was what the dying were supposed to do.

'No, I do not want the sleeping-water,' Sharmali said in a firm voice, next to Tara. 'I do not fear death.' She was standing proud and erect, her red eyes blazing in the flames of the torches that would ignite the many pyres being set up with canopies, their tops spread with flammable twigs and doused with oil. The scorching winds would fan the flames.

'You are brave, Sharmali, just like your mother. She would have been proud of you,' Tara said through barely parted lips to minimise the pain in her aching jaw. She

was aware of her vision blurring and a great weariness
in her limbs. The feeling was not unpleasant, but
soothing, rather like that she had experienced when
Céline had forced her to drink the *bhang*. She thought
she felt the earth rock, but no one seemed to notice and
she assumed that the opium was responsible. Near her,
the young girl fell in an unconscious heap.

The priest who had handed round the sleeping-water
went down on his knees to Sharmali. Placing the tray
to one side, he lowered his head on her feet. 'You are
indeed brave, Rajkumari. The gods Vishnu and Shiva
will welcome you to paradise. We entreat your blessing,
for assuredly you are a *sati*.'

'Blessing?' she sneered, snatching her feet from under
him. 'Do not contaminate me with your vile touch! You
all contrived with Todar Ram to oust my brother,
Rajkumar Nagandra, the true heir to Motipur, and blind
my mother.'

The priest leapt to his feet, fury and awe vying for
supremacy on his face. 'Contaminate you, *Hazrat*?
Brahmans, and especially priests, are never defiled! We
are the chosen of the gods!'

'Murder defiles all. This cruelty of suttee has been
forced on women. Nowhere in the sacred text has it been
authorised.'

'But, *Hazrat*, the ancient scriptures do...'

Tara staggered. She still supposed that it was the effects of the opium and not the shaking floor. And what
was there about this priest? He seemed... He seemed...
But she felt too exhausted to think further.

'The ancient scriptures have been wrongly translated,'
Sharmali interrupted the priest. 'There are religious re-
forms proposed even now to forbid this rite. Enough!
If I am to burn, then burn me first. But beware, when

the flames roar forth, I shall issue my curse!' Her
laughter came shrill and eerie.

'Bring the garlands,' the priest ordered a colleague.
'The royal women must be adorned.'

He brought his head close to Tara as he placed the
rope of marigolds round her neck. 'We'll get you out of
here, Tara, never fear.'

Roger Markham's voice, she thought complacently,
all part of the drug-induced hallucinations. She chuckled
inanely.

'I shall not wait to be led to the pyre. I shall curse
you all now!' Sharmali cried, face and eyes glowing in
cruel triumph. She raised her arms like an ancient
priestess, and the hot wind billowed her sari, caught her
loose hair, swept it up in a white tangled skein. 'Accursed are you who force the burning of innocent
women! May you perish by the hands of the gods!'

The priest put the garland round Sharmali, and Tara
could have sworn she heard him say, 'Well done,
Sharmali Bai!'

First a turnkey and now a priest. What guise would
he assume next?

Sharmali shrilled her curse again, and as she did so,
the hot winds hurled her words round the battlements.
The priests ceased their labours and chanting to gape
aghast at her.

All of a sudden the cannon boomed, and the building
trembled and rocked. Tara swayed and stumbled. This
must be a nightmare! Her stomach churned and she
turned away to retch, bringing up the sweet opium-water
and bile. It seemed to go on for ever. When the sickness
subsided, her head began to throb, and an aching chill
attacked her bones, despite the burning winds.

The once orderly chanting had now been replaced by discordant shouts of dismay, 'Earthquake! Run! Run!' Pyres and women were forgotten, abandoned. Priests, guards and soldiers rolled, stumbled and pushed their way to the only flight of steps leading down.

Tara wondered fleetingly about the cannonade and gunfire directed at the palace. Had the spy not told Delacroix that the enemy had fled? She could see that the unexpected enemy attack, on top of the earthquake, had created more panic on the battlements. Chaos reigned. Screams filled the air-borne dust as enemy musket-balls found their targets. As the hot winds struck her chilled flesh, she felt as though she were indeed being burned on the pyre.

'Hold on to me, Tara.'

Markham's voice reached her, but she could hold on to nothing. The violence of the rocking threw her to the floor, where she lay stunned, in thick dust, hearing only the rumbling that grew to a thunderous roar. In the light of flaming torches she saw part of the battlements break away and land with a resounding splash in the moat below, and people falling to their deaths. Above the swelling clamour she caught the sound of bugles and drums, and knew that the English had at last arrived. But even that sound was swallowed up in the uproar, the upheaval, the howl of the fiery winds.

'Sharmali,' she called feebly, unable to see now, her eyes slitted against the wind and dust.

Beneath her the floor tilted, rose, fell, cracked. The smell of gunpowder, oil, sulphur and dust made her retch again, but this time she brought up nothing.

This was the end.

This was death.

This was hell!

'Tara!' His voice came as though from the depths of hell. He was somewhere close. Surely he would save her?

'Roger?' She forced his name from her dry and sore throat. 'Where are you?'

Booted feet ran up and down, guns exploded, swords clashed and rang. The bloodcurdling screams of wounded and dying men mingled with the roar and the scorching winds. Why were they fighting? They should be fleeing for their lives. Could they not feel the quaking earth? They were all in hell together. But where was Roger?

'Tara! Oh, Tara, at last!'

Strong arms wound round her; someone lifted her. Smells of sweat and sandalwood oil assailed her nostrils. Bristling skin scraped her good cheek. Roger! she called silently, the word locked in her choked throat.

He was running with her, down steps, through courtyards, across the drawbridge, out on to open ground. She glanced down to see the earth cracking and the chasm widening. On the opposite side of the abyss stood her mother, father, and the Jesuit priest of her youth. They were waving her back. 'Not yet! Not yet! Return!'

The vision vanished, and simultaneously the rumbling, rocking and the wind stopped. The sounds of battle receded; a hush fell. Tara opened her lids to see green eyes. Roger!

She felt herself sinking into coolness, softness.

CHAPTER SIXTEEN

ROGER LAID Tara gently on the divan in the tent and gazed tenderly down at her. In the light of the lantern she looked dishevelled, hair loose and tangled, her coarse gown dirty, her cheek swollen and showing signs of purpling. He had wanted to kill Delacroix when he had brutally struck her, but had forced himself to practise restraint if his plan was to succeed. Enough time had already been lost by the time he and the prisoners had unexpectedly confronted Delacroix and his men. Thanks to his Blue Cloak spy, he had managed to get his false message across to the French bastard.

His aim had been to keep the doomed women away from the parapet and safe from the cannonade, and to delay the *jauhar* until the French rat had sent up his 'victory' rockets, the signal for the Blue Cloaks and Prince Nagandra's forces to storm the palace. Sharmali had played her part admirably. She had timed her curse to coincide exactly with the earthquake, which was not totally unexpected since the tremors had become more frequent and increased in intensity.

His mouth tightened into a grim line. He could not think what spell Tara had woven over him. He must have been crazy to have actually married her, considering his attitude towards women in general: they were on the whole mercenary and cruel like his stepmother. Women were playthings to satisfy his lust, and then to be paid handsomely and tossed aside.

Tara was no better than the rest: she had played him false on their wedding night. Undoubtedly this girl had hired thugs to knock him out and then made her escape. But why had she returned to Motipur? He had ignored Todar Ram's demand for another ransom for her and had bombarded the palace, which had resulted in the raja's and Dupont's deaths. He had decided on a different strategy when his suwars, who had escaped from the Motipur dungeons and the deserting turnkey, had fled to his encampment and told him of Tara's imprisonment. He had been devastated, had tried every trick to get her out.

Markham removed his gaze reluctantly from Tara. Soon his risaldar major and his suwars would be here to collect him for the victory march into Motipur. He washed his face, exchanged his *dhoti* for breeches and boots, and the Brahman sacred thread for a shirt and gold-corded blue coat. The priest's wig he tossed aside in favour of a blue cocked hat.

'Sikandar Sahib!' the risaldar called.

Markham gave Tara one long look before lifting the tent-flap and striding out.

In the pink and gold light of early morning, Tara opened her eyes and gazed through an open window that revealed only the sky. Cool, sweet air brushed her face. The deep blue *punkah* was waving back and forth, back and forth, squeaking in irritating monotony. Where am I? She saw a woman sitting on the floor pulling the fan, the rope caught between her toes, while she treated herself to *pān* from a small box. Tara had never acquired a taste for such, but now she could eat anything.

She ran her tongue over her paper-dry lips. 'Give me some, please?' Raising herself a little, she pointed to the box and fell back weakly with an exhausted moan.

Her sudden voice seemed to startle the servant, who released the rope from between her toes and shot to her feet. 'Are you hungry, *Hazrat*?'

'I'm ravenous, good woman.' It was debilitating even to talk! 'May I have some *pān*?' An irrational impatience assailed her. How many times must she keep repeating herself?

'*Nahin, Hazrat,*' the servant said apologetically, 'Sharmali Bai ordered that I tell her when you awake.' She fled, her sari billowing with the swiftness of her movements.

Tara became fretful. Why does the woman not give me *pān* and explain why I am in this vast chamber all by myself? This was no room in Chiriabagh Palace, she observed grumpily. So where? She tried to sit up, but the room began to reel and hastily she flopped back, closing her eyes, surprised at the weakness so slight an exertion caused.

A swishing of garments compelled her to open her eyes, and Sharmali entered, squinting and shading her eyes, but smiling happily. 'Leeta tells me you are hungry, Tara Bai. Would you like a bowl of curds and mango?'

'Sharmali,' Tara found it an effort to speak, her voice breathless, 'I'm so hungry! Yes, curds and mango sound delicious.'

The albino's smile broadened, and she caught Tara's hand. 'My friend, you have slept two nights and a whole day. It was the effect of the opium-water drunk on an empty stomach. Perhaps you would have slept longer had you not been sick. After you have eaten, I have many surprises for you.'

Surprises could wait, Tara thought, feeling like weeping. 'How did I come to be here?'

'Sikandar Sahib brought you.'

Tara stiffened on hearing her husband's name. She recalled his callous behaviour when he made no effort to protect her from Delacroix's blow. Disinclined to discuss him with Sharmali, she asked, 'What is this place and where is it?'

'This is a chamber in the Tower of Winds in the Motipur Palace.'

Tara frowned quizzically. 'From what I can remember, Colonel Markham carried me out of the Motipur Palace.'

'Yes, first he took you to his tent in the army encampment on waste ground beyond the moat. Then, when the fighting and earthquake had ceased, he brought us to this tower,' Sharmali said. 'It is cool, and one of the few buildings left standing within the palace walls.'

Tara managed a wan smile. 'I'm so pleased you are safe and well, Sharmali.'

She nodded and patted Tara's hand. 'Enough of talk. First you must eat . . .'

'And bathe also. I feel dirty.'

'Assuredly, Tara. Now I will arrange for your food to be brought up here,' Sharmali said, gliding out of the chamber.

After consuming all her breakfast, she ambled to the adjoining bathroom decorated with lapis lazuli tiles, and sank into the cool depths of a gilded bathtub. Instead of invigorating her, the bath made her feel drowsy, so she returned to the divan and relaxed on it, marvelling at the potency of the opium-water she had swallowed on the battlements all those hours ago. In moments she lapsed into dreamless slumber. When next she woke, she looked straight into Roger Markham's carved face and unreadable green eyes. Her heart gave an unexpected lurch.

'Sharmali tells me you have recovered enough to eat and bathe,' he said, 'but when I arrived, you were asleep. So I waited. How do you feel?'

The unexpected joy she experienced on seeing him was instantly suppressed by the cool timbre of his voice. His presence evoked in her a vibrant awareness of him. He smelt fresh and looked neat and cool in a white shirt with a lace cravat, white breeches that emphasised the bulge of powerful muscles on his shapely legs and patent shoes with silver buckles. The sun shone through the open window on his copper-gold hair tied back in an elegant black riband. The air seemed to be charged with an intangible, alluring force that radiated from him. His potent masculine attraction threatened to undermine her defences, which he had successfully breached on their wedding night—though, she was compelled to admit, with her full consent. And he had proved to be an exciting lover. The recollection sent a melting heat pulsing in her loins and high colour rushing to her cheeks.

He gazed at her curiously. 'I asked how you felt.'

'I—I'm well enough, thank you.' To excuse her flush, she added, 'It's rather hot in here. I fear, sir, I'm ill groomed to receive visitors. Alas, my hair is in a tangle and this cotton shift is too large and dowdy.'

His eyes raked her up and down while a faint smile touched his well-shaped lips. 'You look beautiful in anything, but best of all in nothing.'

She raised herself on one elbow and stared at her small hands. With a secret amusement, she felt tempted to say, So do you, and observe his reaction to so outrageous a remark. But she refrained from what she considered ill-bred brashness and remained silent.

'You don't have to feel embarrassed, lady. I think you need to be reminded that we are married.'

She lifted her long-lashed lids to look squarely at him. 'I can scarcely forget, sir, that it was a marriage of convenience for both of us.'

He had remained standing as they conversed. Now he stared down his nose at her, eyes opaque, face wooden. 'Lady, I advise you to speak for yourself,' he told her coldly. 'However, this is hardly the time and place to continue the discussion. Come and dine with me tonight. Then you'll have had the opportunity to groom yourself to your satisfaction.' He lifted her hand to brush it with his lips.

She knew he observed conventional courtesy by his action, but what surprised her was her own reaction to the light unemotional kiss. A strange, pleasurable jolt streaked up her arm, and for some time she gently rubbed the back of her hand where his lips had been.

Fear and worry badgered her brain; she felt disturbed that, despite her resistance, she was becoming increasingly emotionally involved with Colonel Markham, whom she had branded a philanderer. What had happened to his mistress, Céline Dupont? She must question him tonight. Meanwhile, she should do something about her hair....

Sharmali sent word by the servant who brought in Tara's lunch that she regretted her inability to come herself, because with the arrival of her brother Prince Nagandra, the new ruler, and his family, she had to look after them. Soon, however, Tara would receive a pleasant surprise.

Tara was not excessively curious about the surprise, but puzzled over her husband's cold and condemning manner towards her, considering it was *she* who had been wronged, snatched away by his mistress, drugged and imprisoned. And though he had tried to save her from the pyre, she felt aggrieved at his cowardice in allowing that evil French devil to hit her. What had ruffled Markham's peacock feathers? Even so, she was heartened to observe that her resentment had no effect on her appetite; she enjoyed a lunch consisting mainly of lightly cooked vegetables, wholemeal pancakes, a large mango and plenty of refreshing lime-juice. The food brought a resurgence of strength to her mind and body.

Tonight, when she dined with Colonel Markham, she would be in command of herself and ignore his powerful attraction, question him firmly on his baffling behaviour. Moreover, she would insist on returning to Chiriabagh. If he refused to take her, she would have to approach Prince Nagandra. Then she remembered that during the battle for Motipur, she had heard the sounds of European drums and flutes and had assumed that the English had arrived. She sighed. That might well have been a fanciful flight of imagination.

She was pleasantly distracted when servants carried in a pile of the clean garments that Markham had promised her. To her delight, they were her mother's clothes; outmoded in fashion, she knew, and adapted to the hot climate by the absence of hoops, stays or padded rolls. She had a choice from half a dozen dresses and selected her mother's favourite yellow muslin lined with satin. The low-cut bodice was enhanced with two tiers of delicate lace, and the wide skirt fell in graceful folds. The servants helped her with her toilet. They were a pleasant, cheery lot of women who, like her, considered themselves lucky to have escaped the pyre.

After she had dressed, she picked up a hand mirror to view her face. Ruefully she regarded the bruise on her cheek, which had turned a dark yellow, but at least the swelling had disappeared. Her eyes sparkled with excitement, and the black pigment lining her lids emphasised the sapphire of their irises. She felt particularly pleased with her now tangle-free hair, which she twisted into a burnished coil on the top of her head. The only thing she lacked was jewellery. It made her feel a trifle bare.

Scarcely had the women left than she heard a peremptory knock on the door. 'Who is it?' she asked, nervously twiddling the wide fall of lace edging her elbow-length sleeves.

'Your husband, Tara.'

She started. His bald announcement had shaken her. This is ridiculous! she chided herself. They had consummated their marriage fully and enjoyably, hence he was entitled to call himself her spouse. Yet she had thus far identified him only as Colonel Markham. 'Come in, sir.'

As he entered, he halted suddenly, viewing her from head to toe, admiration glowing in his green eyes. His gaze stopped short at her revealing cleavage, and he watched, with a slow smile, the flush colour her cheeks.

In his green cutaway silk coat, matching knee breeches, white stockings and lace cravat, he looks the most handsome man in the world, she thought fancifully, but instantly checked any further meanderings of her brain. She noticed then that he carried a flat case in his hand.

He gave it to Tara and urged her to open it. She drew in a sharp breath on seeing nestling in cream satin a set of necklace, earrings, bracelets and a ring in cornflower-blue sapphires, the exact colour of her eyes. For a moment she stared up at him, her face radiant. 'These—these must be priceless,' she breathed in awe. 'I see the setting is European, and the stones cut in the new style to heighten the brilliance of the gems. They're superb!'

He smiled easily. 'You're right, Tara. I see you know quite a lot about gems.'

Her face clouded, and she dropped her lids. She did not really want to accept jewellery from him. All she wanted was to return to Chiriabagh and its people. On the other hand, it would certainly be ill mannered of her to return the gift; he was her husband, whether she liked it or not. 'How did you come by so exquisite a set?' she asked, lifting out the necklace and admiring its blue fire.

'A grateful nawab gave them to me. The Kashmir sapphires, I mean, and I had them cut and set by his French jeweller. I had no idea I would marry a lady whose eyes would match the gems perfectly.'

'Thank you,' she said simply.

He moved to stand behind her. 'Give me the necklace.'

Without physical contact, his proximity alone increased the tempo of her heart; however, the casual touch of his hands as he manipulated the clasp created a minor upheaval of her system.

He remained standing behind her after completing his task. Then, with slow deliberation designed to provoke, he traced the fingers of both his hands along the edge of her neckline, moving round over the swellings of her breasts until his hands stopped at her cleavage.

The effort she exerted in controlling her rapid breathing sent blood pounding in her head. Where his fingers had touched her, her skin burned with a sensual ecstasy that caused her nipples to tingle. And then she was free.

She heard his sigh and closed her eyes in disappointment, but opened them swiftly when he came round to face her, and assumed a serene expression. It belied her inner arousal, which she knew would stay with her while she remained in his company.

He looked flushed, as though he had been drinking. Clearing his throat, he offered her his arm. 'I think it's time we dined,' he said, his voice husky.

Tara nodded, picked up a lace shawl from the bed, draped it round her shoulders and took his arm.

For a moment he hesitated. 'Do you wish to put on the rest of the jewellery?'

Distractedly she looked at him, then at the case lying on the fretted sandalwood table. 'Perhaps it would be wise to wear the full set and not to leave it lying around in an empty room,' she said, a little unsteadily.

He did not help her this time, and she was relieved lest he guess her turmoil. His smile and his admiring eyes told her she had made the right decision.

She was a little surprised when he guided her into a large chamber on the floor below her room. She had presumed they would be dining in his encampment outside the palace walls; however, she made no remark. She had also imagined that there would be other guests, but from the two places laid on the European-style rectangular table she was glad that they would enjoy a tête-à-tête; there were so many questions she wished to ask him. Where was his mistress? What did he intend doing with herself? She curbed her impatience until they had eaten.

Liveried retainers served them with a simple, tasty dish of potato chops, which were different from European chops in that the meat was chopped finely, seasoned and cooked to a dry consistency. Then a blob of the meat was placed on a flat round of mashed potato, covered over, rolled in flour and fried to a golden brown in *ghee*. These were served with carrots and spinach. As they sipped their drinks and ate, they talked. At first their conversation was desultory, praising the food until dessert had been served. Markham then thanked the retainers and dismissed them.

'How much damage did the earthquake do, sir?' Tara asked after dabbing her mouth with a white napkin.

His thick brows lowered in a frown. 'Is it so difficult to call me "Roger"?'

She stared at the flickering flames of the perfumed candles, and said nothing. She preferred to address him formally until he had explained his behaviour.

He shrugged his broad shoulders and pushed away his dessert bowl without touching the delicious mango fool. 'The earthquake did a lot of damage. Apart from this tower, the marble buildings comprising the audience hall, the raja's apartments, including the treasury and Sharmali's *tehkhana*, most of the other buildings were destroyed. Fortunately, too, the granaries are intact, so that survivors and refugees from outlying villages that have been annihilated can at least be sure of a few days' sustenance.'

'Were there many deaths?'

He nodded grimly. 'Many people perished. Prince Nagandra's troops and mine are still searching for survivors beneath the débris.'

'I suppose you have now moved into the palace as a guest of Prince Nagandra,' she said, maintaining a haughty coldness. She derived a modicum of pleasure on observing that she was disconcerting him by her manner.

'No, I'm still out there in my tent.' He poured himself another glass of claret, swallowed half of it, and continued, 'What's the matter, Tara? Why are you so stiff? What have I done to deserve your censure?'

That was all she waited for, and her eyes flashed blue anger. 'Well might you ask, sir! I disapprove of cowards!'

'Cowards? What the devil are you implying?'

She stroked the bruise, drawing his attention to it. 'I'm not implying. I'm telling you bluntly that I consider you a coward, Colonel!'

Glancing at her bruise, he nodded. 'I see. I didn't save you, or attempt to do so, from Delacroix's blow. Am I right?'

'Precisely.'

He swallowed the remainder of the claret and slammed down the glass. 'You should have asked for an explanation instead of blindly accusing me!'

'What explanation could you give, Colonel? You stood beside me like Medusa turned to stone and made no effort to punch that bully. He could have killed me!' She glared at him, while absently rolling and unrolling her napkin, then flung it down. 'Or perhaps that's what you hoped.'

He swallowed a laugh. 'You talk without thinking. Damn it, woman, would I have risked my life to save you from burning if I'd wanted you dead?'

'You didn't save me, sir. The earthquake did.'

'An act of God helped, I don't deny. But if I'd played the gallant and got into a fight with Delacroix, you can be certain, lady, we'd all be in the hereafter. Did you not notice that his men had us covered with pistols? Though he hurt you a good deal, I could see he hadn't killed you. And, whatever you believe, I yearned to take the skin off his accursed back,' he snapped, ending with an exasperated click of his tongue.

At her disbelieving 'Huh!', Markham pushed himself out of his chair, strode to the window and stared down on the courtyard. He looked tall and lean, and so elegant in his modish attire. Tara quelled her wayward thoughts and pondered on what he had said. It sounded truthful, or at least plausible.

He spun away from the window, returned to the table, placed his palms on it and leaned towards her. Dangerous sparks glinted in his eyes, the candlelight heightening the gold tints in his neat hair. 'It is you who have much to answer for.'

Tara blinked. 'What are you talking about?'

'One of my trusted officers heard you bribing Céline Dupont to help you escape to the British. At first he thought you were offering gold to one of the suwars.'

'Then why didn't he report it to you?'

'Alas, he had had a sip too many of grog, and dismissed what he'd heard as a figment of his imagination, especially when you went through with the marriage ceremony. But, with Céline's help, you managed to abscond on our wedding night. Except that she hoodwinked you and took you back to Motipur to be thrown in the dungeons.'

She licked her lips and swallowed. 'I—I...'

He caught her by the shoulders and hauled her out of the chair. 'Did you or did you not try to bribe Céline?' Her cheeks burned in shame as she averted her eyes from his. Giving her a little shake, he insisted, 'Look at me, Tara! Did you bribe her?'

Her head snapped up, eyes glaring defiance. 'Yes, she threatened my life if I married you. She also ordered me to ask you for money. Instead, I offered her gold if she would take me to my mother's cousin in Calcutta. Uncle Thomas would have given Céline the money and would have asked Governor Hastings to march on Motipur.'

'So you don't consider I'm equal to the task?'

She fought to wriggle out of his grasp, but he held her fast. 'You wanted conditions...'

His voice softened a shade. 'I wanted you.'

Closing her eyes to prevent him from bewitching her, Tara said, 'What happened to my parents' killer, Captain Delacroix, and your—your erstwhile mistress Mademoiselle Dupont?'

'They're dead.' Her eyes flew open. 'The parapet gave way and they both crashed into the moat, pinned down by slabs of concrete.'

All she could say to that was 'Oh.'

'And what happened to the other Frenchman? André I believe was his name.'

'Captured by the British. France and Britain are presently at war with each other. But Todar Ram's French mercenaries are deserters, and they'll be returned to French Pondicherry. Beyond that, I don't know. I don't care. All I want is you.'

'I dare say, because of Chiriabagh. You want to be the new ruler.' She paused, waiting for him to vociferate protests and denials, but none came.

He released her, sat down and gave a bored sigh. 'Go on,' he said, as though he had heard it all before, which he had.

Oh! She would shake him out of his complacency. 'Marriage with the heiress would establish your power there and the British would acclaim you as the White Zemindar. Hmm?' She swallowed to relieve the choking thickness of her voice, so incensed was she. 'You married me to further your ambitions, knowing full well that a woman ruler would be acceptable neither to the British nor to the Indians. I'm an oddity in a masculine world.'

At last she had succeeded in making an impact on him, but her outburst brought her no satisfaction. His eyes hardened to resemble green ice that seemed to freeze her to the marrow.

Slowly he rose to tower over her. 'You haven't a trusting bone in your body! You base your wild conclusions on mere shaky conjecture. Did it not occur to you to find out first?'

'I'm waiting for you to tell me, Colonel,' she sneered, raking him with her fiery blue gaze.

'You wouldn't believe me. The British are here, so why don't you ask them?'

So she had not been deceived about the British arrival. For a moment, she experienced delight. 'I'm asking you, Colonel,' she said, aware that she could ask the British to verify his statement.

'And afterwards have it confirmed?'

She did not reply.

'Very well. When I first arrived in Chiriabagh, I sent word by courier to Fort William to tell the Governor about the massacre—I didn't know at that time that you were alive—since he had a right to know, Bihar being in the East India Company's domain. As you know, it takes months for news to travel to Calcutta and for a contingent of dragoons and sepoys to march to Chiriabagh. On arrival there, they read the letter I'd left explaining the situation to them.' He paused, swallowed a deep breath, and continued, 'I did not recommend myself for the rulership. And I did not marry you for your domain.'

'Really?'

'You're not in the least convinced.'

'Should I be, Colonel?'

'You will be, lady.'

'Why?'

'Because Chiriabagh no longer exists.'

She eyed him with scepticism. 'No long——? This is no time for jesting, sir!'

He sighed. 'Ever a doubter, Tara? The earthquake that you claim saved you took your beloved palace. Eye-witnesses, the few that were left, saw the ground crack open and...'

As she swayed, he caught her to him. With a strangled cry she buried her face in his chest. 'Don't say more. I—I... Oh God,' she sobbed, 'I've lost everything: my people, the palace and my chance to prove that if I were the Ranee of Chiriabagh, queen of the Emerald Throne, I could have made the realm as prosperous as my father left it.'

He gathered her closer. 'You've got me, Tara. I'll take care of you.'

She raised her tear-stained face and saw the brilliance shining from his eyes.

'Lady, I married you because I love you.'

She shook her head, not quite convinced, and tried to push out of his arms, but he refused to let her go.

'I seem to have lost my very identity. I—I... Who am I?'

'You're still a princess, and my wife. You'll have to accept the loss of the palace.'

She nodded and in despair sagged against him. 'I don't know what to do.'

Roger lifted her chin. 'You can kiss me,' he said softly.

His eyes were working their magic on her, drawing her into their endless green depths. 'The servants might walk in,' she whispered shakily.

Sweeping her up, he carried her to the bedchamber above. Lamps burned low in scalloped niches on either side of the divan. To her surprise he continued past the bed and stepped into an alcove, where she spotted another flight of stairs. He leaped up these to a flat roof supporting small booths at the four corners and a large, open-sided, one in the centre. It was to the middle one that he carried her and laid her on the wide, silk-covered divan. Absently she glanced up at the huge stars like glittering pendants hooked to an indigo shawl. The breeze ruffling through the arches was cool enough for comfort and strong enough to discourage mosquitoes.

But her attention focused on the man who flung off his coat and tossed it over a fretted rail. He towered over her, clad only in his shirt and breeches. So devastating did he look that her heart began a rapid drumming, arousing fully her sensations that were simmering beneath the surface.

Roger lowered himself sideways next to her, reclining on the satin bolsters, and he positioned her so that her back rested against his chest. His long fingers caught her chin and turned her face up to him. 'Kiss me,' he urged her again, his lips just touching hers.

She could not resist his allure had she wanted to, and she did not want to; she ached for him; ached to love him. She believed she needed the lovemaking of this virile, attractive man in order to expunge her terrible loss. In his strong embrace she would feel protected and could escape from the harsh reality of life.

Her mouth opened beneath his to receive his insistent kiss. At the same time his caressing hands were stroking her throat, the bare skin under the necklace and the voluptuous swell of her breasts above her low-cut dress. He lifted his mouth suddenly, and her breath caught. Did he think her brazen?

'How do you undo this dress? Too many clothes! Too much jewellery! I want you as naked as Venus rising from the ocean.'

He helped her to remove the sapphire set and stretched out to place it in the inner pocket of his coat. 'Now the dress.'

'It laces in front,' she said breathlessly, sitting up. With unsteady hands she undid the tapes. From the back he eased the garment from her, planting feather-light kisses on her shoulders and down her spine. She shivered, goose-pimples of pleasure rising on her skin.

A short while later he pulled her against him, her back resting on his furry chest, and she knew he had discarded his clothes. This time, it was she who whispered, 'Kiss me.'

He gave a soft laugh before his mouth came down on hers. Still kissing her, he lifted her hands to clasp the back of his neck. Slowly his fingers trailed down her arms, up the front of her ribs and circled the pink aureoles of her breasts. She drew in a sharp breath of ecstasy, as fiery jolts of rapture radiated through her until she was throbbing for fulfilment.

Breaking the kiss, he rubbed his jaw, hard and slightly prickly, against her soft face, and whispered, 'Are you enjoying what I'm doing?'

Unclasping her hands from behind his neck she looked with a straight face at him. 'No!' she said, and he laughed.

He let go of her breasts, now pleasurably tingling, and turned her to face him. 'Pleasure me, darling,' he said, his voice husky.

Guided by instinct alone, Tara pushed him gently until he lay flat on his back. For a few seconds she gazed into his eyes, seemingly bottomless, black, drawing her into their abyss of power. Lightly she kissed his mouth, traced her lips along his square chin, down the strong column of his throat and nibbled the deep hollow. He released a sighing moan. Gently he tipped her on her back, and she whispered, 'Take me, Roger.'

'We're both ready, my love,' he said, and hungrily his mouth sought hers again. Then his arms tightened, crushing her to him as they rode to the stars, there to climax in a glorious explosion.

She was in love.

No other condition would have tempted her to respond with such wanton passion to Roger's lovemaking, she reflected in the dreamy aftermath. Twice more during the night he took her, and each time proved more exhilarating than before. As yet she had not declared her love; he might think she was doing so for convenience, as a form of compensation for her loss of Chiriabagh. In time she would convince him!

The following evening they attended the glittering reception held in the Hall of Public Audience. On the arm of her husband, now in uniform, Tara lifted the bell-shaped skirt of her sapphire blue dress to just above her gold shoes and mounted the steps draped in silver cloth to the gem-encrusted throne partly hidden by the new Maharaja of Motipur, his Highness Nagandra Ram, who stood in front of it to welcome his guests.

Unlike his brother, the new ruler was a slender young man, elegantly attired in knee-length *achkaan* of gold cloth and narrow draped trousers. On his gold turban, an emerald shaped like a falcon supported a stiff aigrette. Gold chains studded with pearls, and jewels round his neck, clinked as he moved.

As the resplendently garbed usher announced the couple, Nagandra's large brown eyes looked kindly on Tara as she honoured him with a curtsy, and smiled in delight at Roger's smart salute.

'Welcome, good friends. I think you would like to greet a very brave lady. Sharmali Bai tells me that here is the surprise she promised you.' Mischief sparkled in his eyes as he stepped to one side.

Tara drew in a shocked breath. On the throne lounged Uma, a golden mask concealing her eyes, and a gold-braided, indigo sari draping her frail figure.

'Ah, Tara my child, you thought old Uma was ashes?' She chuckled at her own black humour. 'I have defeated death itself, have I not?' She held out her hands, fingers ablaze with rings.

Tara gave a soft cry of joy and bent to clasp the old lady. 'Oh, Uma Bai, I'm so—so happy that you escaped that dreadful pyre. Sharmali's surprise, I swear, is beyond all my expectations!'

'My good daughter did not wish to excite you while you were recovering from the effects of the opium-water. I shall tell you what happened, hey?' She sucked her lips thoughtfully, and went on, 'The priests decided to burn me last. They still feared me because I told them I had cursed Todar Ram and that was why he died. They locked me in a chamber, and there the good Pullen Sahib found me.'

'I'm overjoyed to see you looking so well and happy, Uma,' Tara remarked, glancing round. 'But where is Sharmali? She should be here to celebrate.'

'If you remember, Tara, she does not like the bright lights and entertainment. But tomorrow you and your good husband must dine with us. I hear he is great at masquerades! Now let me greet the noble Sikandar Sahib.' She clicked her tongue, and admonished Tara playfully, 'You are surely a sly one, Tara Bai, not telling us that you married him!'

'Tara is not quite used to the idea of being my wife, ma'am,' Roger said, lifting Uma's hand and kissing it, and Tara laughed.

Then, to everybody's shocked amusement, the old lady disgraced herself by demanding her hookah.

The usher rapped his jewelled mace for attention. 'His Honour Thomas Orme Sahib, envoy to his Excellency Governor Warren Hastings Sahib!'

Tara's eyes widened with astonishment and happiness. Her uncle Thomas, rotund, powdered wig too far forward, his waistcoat too tight, puffed up the steps, mopping his red face and bowing to the Maharaja. 'Pleasure, pleasure, Highness!'

She called to him as he moved to her side without seeing her, when the next person was announced.

'Why, poppet! Delighted!' he exclaimed, and gave her an affectionate hug. 'Heard of your ordeal, m'dear. Your poor parents. Tragic, tragic! Sorry couldn't get here in time. Courier killed. Carrier pigeons no good. But that blackguard Todar Ram and his devilish mercenaries received just punishment! And is it true you are married to the great Colonel Markham?'

She gazed with starry eyes at her husband, her cheeks dimpling. 'Indeed, uncle.'

He stretched a podgy arm to Roger for a handshake. 'Congratulations, sir. 'Pon my soul, you have a fine lass here! Beautiful, beautiful princess.' He beamed at the young couple.

Roger, who had been conversing with one of his officers, accepted Thomas Orme's hand cordially. 'I agree wholeheartedly, sir.' His eyes locked with Tara's, and the message in them said: I can't wait to be alone with you.

She tore her gaze away. 'I believe, uncle, you are here with the King's Dragoons.'

'True, true, m'dear, the 39th Foot. Travelled with them. Dreadful journey. Monsoon floods, heat, flies, mosquitoes, snakes. But that's over, thank heavens. Now I'll be staying for a while as British Resident. Must safeguard his Highness and his family. Good man, what? Can't have wars of succession and massacres in kingdoms relying on British protection.' He tapped Roger's arm. 'Rumour has it, Colonel, that you're abandoning your Blue Cloaks?'

'Yes. But my officer Captain Pullen here is quite capable of taking over the command. The Blue Cloaks are now part of the Motipur Forces.'

'Splendid, splendid! And now what are your plans, sir?'

'His Highness has presented me with his Himalayan kingdom, and he will be returning the Chiriabagh treasures and the Emerald Throne to my wife. We leave for the Diamond Palace after Nagandra's enthronement. As Chiriabagh is no more, Tara has consented to have the outlying territory annexed to Motipur.'

Thomas Orme raised a grey beetling brow in enquiry to Tara, and she nodded. 'Good, good. Best thing to do, poppet. Want to get far from the tragedy.'

She smiled sadly. 'I hope the Himalayan valley won't be too cold.'

'Nonsense! Nonsense! Air pure. No pests. Best place to rear children.'

'Don't give her ideas, sir,' her husband said, mock-seriously.

Thomas Orme turned his pale blue eyes on Roger. 'Take care of my godchild, Colonel. She's all I've got.'

'You're welcome to visit us in the hot season, sir, when you wish to escape the heat of the plains.'

'Capital, my dear fellow, capital!'

The usher announced that the fireworks were about to begin, and would the honoured guests move to the outer courtyard where the display would be held. Happily they all filed out to watch the spectacular illuminations.

'I've come to the end of my quest, my love,' Roger said, drawing Tara to the back of the crowd.

She gazed at him, as the fireworks lit up his face. How handsome he was, and how she loved him! 'What quest?'

'The quest for the woman of my dreams.'

Tara looked at him in wide-eyed innocence. 'Oh? Where is she?'

'I thought it was obvious, lady. The brave Uma, of course, who else?'

They both laughed.

EPILOGUE

IN THE SPRING of the following year when the Himalayan valley was golden with ripening corn and the mountain spurs abloom with clusters of rhododendrons in crimson, purple, yellow and pink, Tara and Roger, wrapped in woollen robes, stepped out on the marble balcony of their bedchamber in the Diamond Palace. They watched the rising sun touch the rim of the snowy ranges and set them on fire. Tara's nose tingled in the crisp, pure air.

'Abode of Snow,' he murmured, kissing her head. 'Isn't that what "Himalaya" means?'

'Yes, and the Hindus call these ranges "the Abode of the Gods".' Tara snuggled up to him, and added with a rueful sigh, 'But I wonder if such a heaven is for me.'

'Why?' he asked, stroking her dark satin locks.

'A matter of blood, I expect.'

'Then, in truth, we are well matched,' he remarked, a mysterious smile hovering on his lips.

Tara pushed back her head to stare at him. 'In what way?'

'Have you heard of the American Indians?'

Her blue eyes widened. 'You mean...?'

'I mean! But I'm not about to explain my ancestry at the moment. Or the question of heaven.' He swept her up in his arms. 'Let's return to bed, and create our own.'

She laughed. 'Oh, Roger, I do love you.'

'Say that over and over again.'

But, when she tried, he stopped her with his mouth.

The Christmas present you won't want to part with.

Four great new titles in a seasonal gift pack for only £5.00.
Long dark evenings of reading by a blazing fire. Will you
keep it or will you give it away?

TRUE PARADISE	Catherine George
TAKEOVER MAN	Vanessa Grant
TUSCAN ENCOUNTER	Madeleine Ker
DRIVING FORCE	Sally Wentworth

Published October 1988   Price £5.00

The latest blockbuster from Penny Jordan

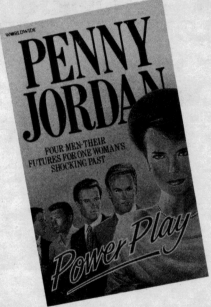

For Pepper Minesse, success as a young and powerful business woman has always been fuelled by one consuming desire – revenge against the 4 men involved in sadistically raping her in her teens.

Now she is ready.

She holds files that could destroy the lives and careers of these prominent men.

Together they must silence her – for ever.

Only one man's love can diffuse the insanity of the situation.

This blockbuster is Penny Jordan's most gripping and dramatic novel to date.
Nothing can beat POWER PLAY

Available: September   Price: £3.50

W❂RLDWIDE

Available from: Boots, Martins, John Menzies, W.H. Smith, Woolworths and other paperback stockists: